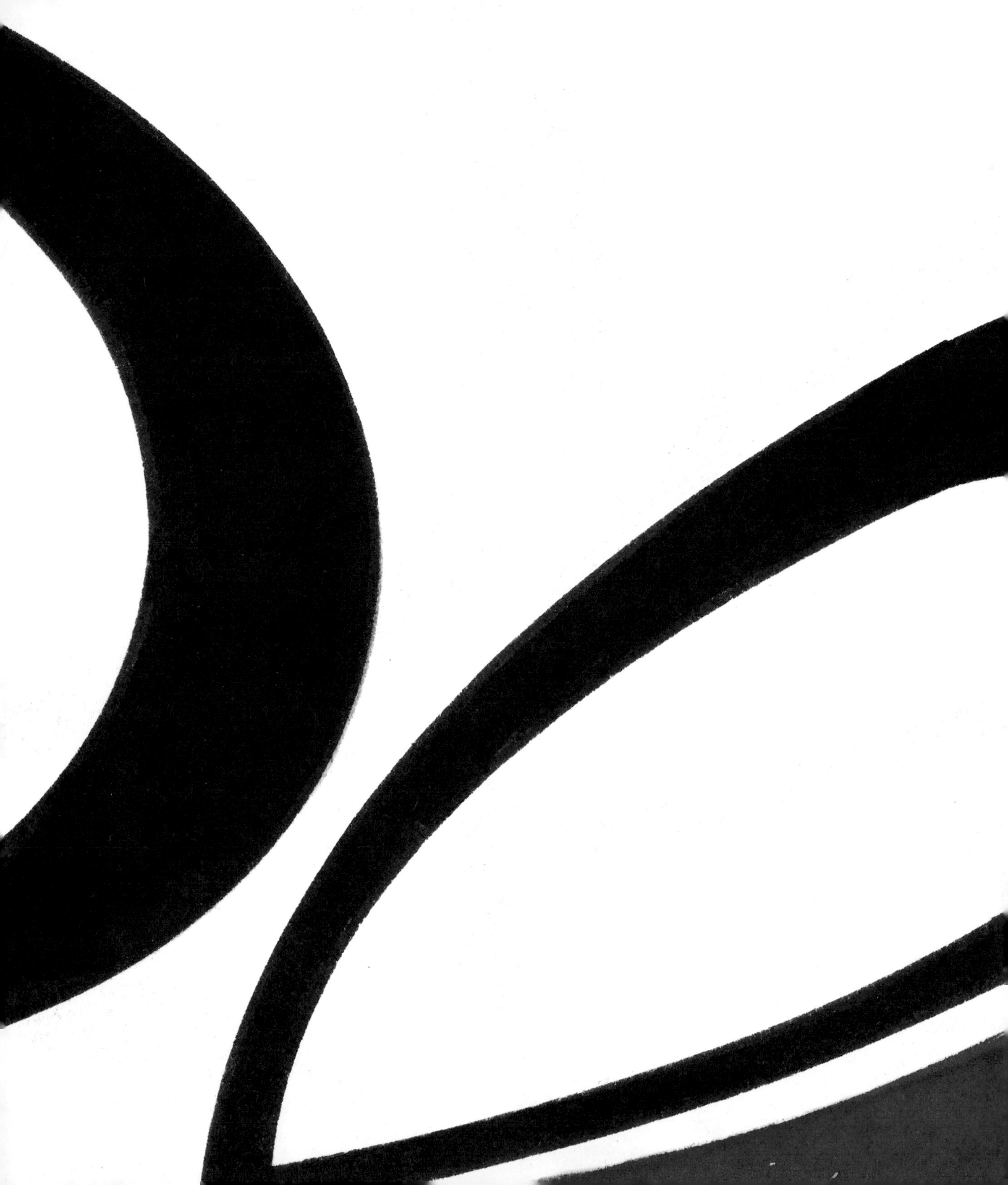

# A HAIDA MANGA

## MICHAEL NICOLL YAHGULANAAS

DOUGLAS & MCINTYRE

FIRST U.S. EDITION 2010, FIRST PAPERBACK EDITION 2014

14 15 16 17 18 5 4 3 2 1

DOUGLAS & MCINTYRE
P.O. BOX 219 MADEIRA PARK, BC, VON 2HO
WWW.DOUGLAS-MCINTYRE.COM

CATALOGUING DATA AVAILABLE FROM LIBRARY AND ARCHIVES CANADA
ISBN 978-1-55365-353-0 (CLOTH)
ISBN 978-1-77162-022-2 (PAPER)

EDITING BY CHRIS LABONTÉ
COVER DESIGN BY PETER COCKING AND MICHAEL NICOLL YAHGULANAAS
COVER ILLUSTRATION BY MICHAEL NICOLL YAHGULANAAS
INTERIOR LETTERING BY ED BRISSON
PRINTED AND BOUND IN CHINA
DISTRIBUTED IN THE U.S. BY PUBLISHERS GROUP WEST

WE GRATEFULLY ACKNOWLEDGE THE FINANCIAL SUPPORT OF THE CANADA COUNCIL FOR THE ARTS, THE BRITISH COLUMBIA ARTS COUNCIL, THE PROVINCE OF BRITISH COLUMBIA THROUGH THE BOOK PUBLISHING TAX CREDIT AND THE GOVERNMENT OF CANADA THROUGH THE CANADA BOOK FUND FOR OUR PUBLISHING ACTIVITIES.

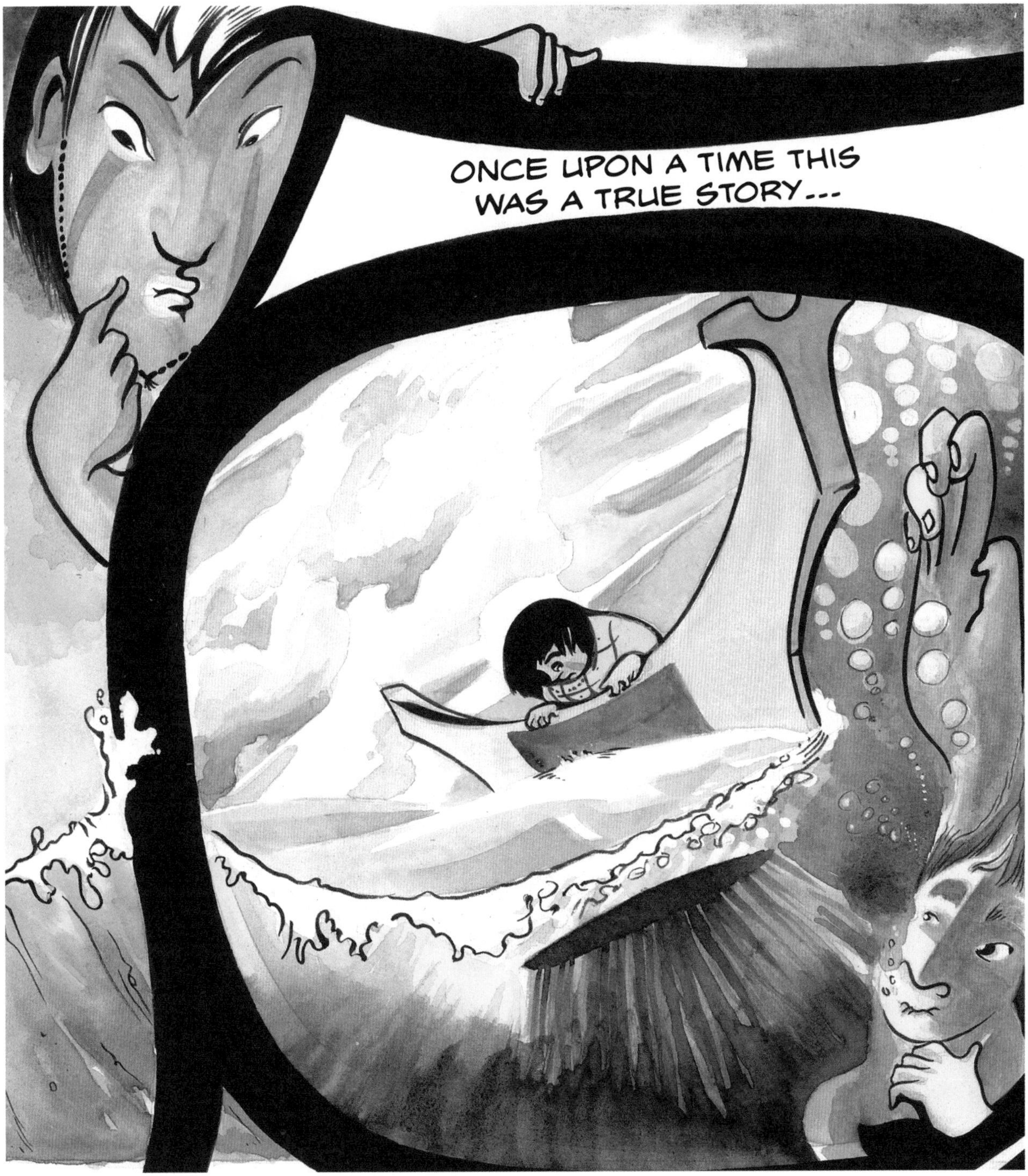
ONCE UPON A TIME THIS
WAS A TRUE STORY...

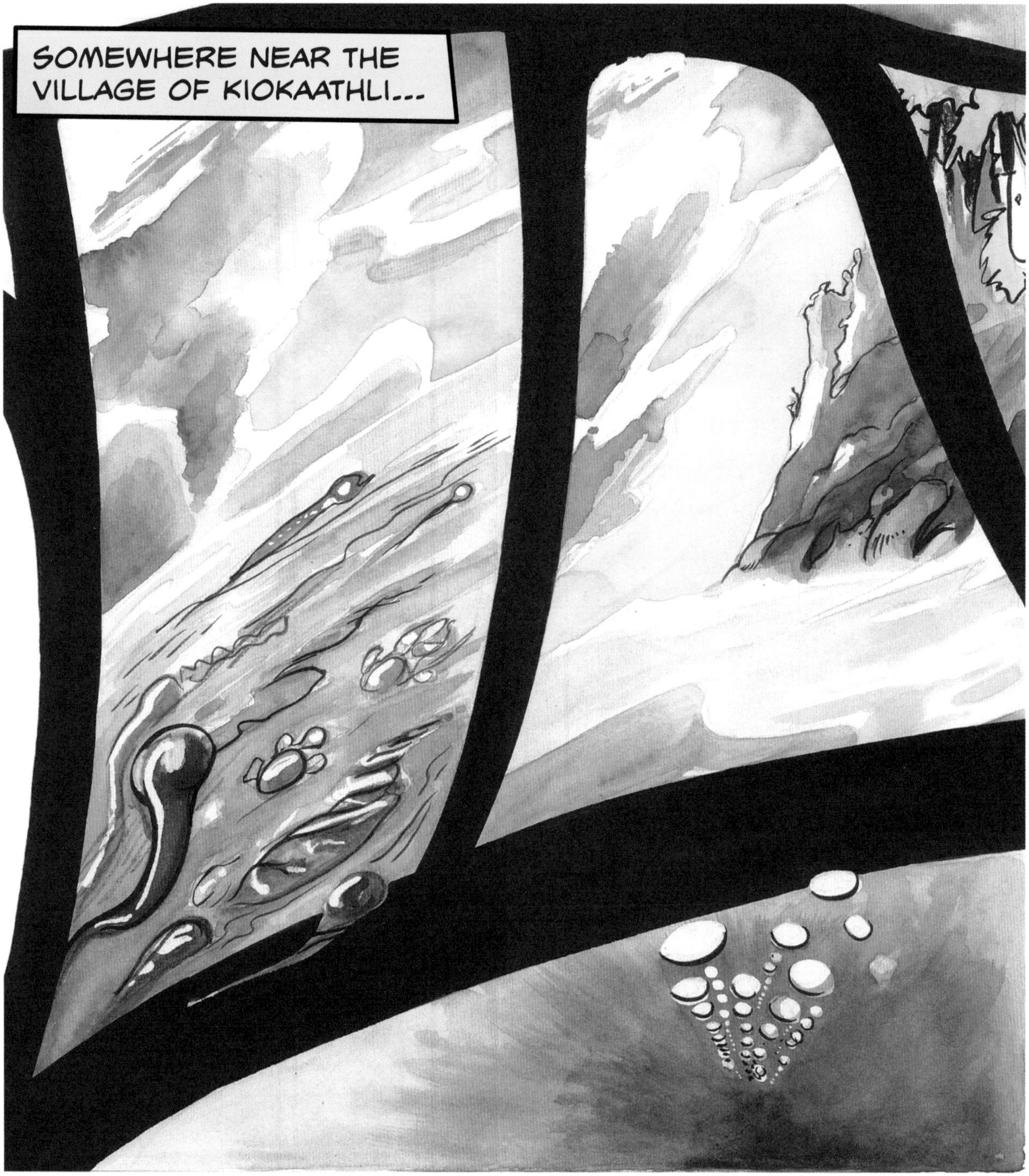
SOMEWHERE NEAR THE VILLAGE OF KIOKAATHLI...

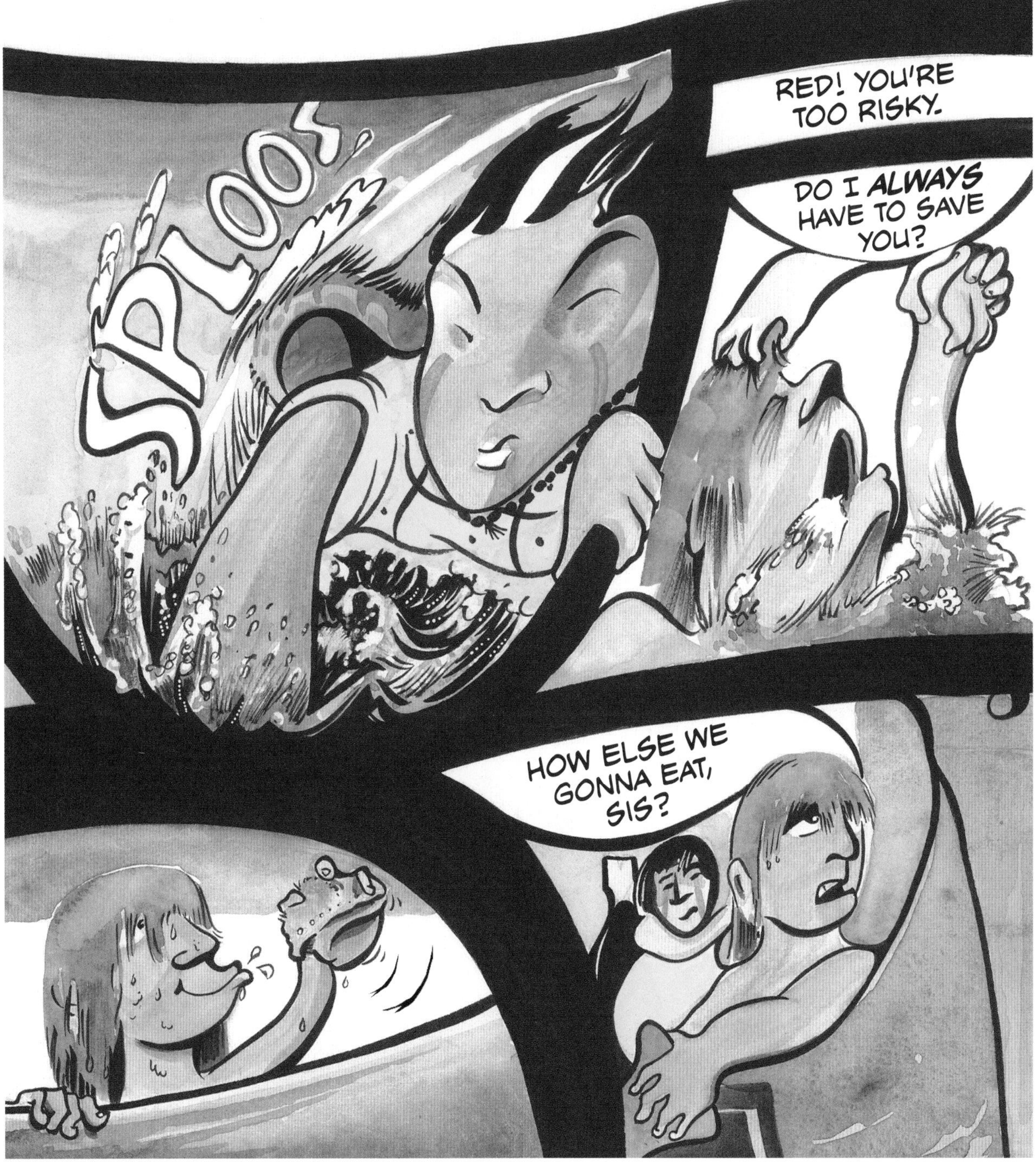
SPLOOSH
RED! YOU'RE TOO RISKY.
DO I *ALWAYS* HAVE TO SAVE YOU?
HOW ELSE WE GONNA EAT, SIS?

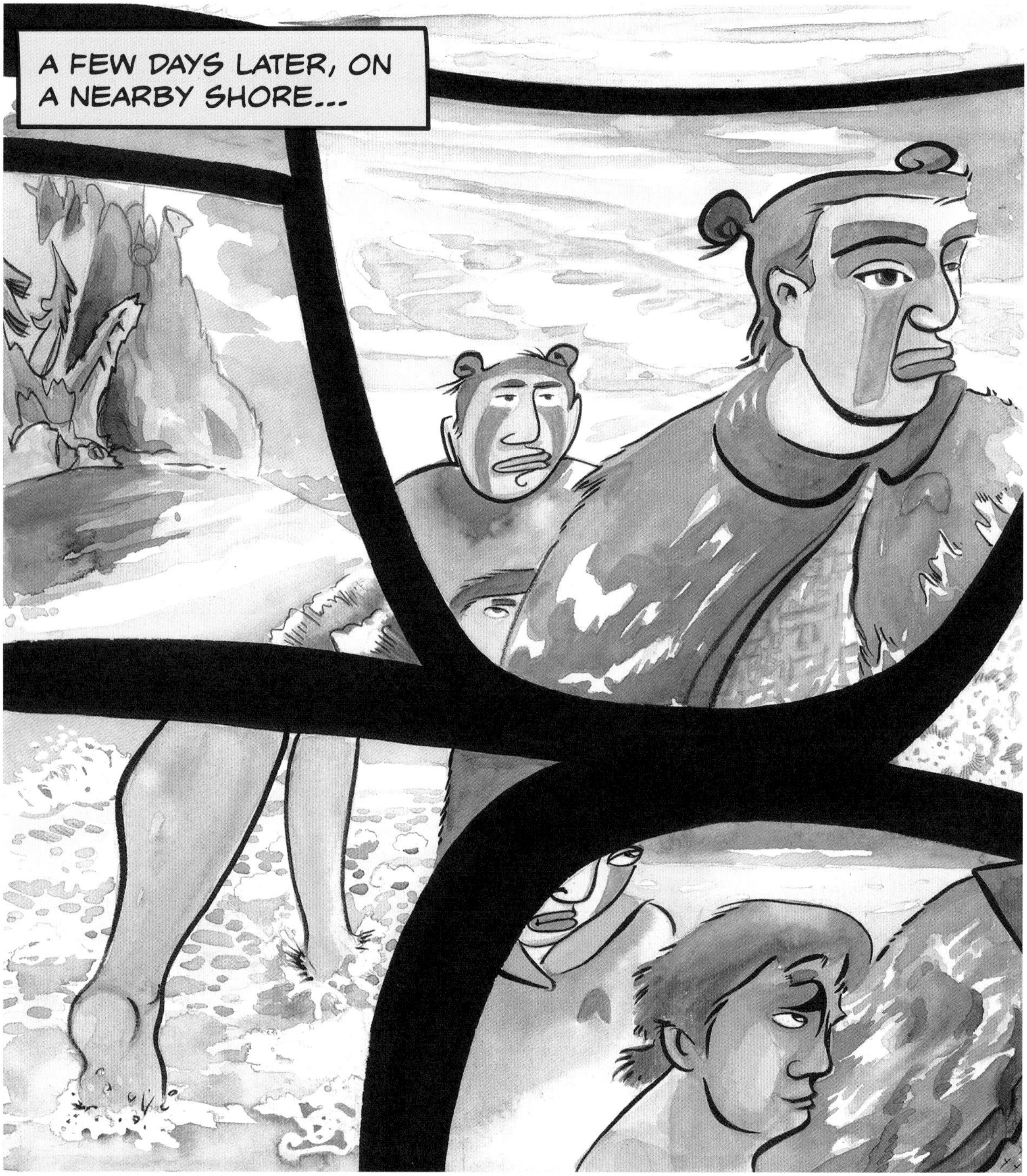
A FEW DAYS LATER, ON A NEARBY SHORE...

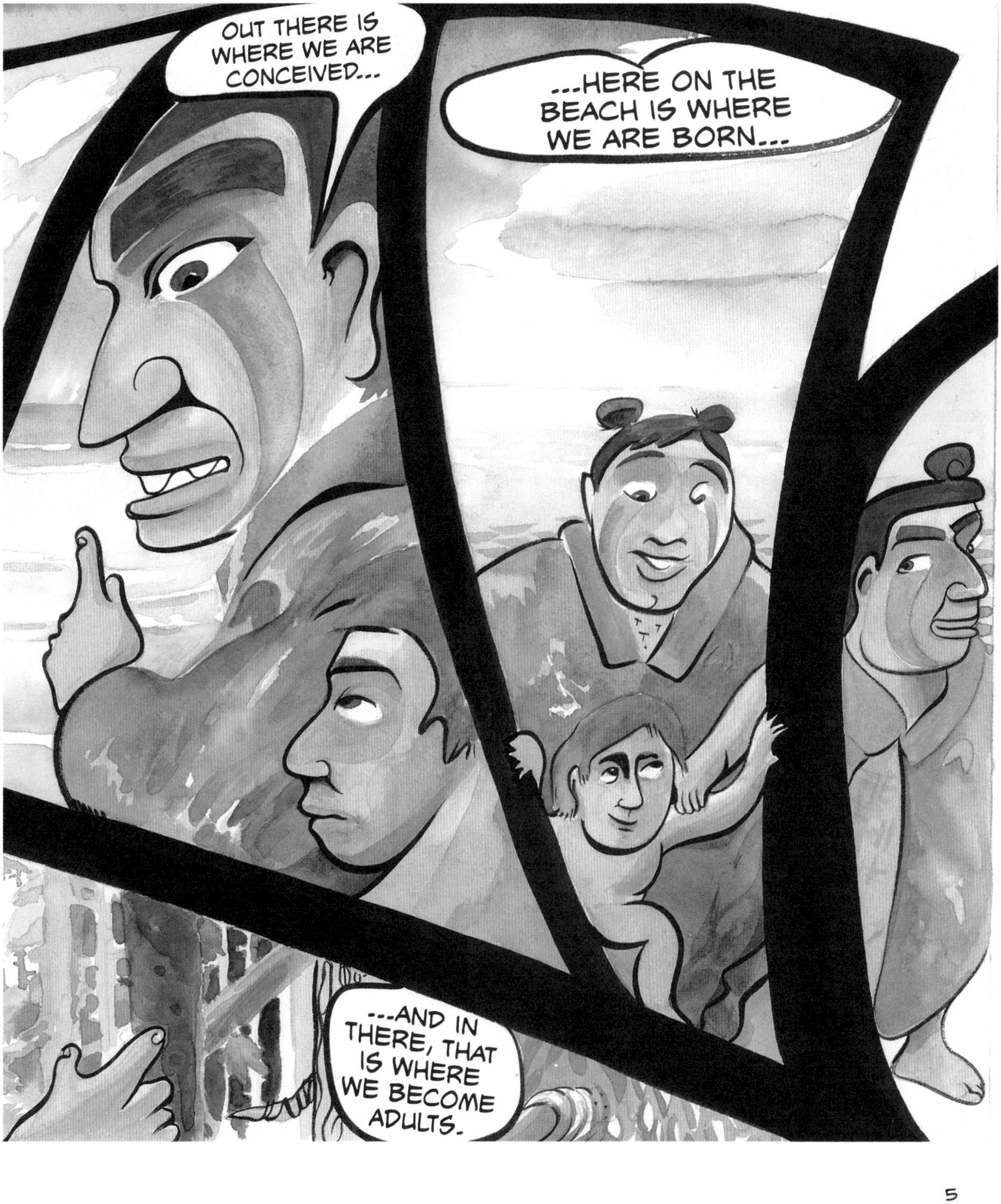
OUT THERE IS WHERE WE ARE CONCEIVED...
...HERE ON THE BEACH IS WHERE WE ARE BORN...
...AND IN THERE, THAT IS WHERE WE BECOME ADULTS.

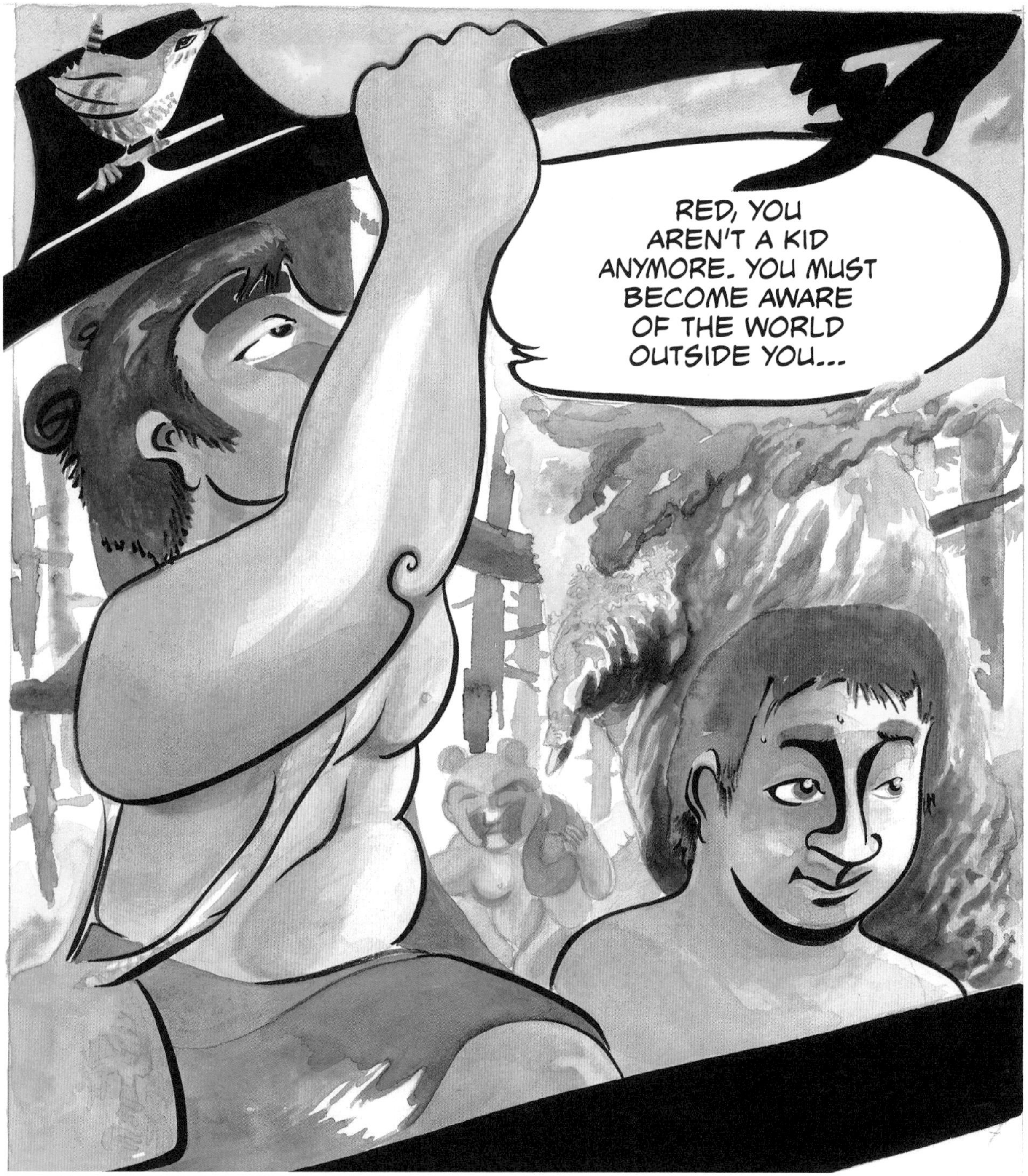
RED, YOU AREN'T A KID ANYMORE. YOU MUST BECOME AWARE OF THE WORLD OUTSIDE YOU...

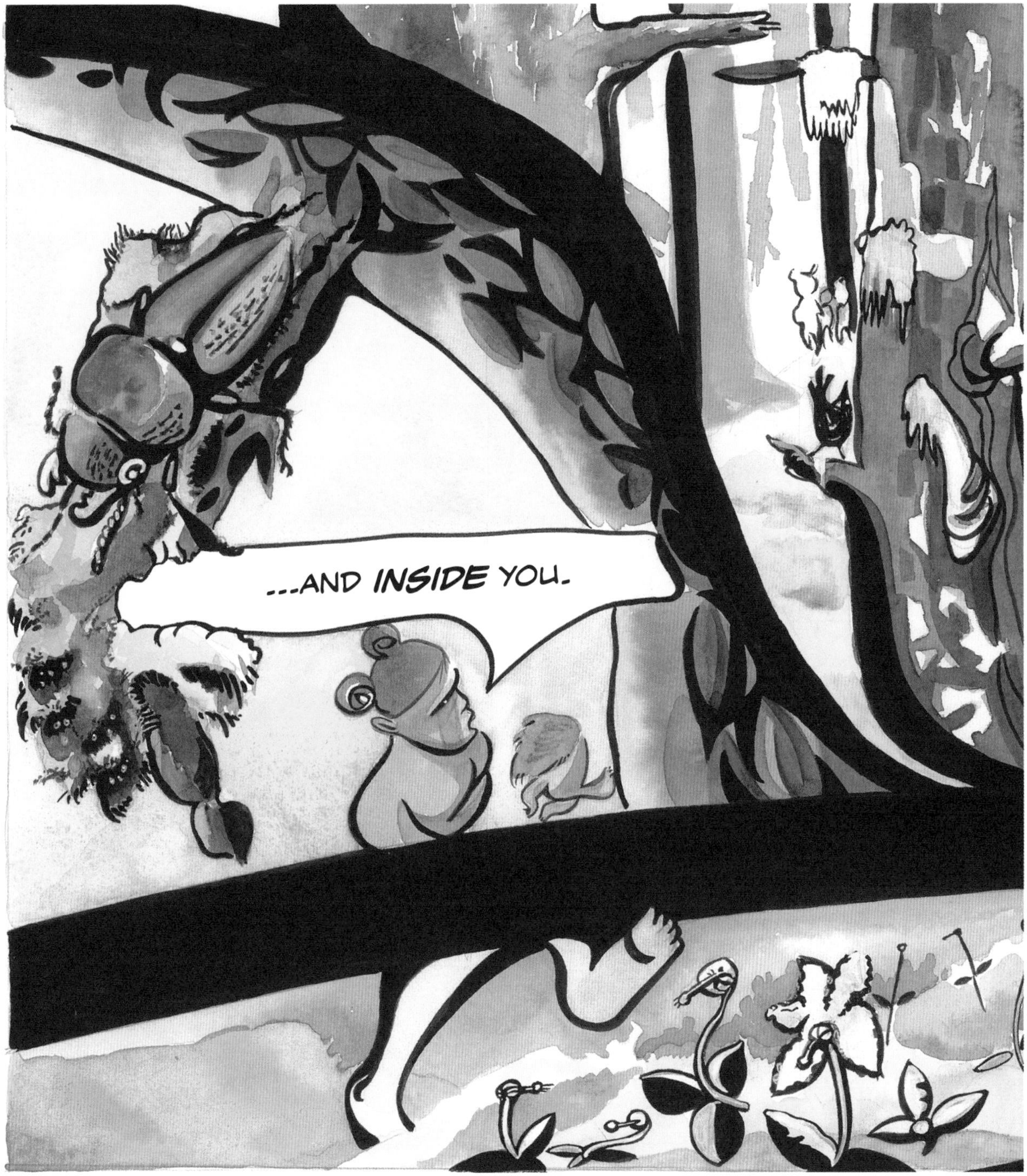
...AND **INSIDE** YOU.

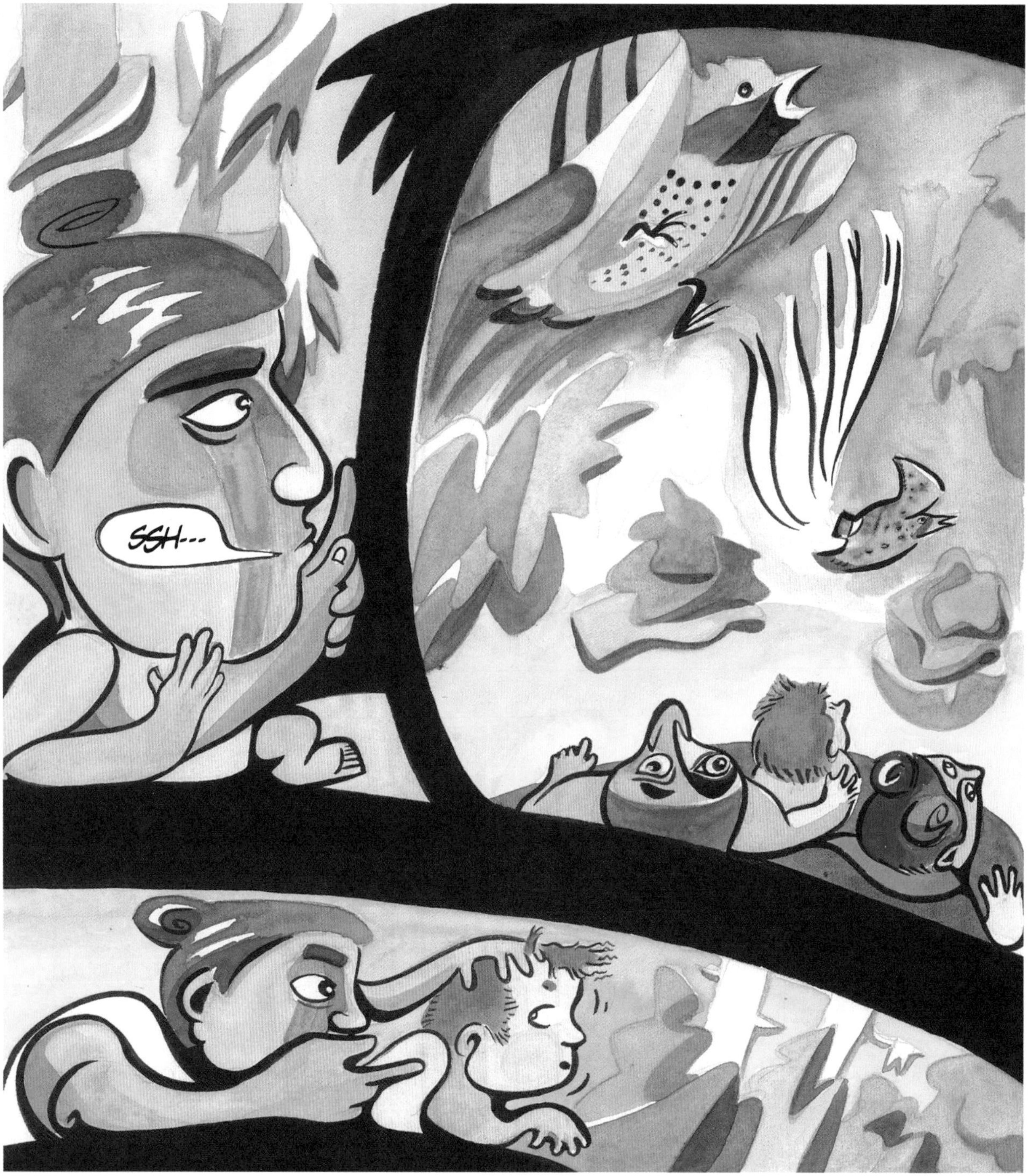
SSH---

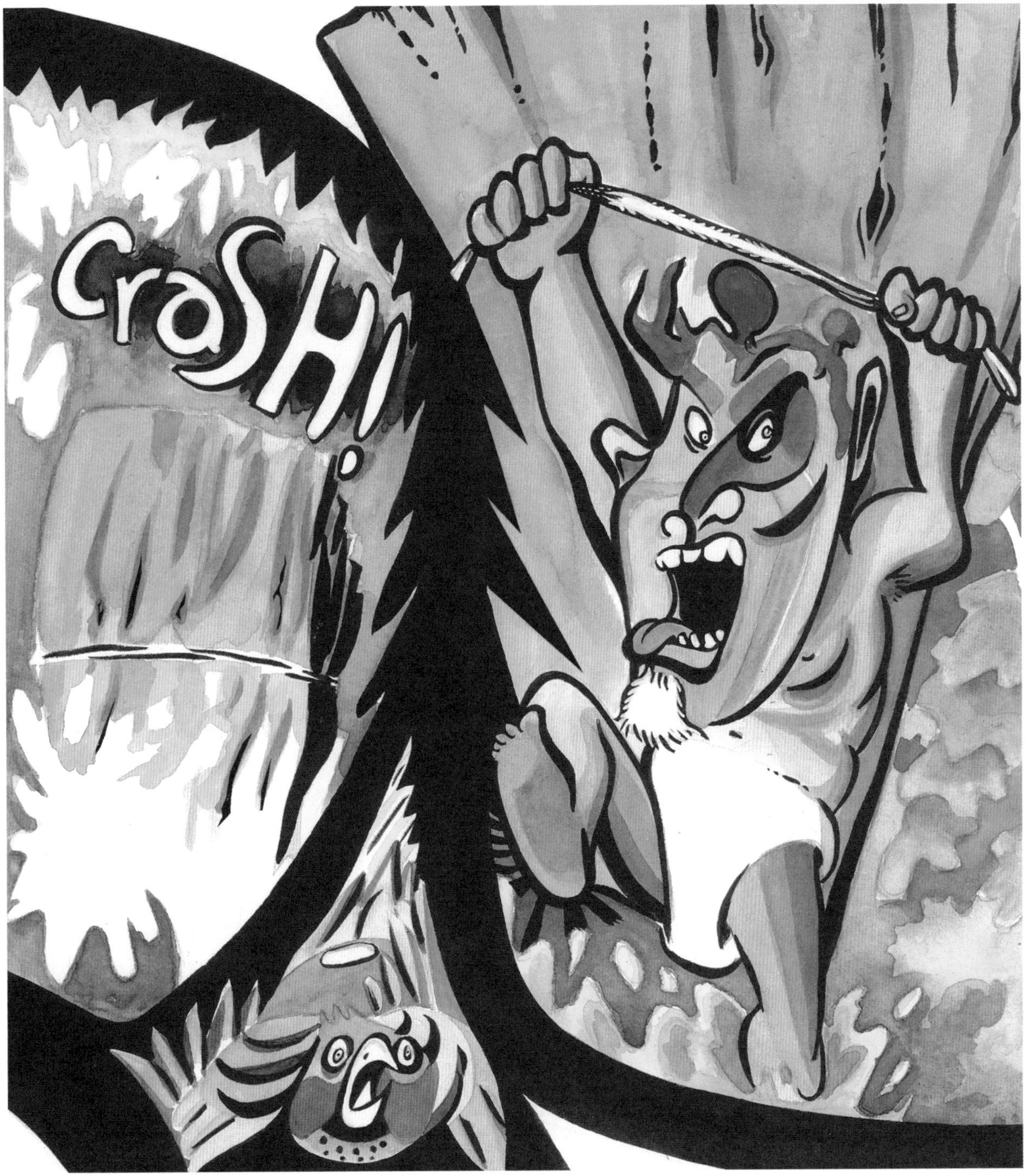
CraSH!

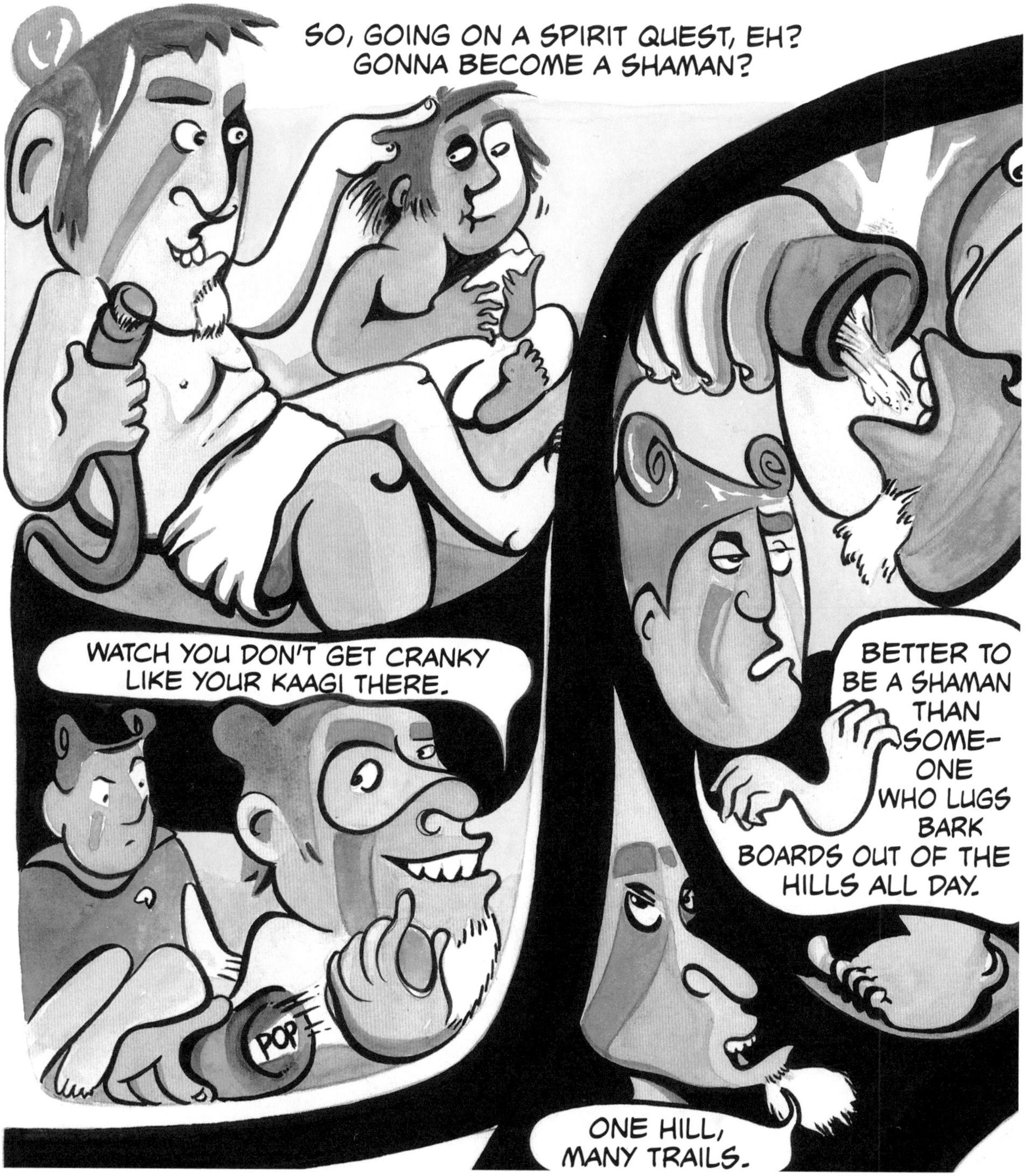
SO, GOING ON A SPIRIT QUEST, EH? GONNA BECOME A SHAMAN?
WATCH YOU DON'T GET CRANKY LIKE YOUR KAAGI THERE.
POP!
BETTER TO BE A SHAMAN THAN SOME-ONE WHO LUGS BARK BOARDS OUT OF THE HILLS ALL DAY.
ONE HILL, MANY TRAILS.

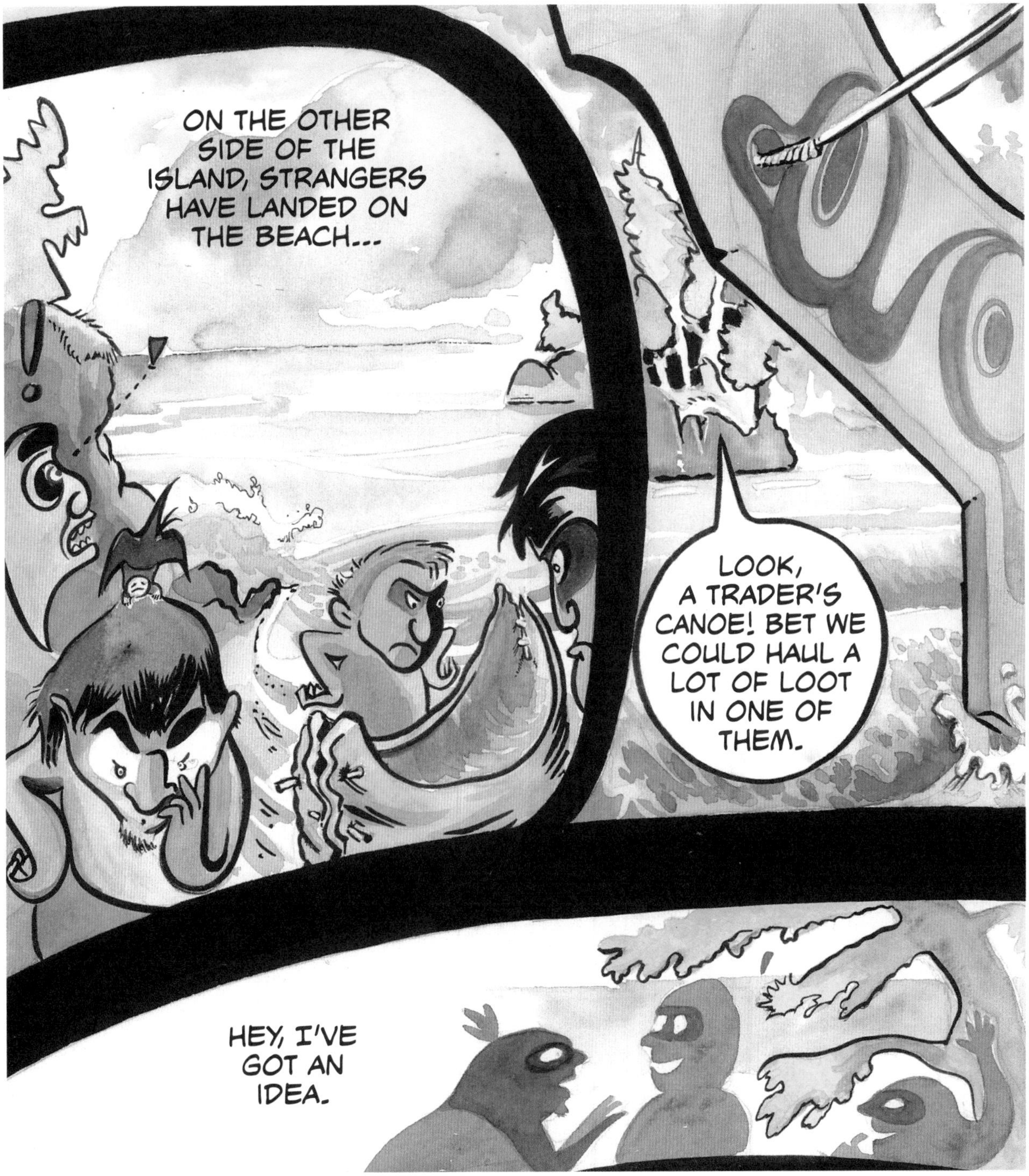
ON THE OTHER SIDE OF THE ISLAND, STRANGERS HAVE LANDED ON THE BEACH...
LOOK, A TRADER'S CANOE! BET WE COULD HAUL A LOT OF LOOT IN ONE OF THEM.
HEY, I'VE GOT AN IDEA.

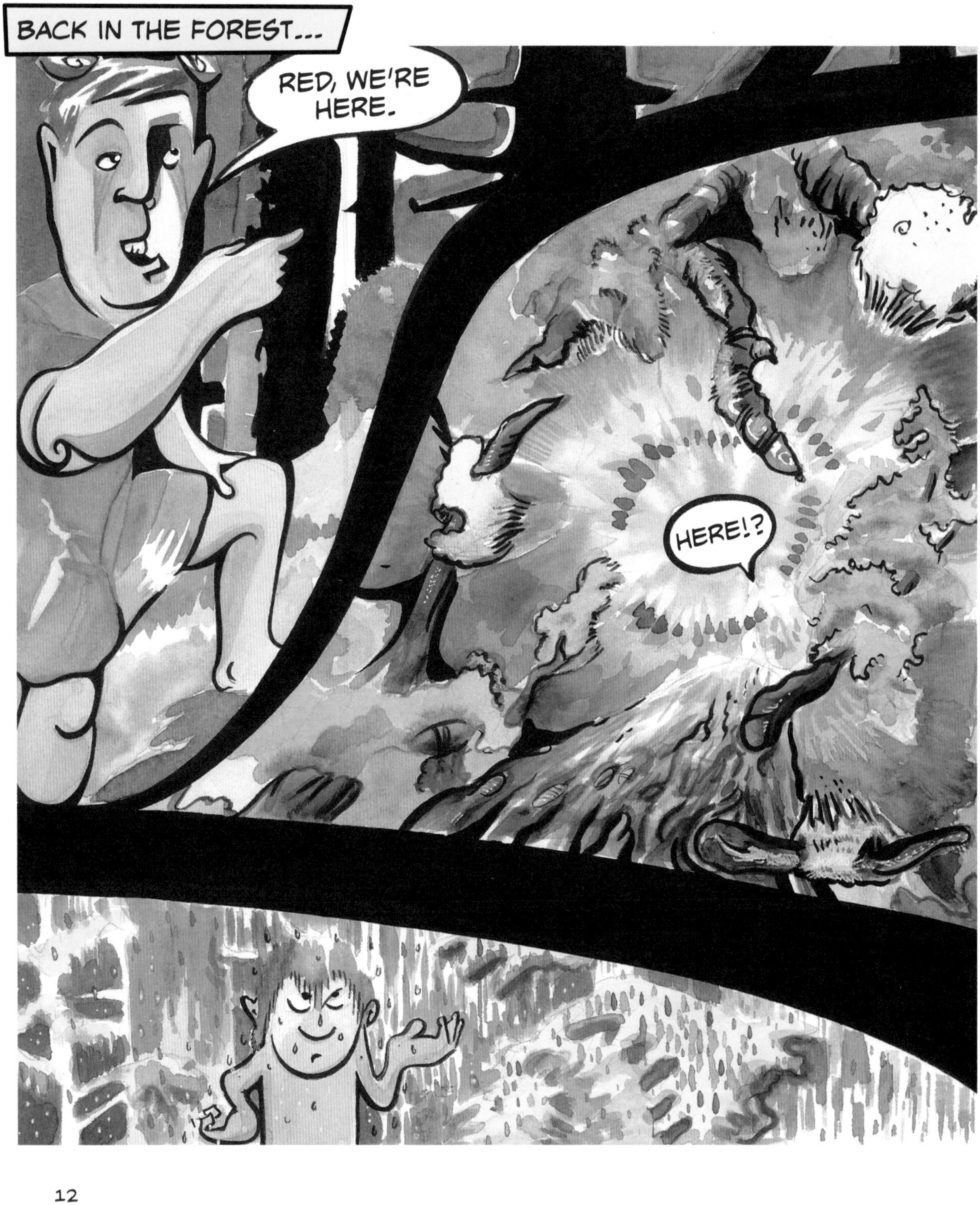

BACK IN THE FOREST...
RED, WE'RE HERE.
HERE!?

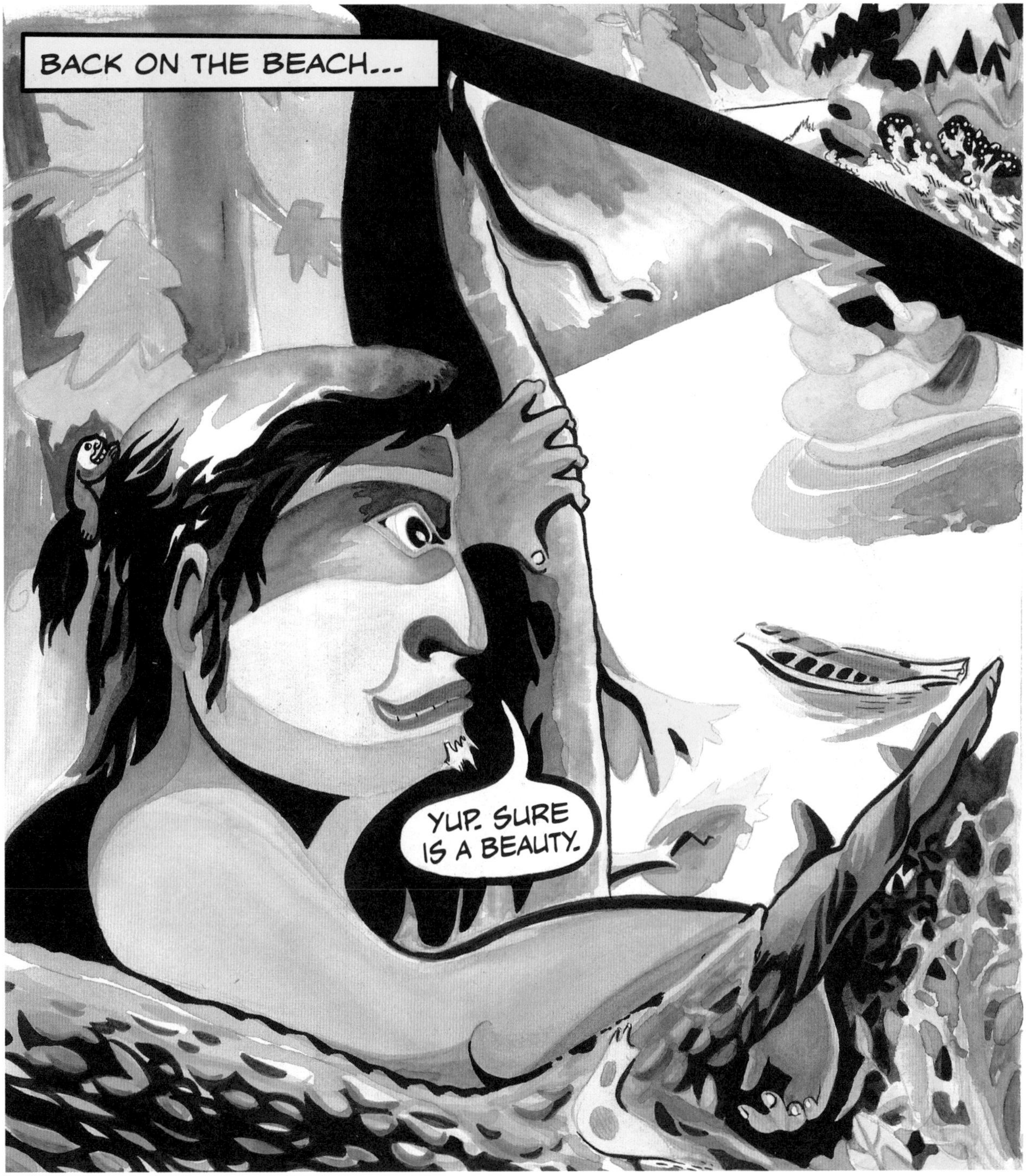
BACK ON THE BEACH...
YUP. SURE IS A BEAUTY.

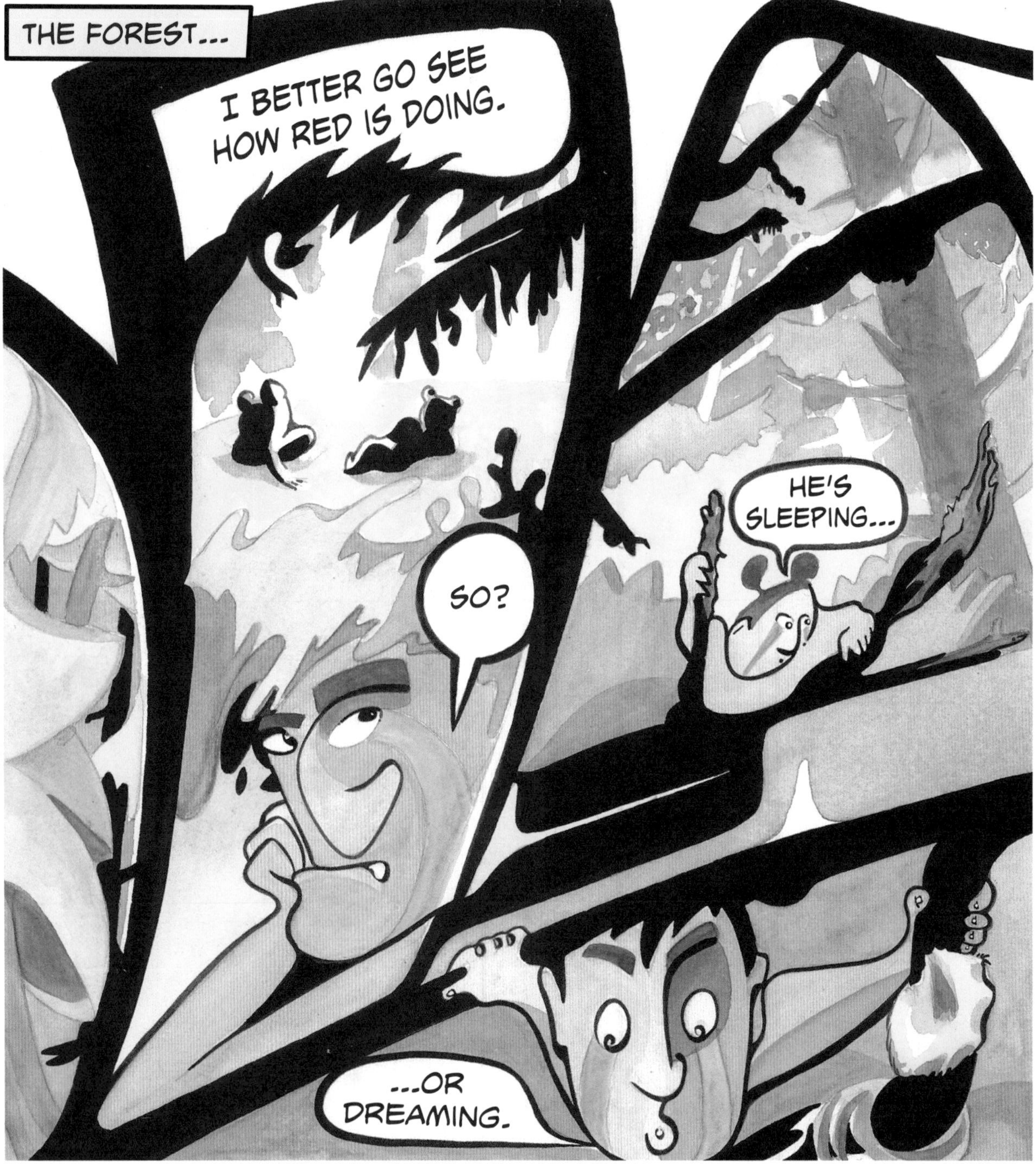
THE FOREST...
I BETTER GO SEE HOW RED IS DOING.
HE'S SLEEPING...
SO?
...OR DREAMING.

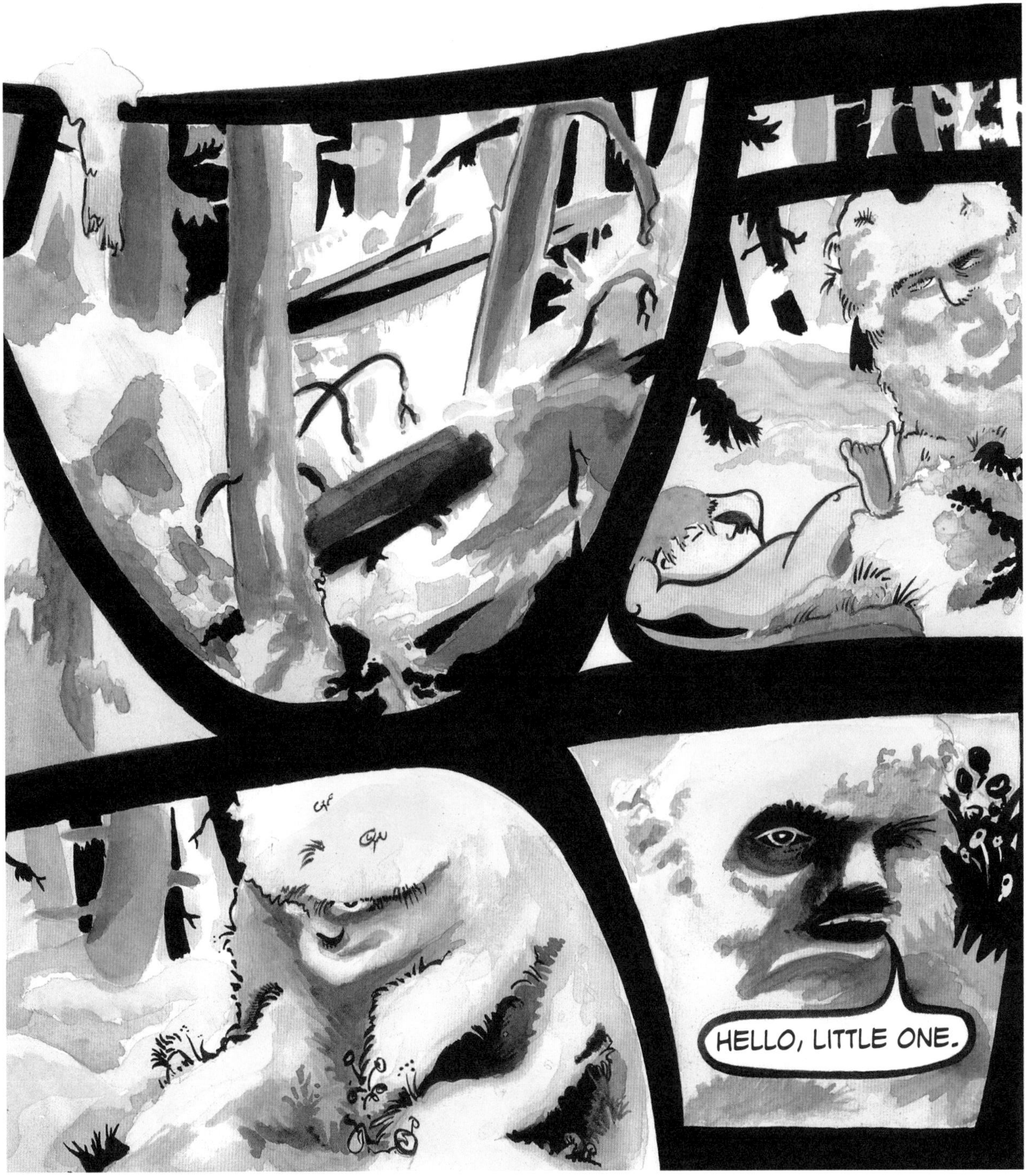
HELLO, LITTLE ONE.

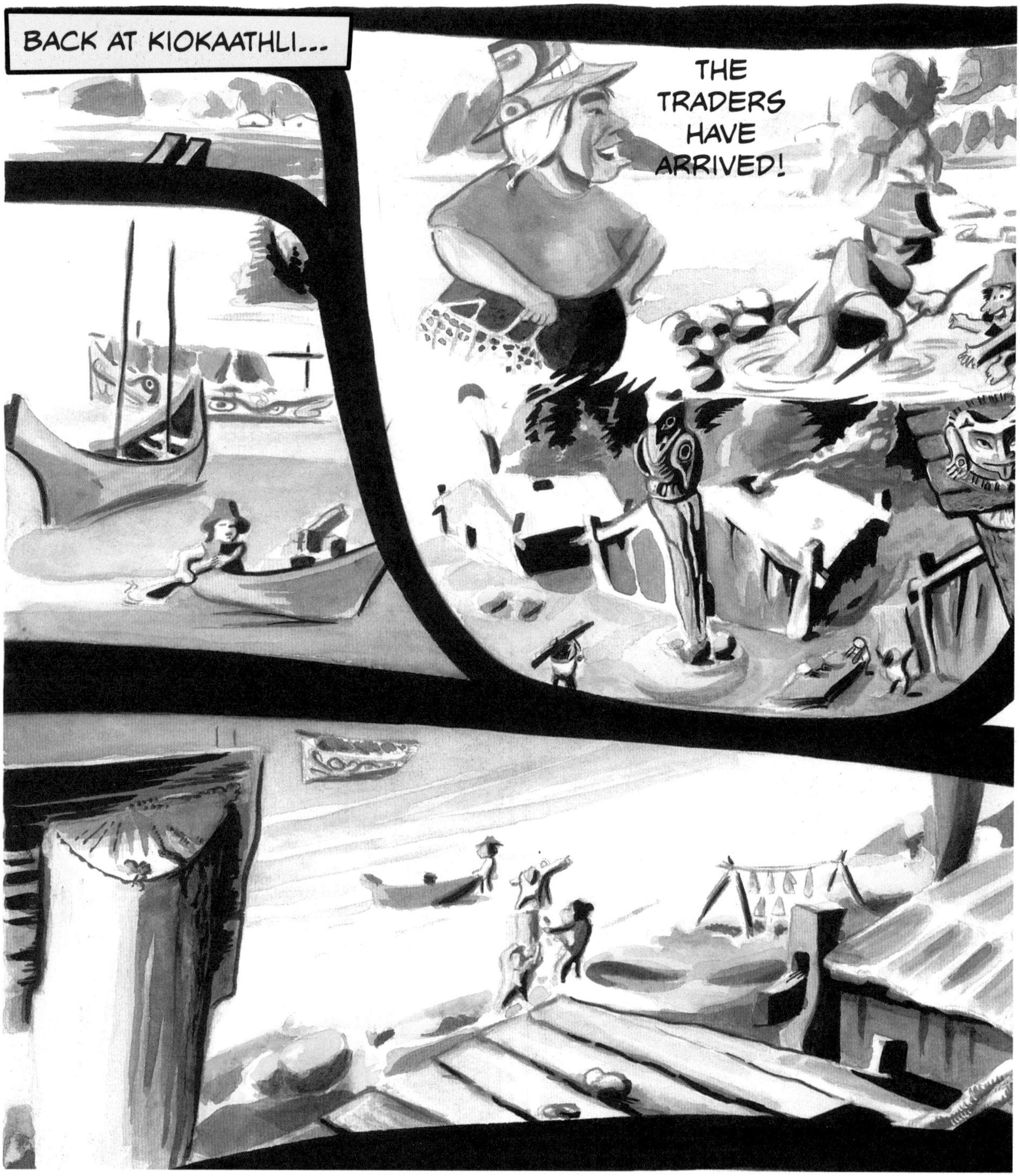
BACK AT KIOKAATHLI...
THE TRADERS HAVE ARRIVED!

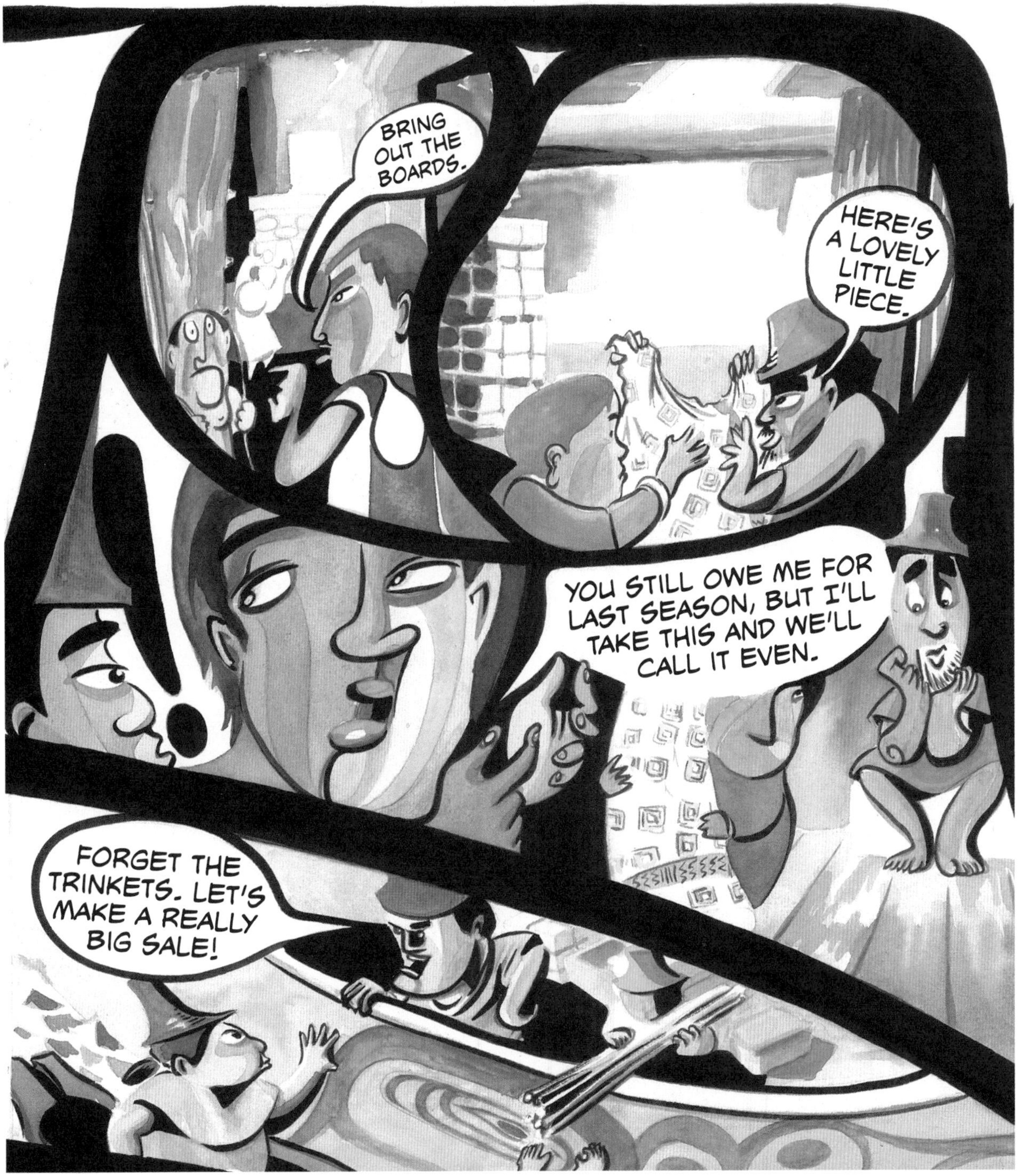
BRING OUT THE BOARDS.
HERE'S A LOVELY LITTLE PIECE.
YOU STILL OWE ME FOR LAST SEASON, BUT I'LL TAKE THIS AND WE'LL CALL IT EVEN.
FORGET THE TRINKETS. LET'S MAKE A REALLY BIG SALE!

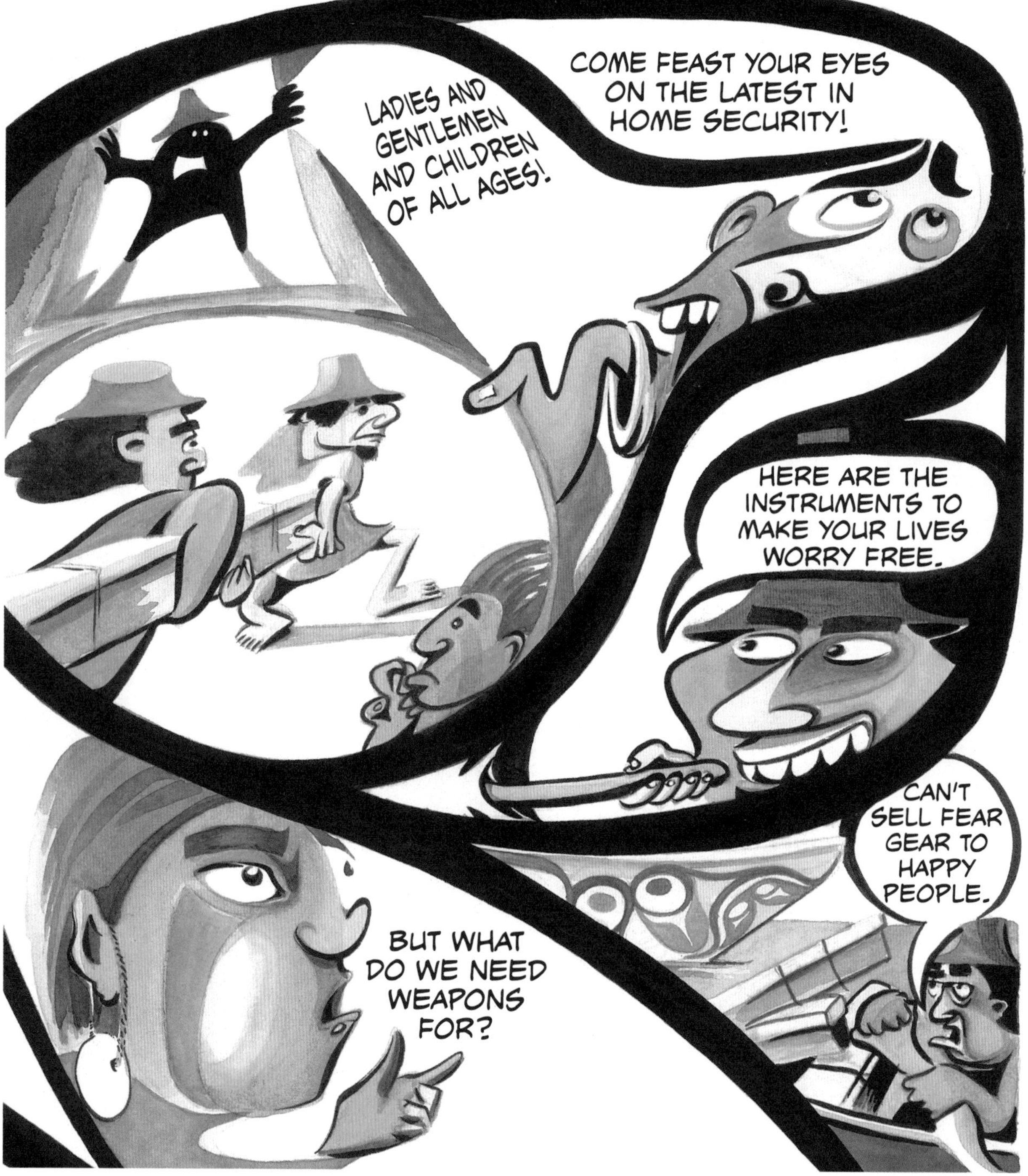
LADIES AND GENTLEMEN AND CHILDREN OF ALL AGES!
COME FEAST YOUR EYES ON THE LATEST IN HOME SECURITY!
HERE ARE THE INSTRUMENTS TO MAKE YOUR LIVES WORRY FREE.
BUT WHAT DO WE NEED WEAPONS FOR?
CAN'T SELL FEAR GEAR TO HAPPY PEOPLE.

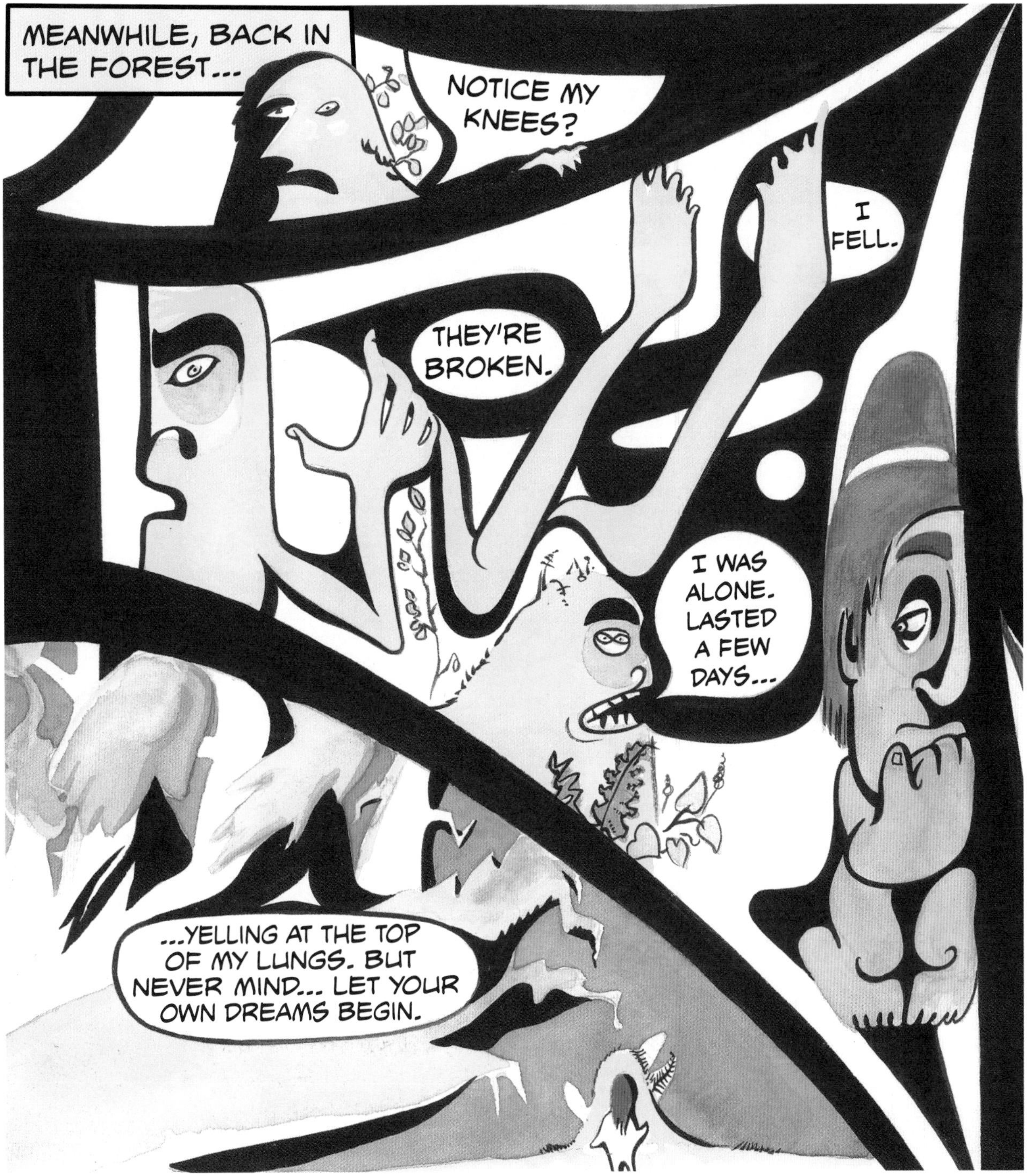
MEANWHILE, BACK IN THE FOREST...
NOTICE MY KNEES?
I FELL.
THEY'RE BROKEN.
I WAS ALONE. LASTED A FEW DAYS...
...YELLING AT THE TOP OF MY LUNGS. BUT NEVER MIND... LET YOUR OWN DREAMS BEGIN.

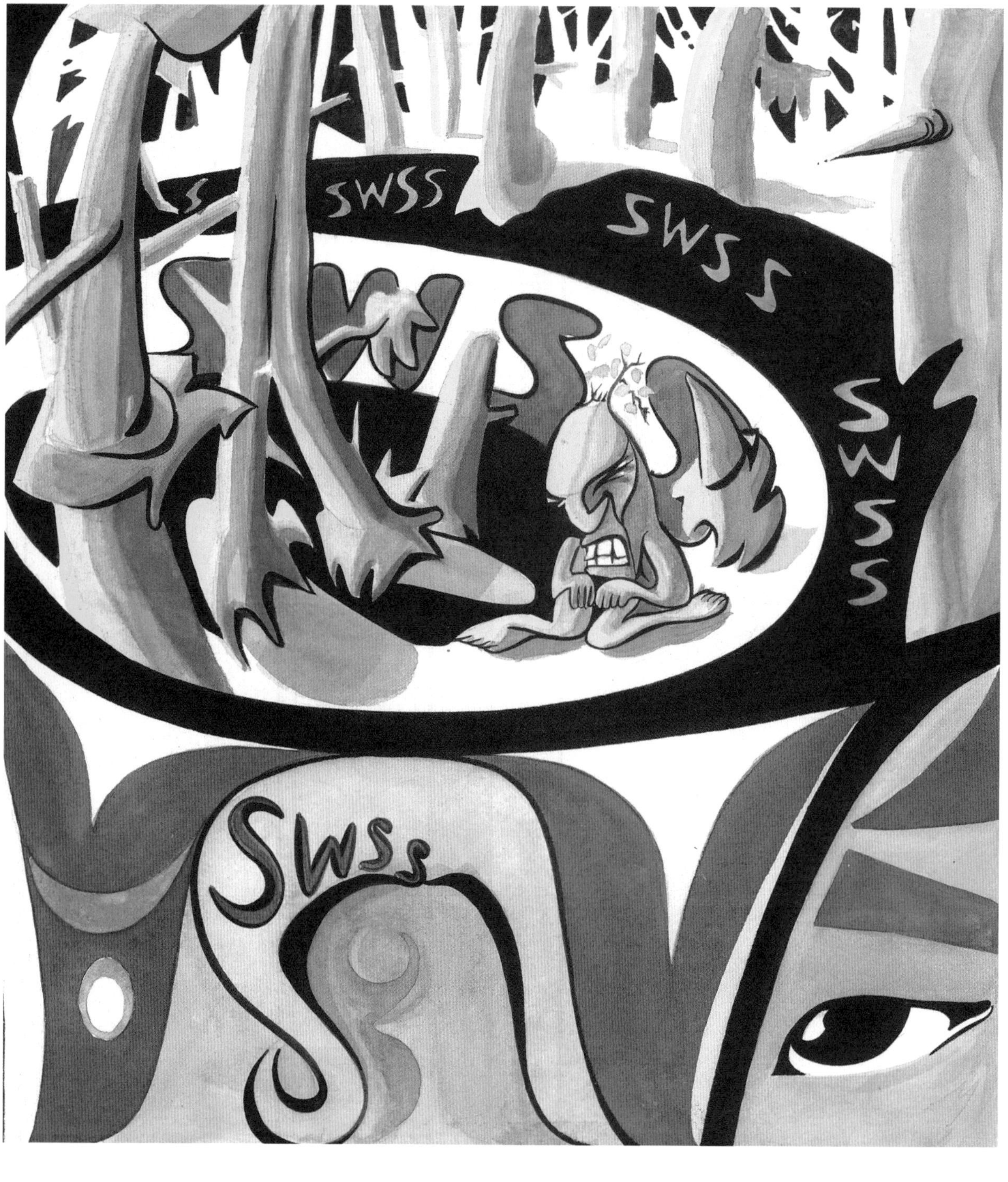
SWSS
SWSS
SWSS
SWSS

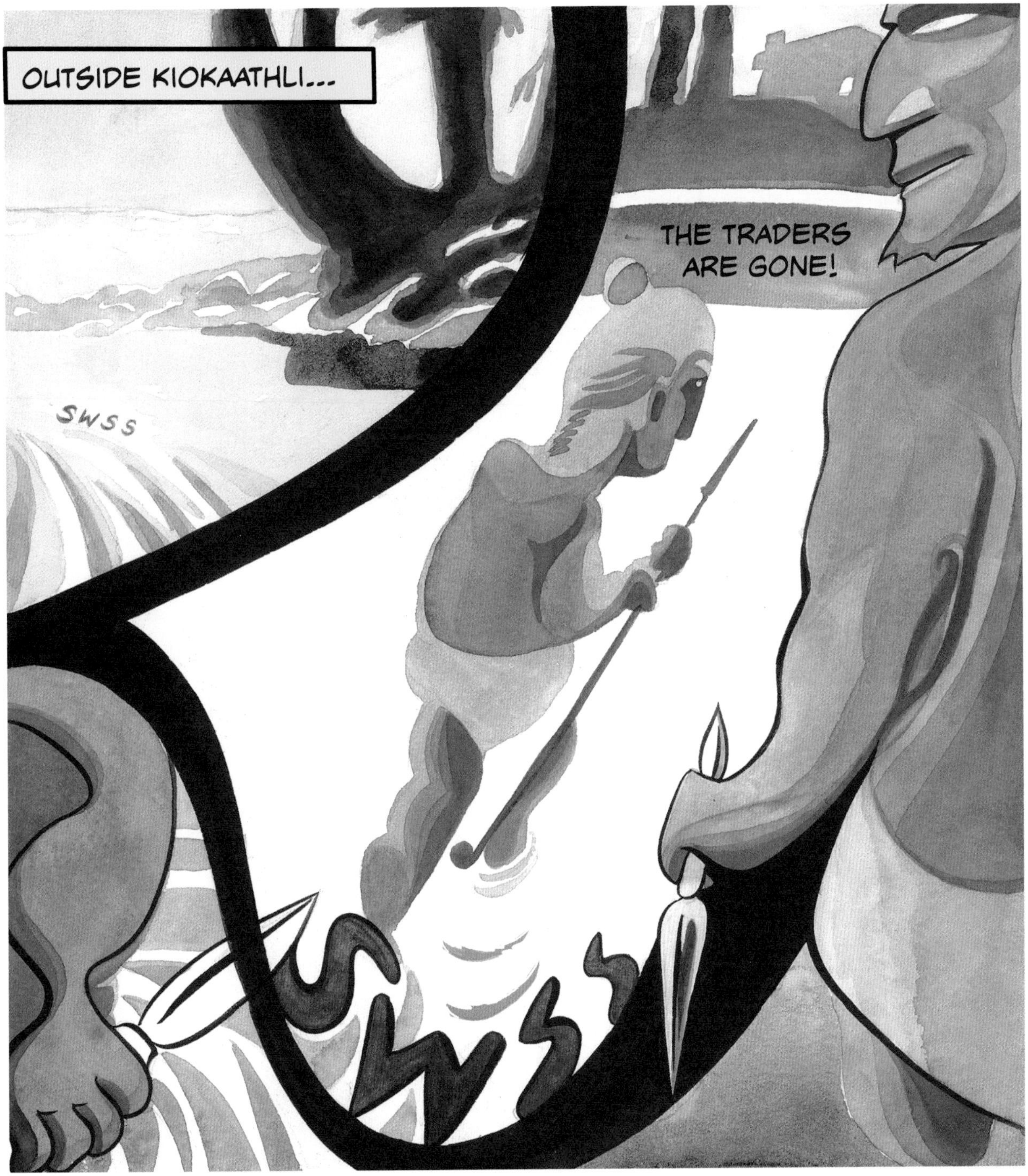
OUTSIDE KIOKAATHLI...
SWSS
THE TRADERS ARE GONE!
SWSS

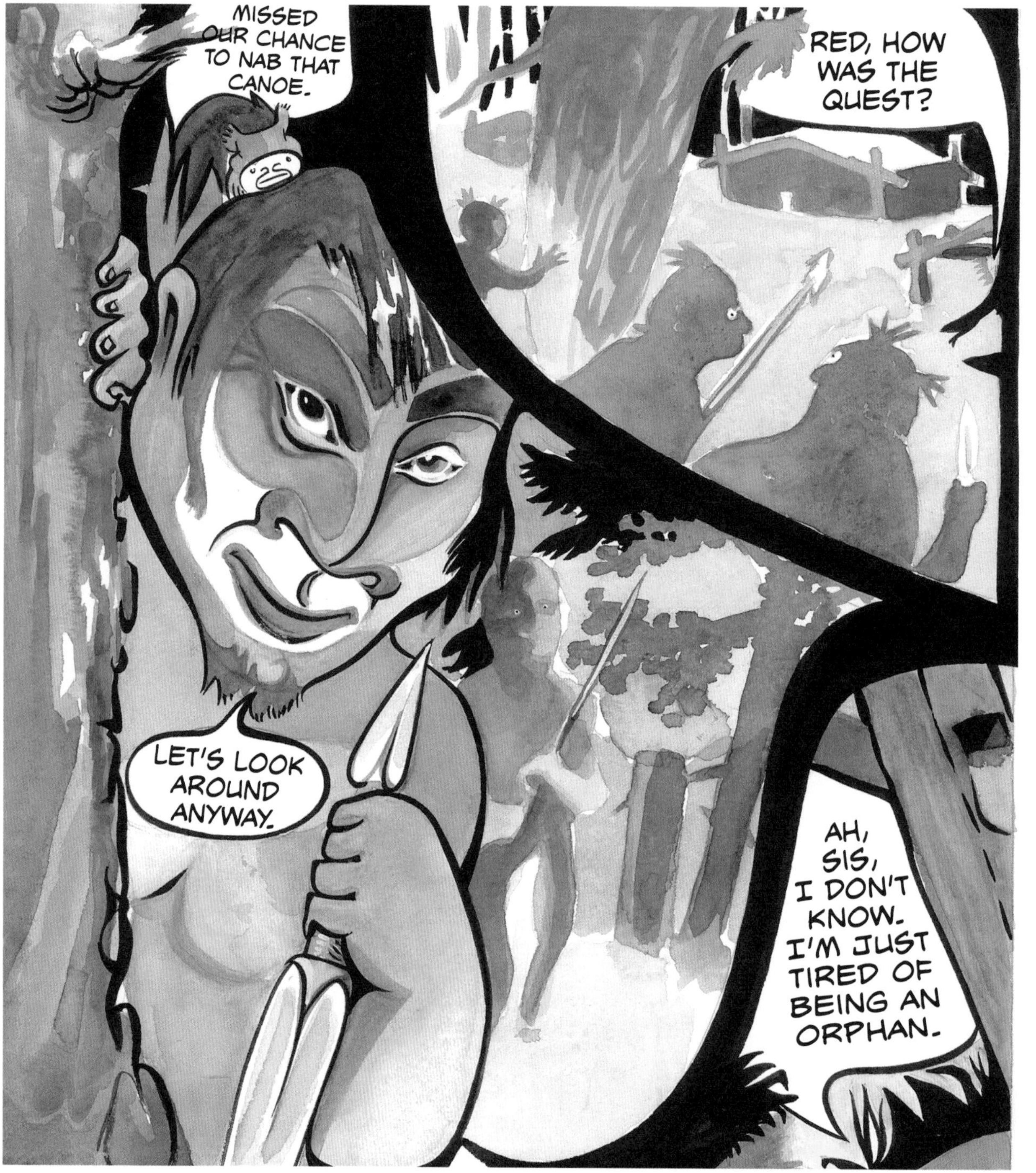
MISSED OUR CHANCE TO NAB THAT CANOE.
RED, HOW WAS THE QUEST?
LET'S LOOK AROUND ANYWAY.
AH, SIS, I DON'T KNOW. I'M JUST TIRED OF BEING AN ORPHAN.

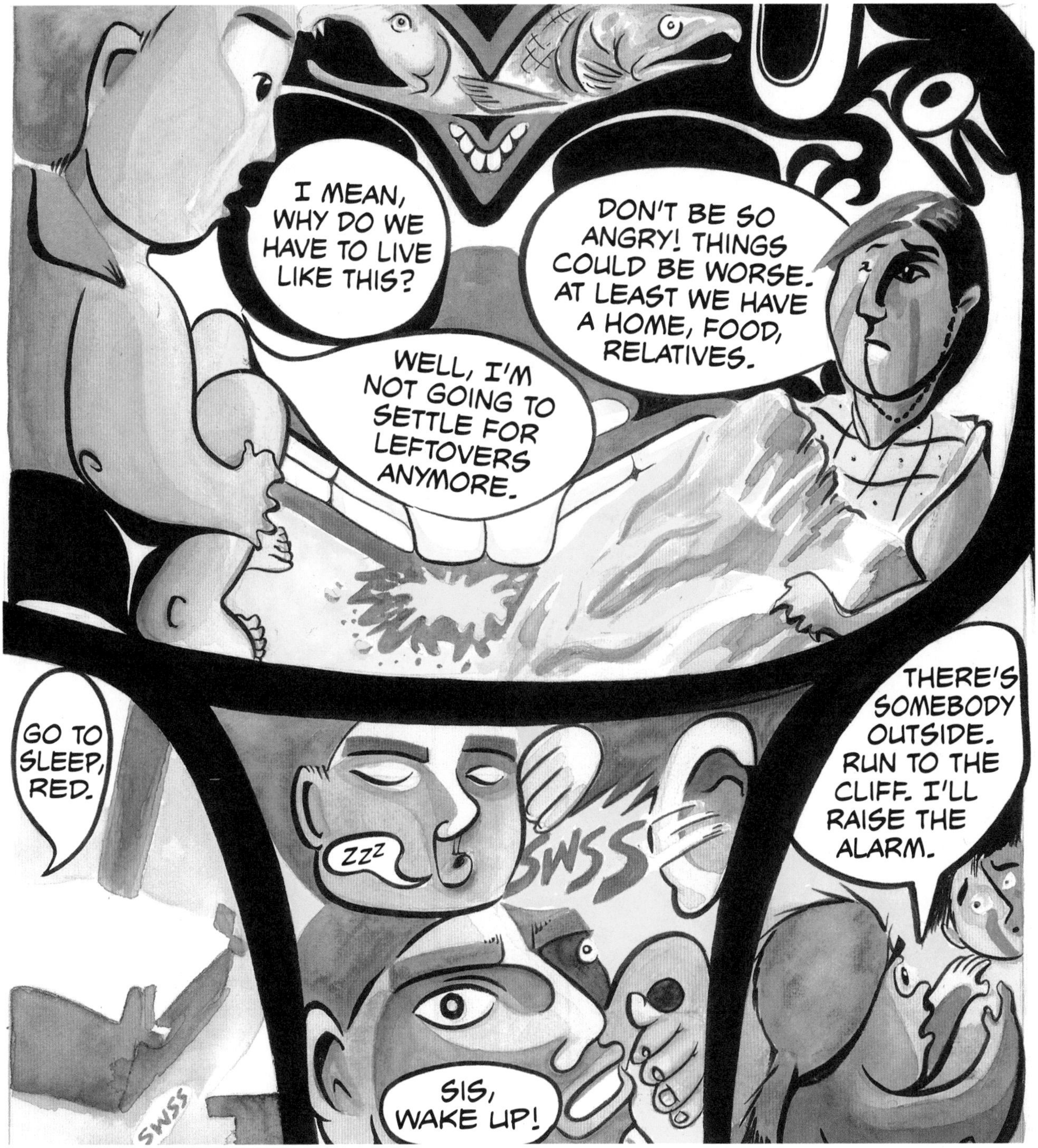
I MEAN, WHY DO WE HAVE TO LIVE LIKE THIS?
DON'T BE SO ANGRY! THINGS COULD BE WORSE. AT LEAST WE HAVE A HOME, FOOD, RELATIVES.
WELL, I'M NOT GOING TO SETTLE FOR LEFTOVERS ANYMORE.
GO TO SLEEP, RED.
ZZZ
SWSS
THERE'S SOMEBODY OUTSIDE. RUN TO THE CLIFF. I'LL RAISE THE ALARM.
SIS, WAKE UP!
SWSS

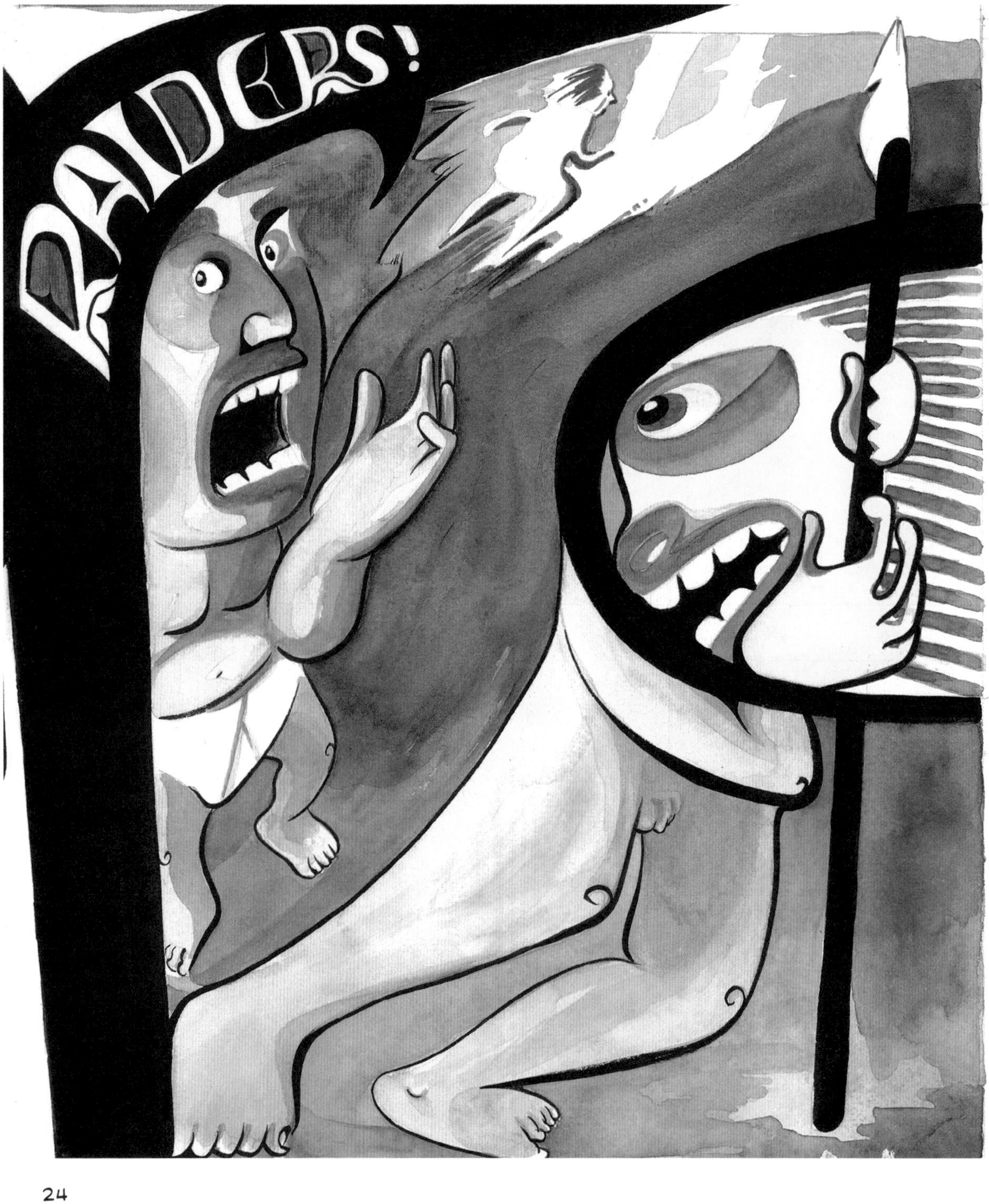
RAIDERS!

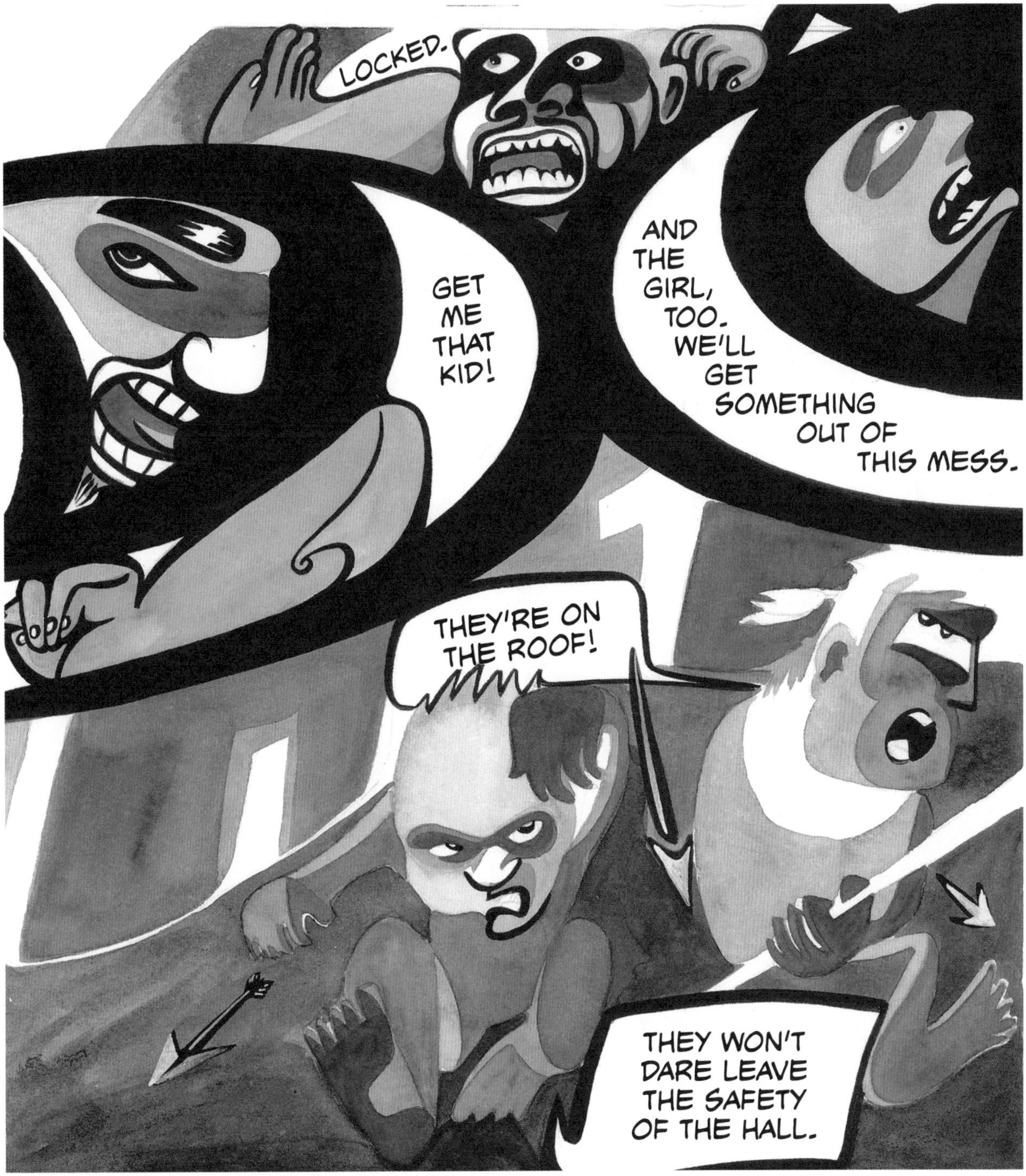
LOCKED.
GET ME THAT KID!
AND THE GIRL, TOO. WE'LL GET SOMETHING OUT OF THIS MESS.
THEY'RE ON THE ROOF!
THEY WON'T DARE LEAVE THE SAFETY OF THE HALL.

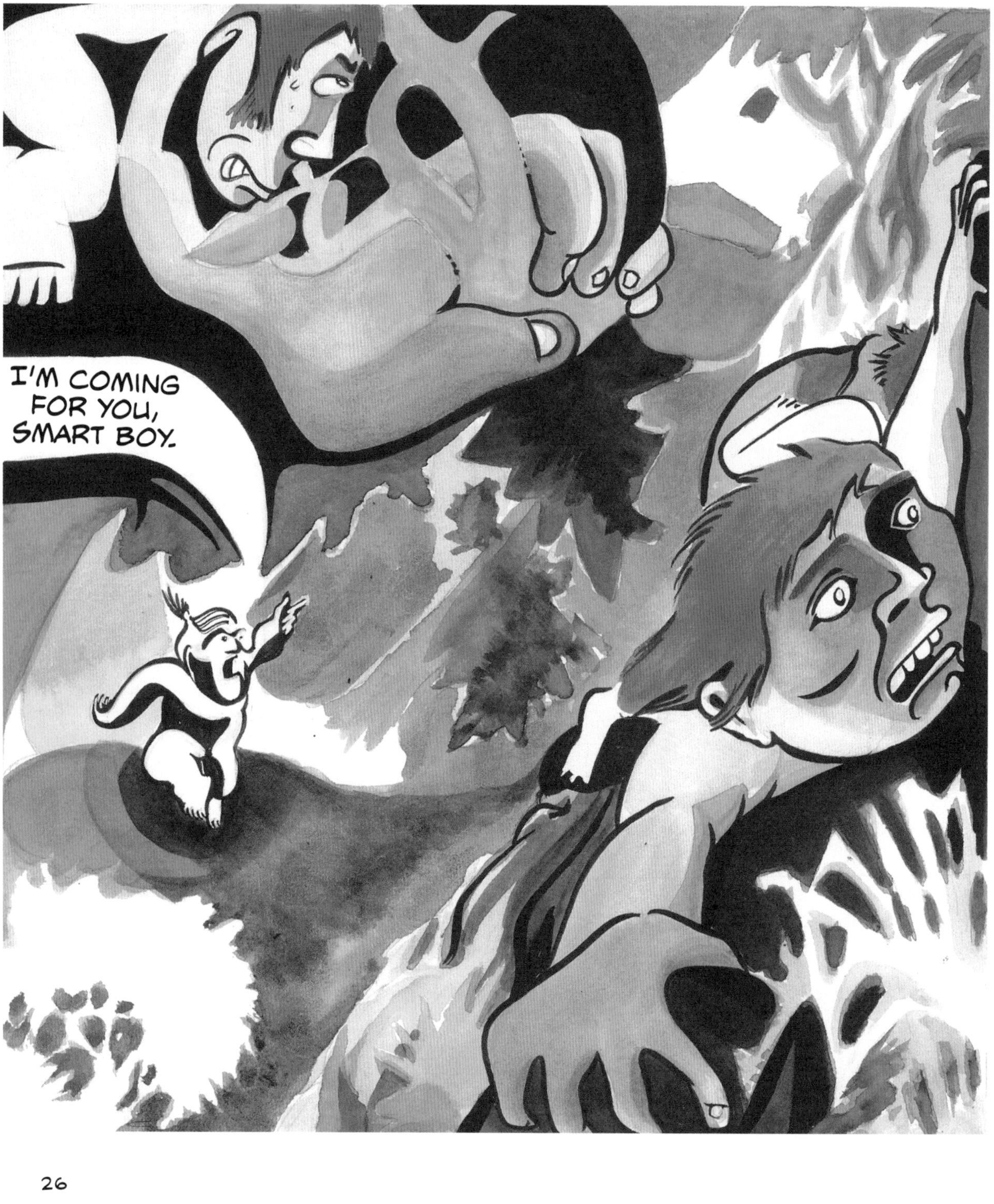
I'M COMING FOR YOU, SMART BOY.

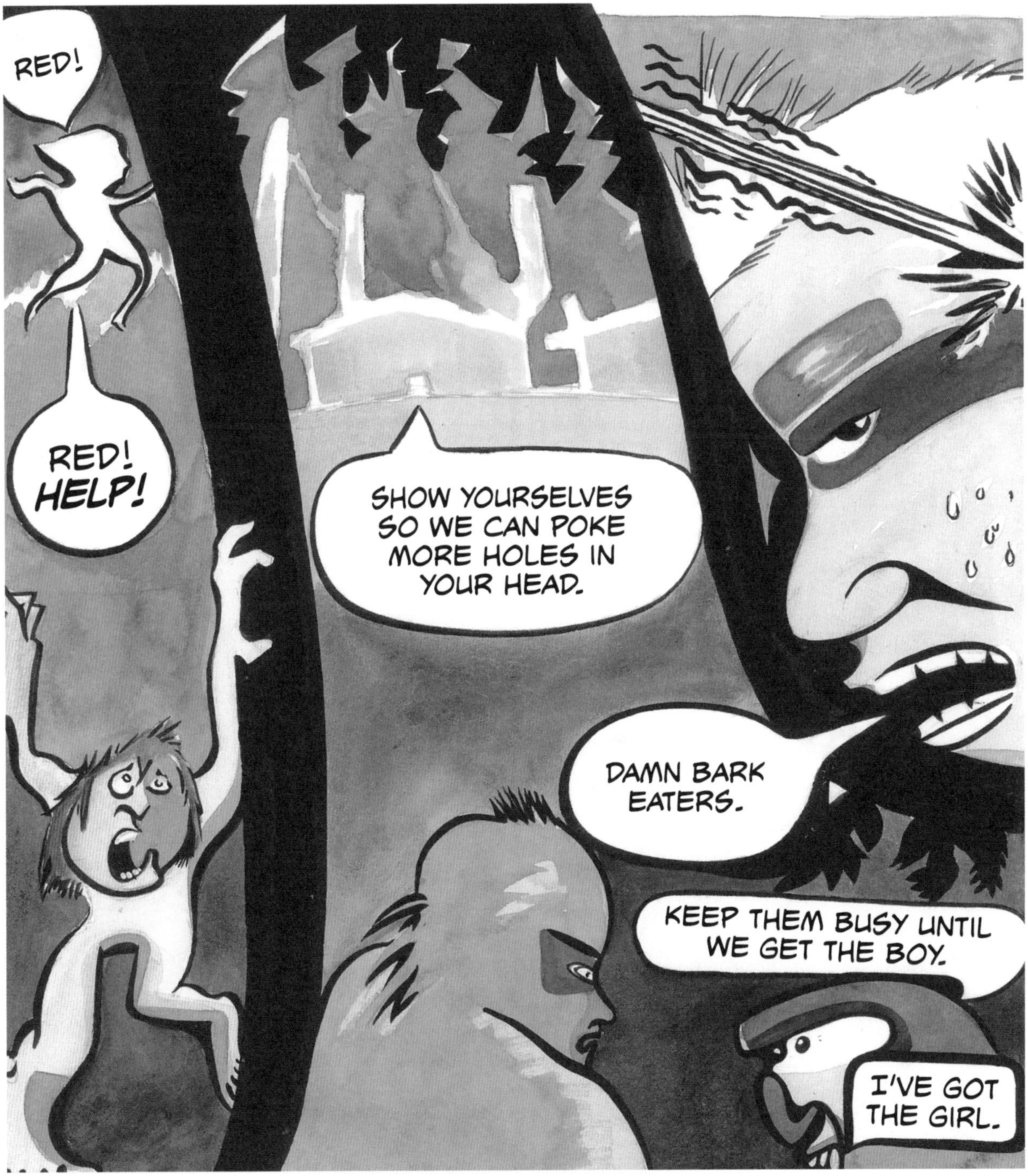
RED!
RED! HELP!
SHOW YOURSELVES SO WE CAN POKE MORE HOLES IN YOUR HEAD.
DAMN BARK EATERS.
KEEP THEM BUSY UNTIL WE GET THE BOY.
I'VE GOT THE GIRL.

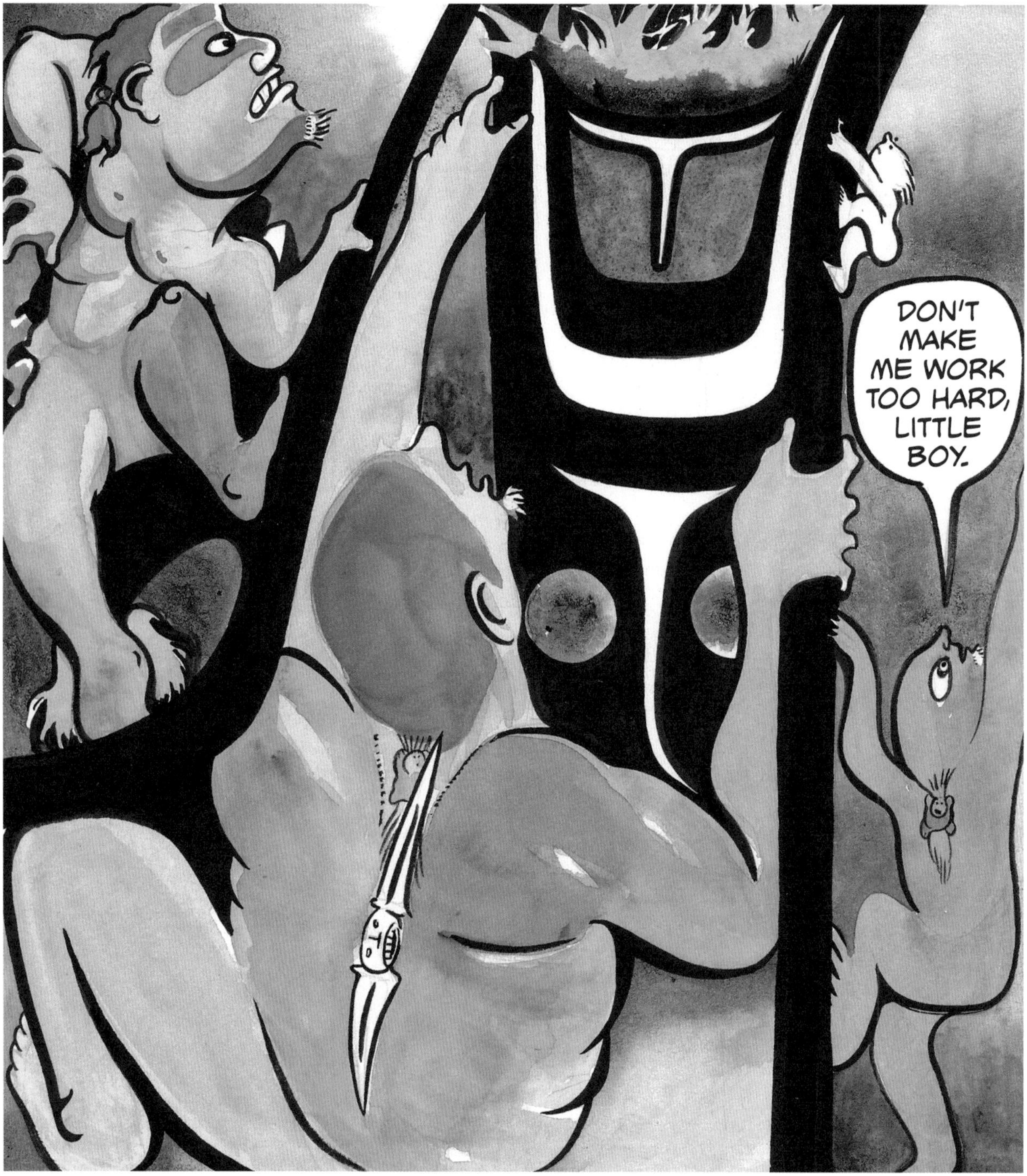
DON'T MAKE ME WORK TOO HARD, LITTLE BOY.

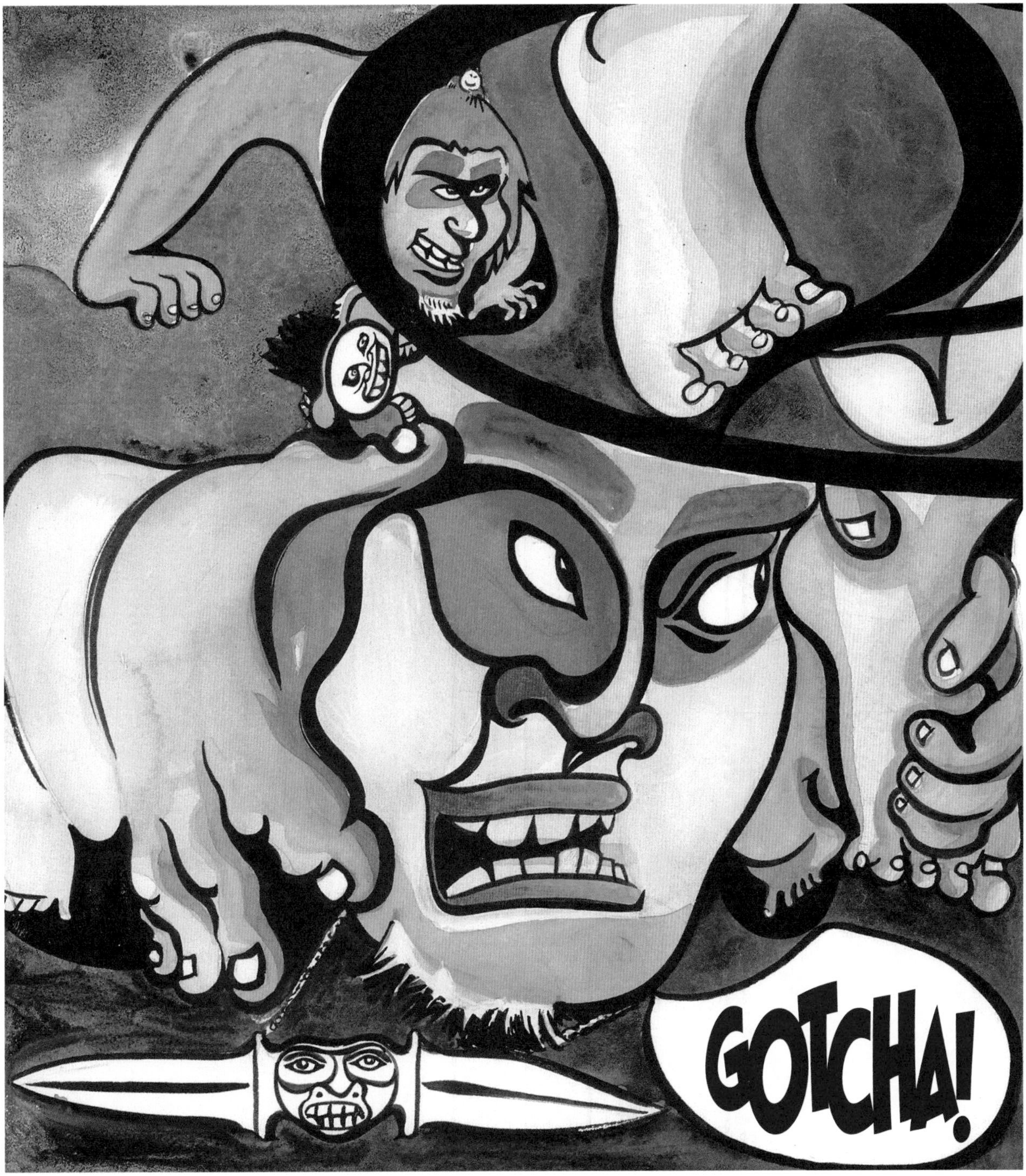
GOTCHA!

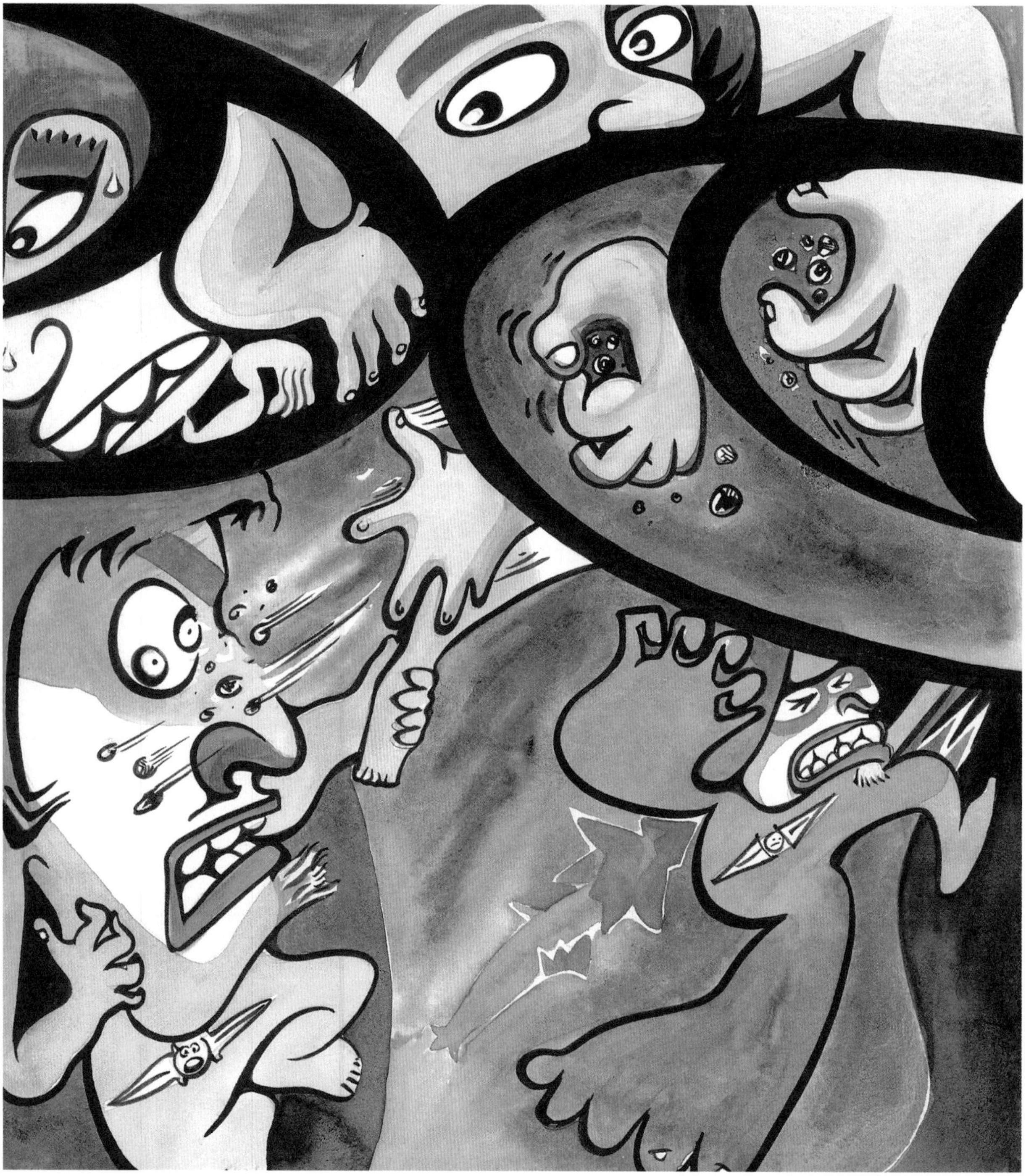

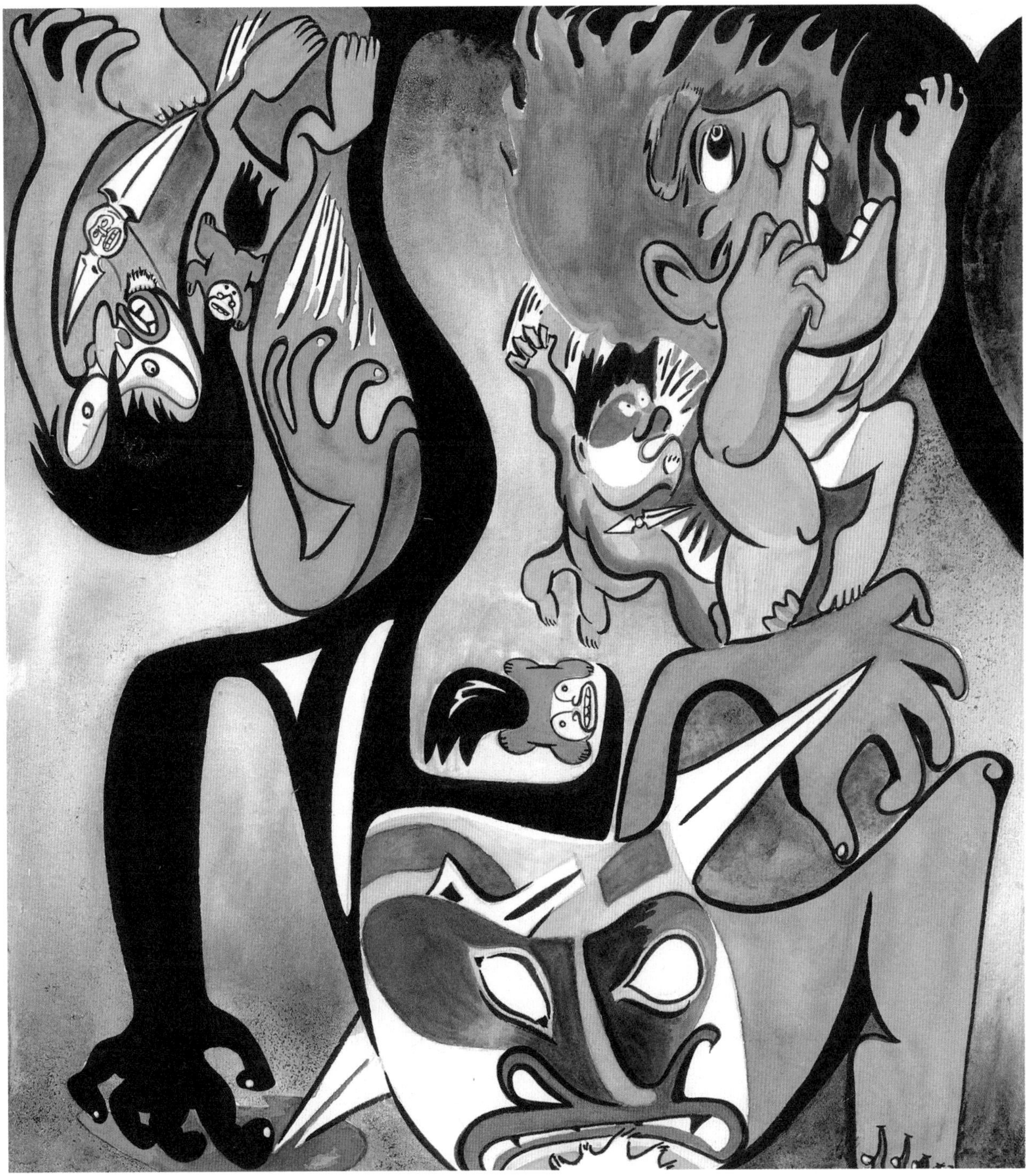

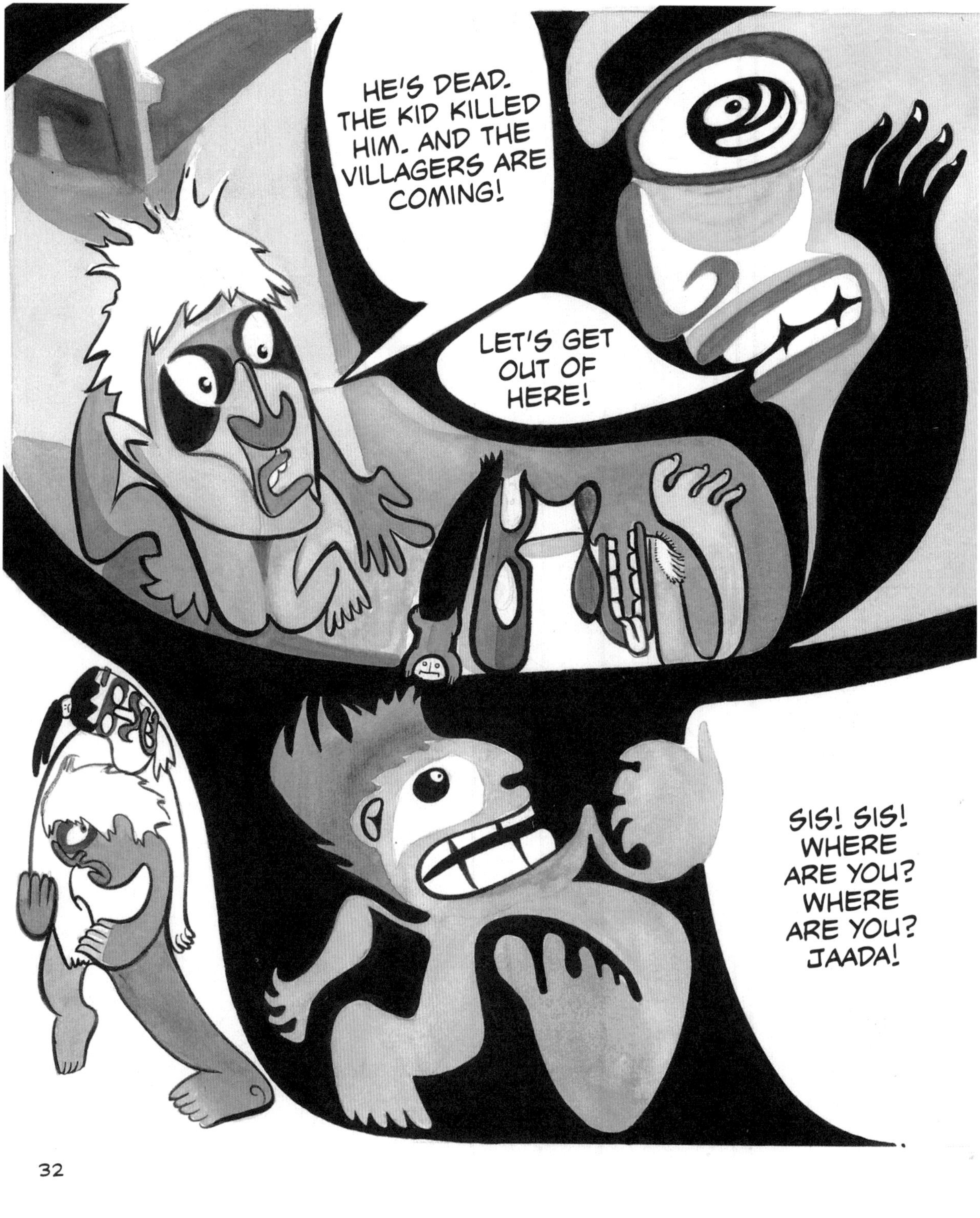
HE'S DEAD. THE KID KILLED HIM. AND THE VILLAGERS ARE COMING!
LET'S GET OUT OF HERE!
SIS! SIS! WHERE ARE YOU? WHERE ARE YOU? JAADA!

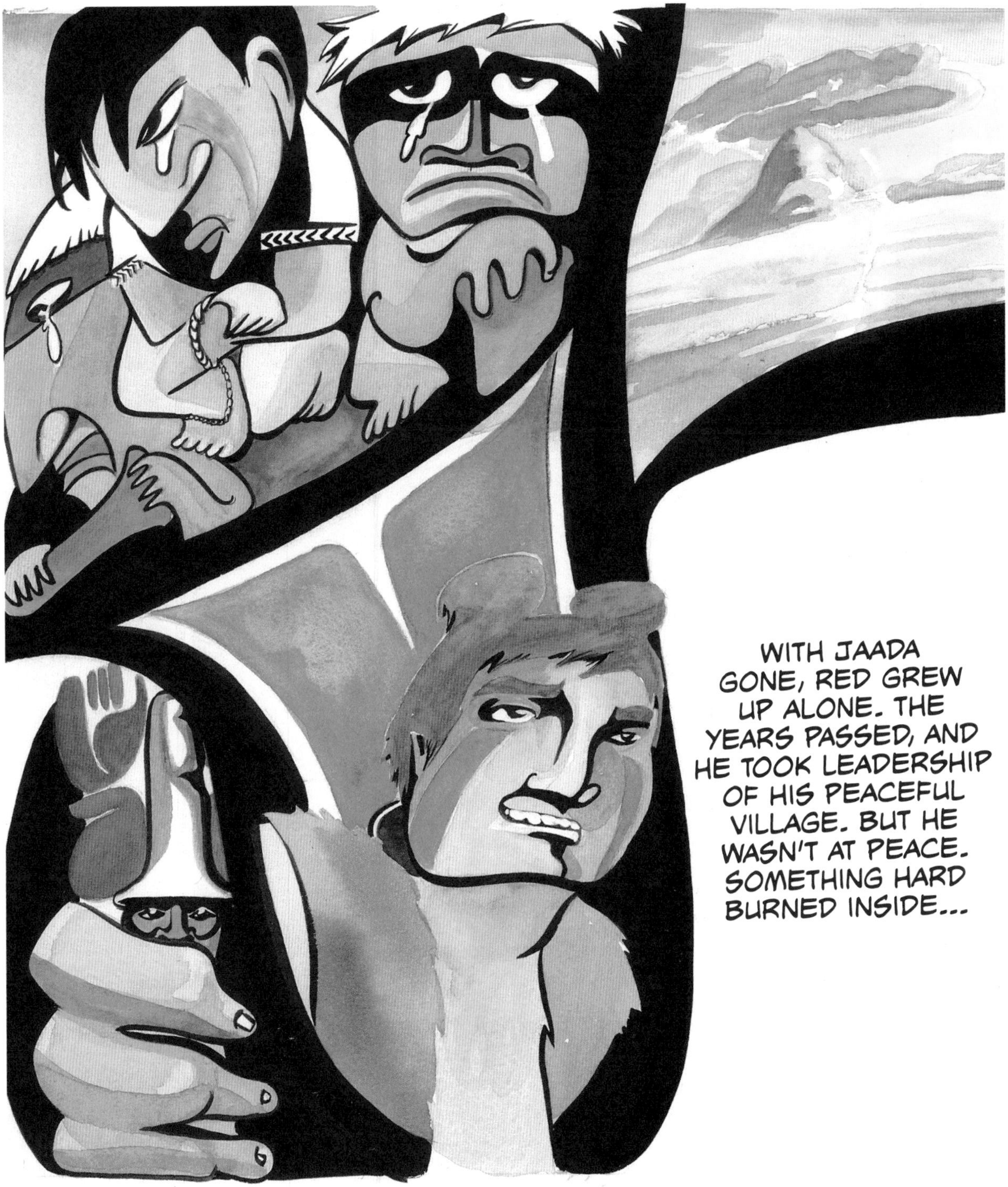

WITH JAADA
GONE, RED GREW
UP ALONE. THE
YEARS PASSED, AND
HE TOOK LEADERSHIP
OF HIS PEACEFUL
VILLAGE. BUT HE
WASN'T AT PEACE.
SOMETHING HARD
BURNED INSIDE...

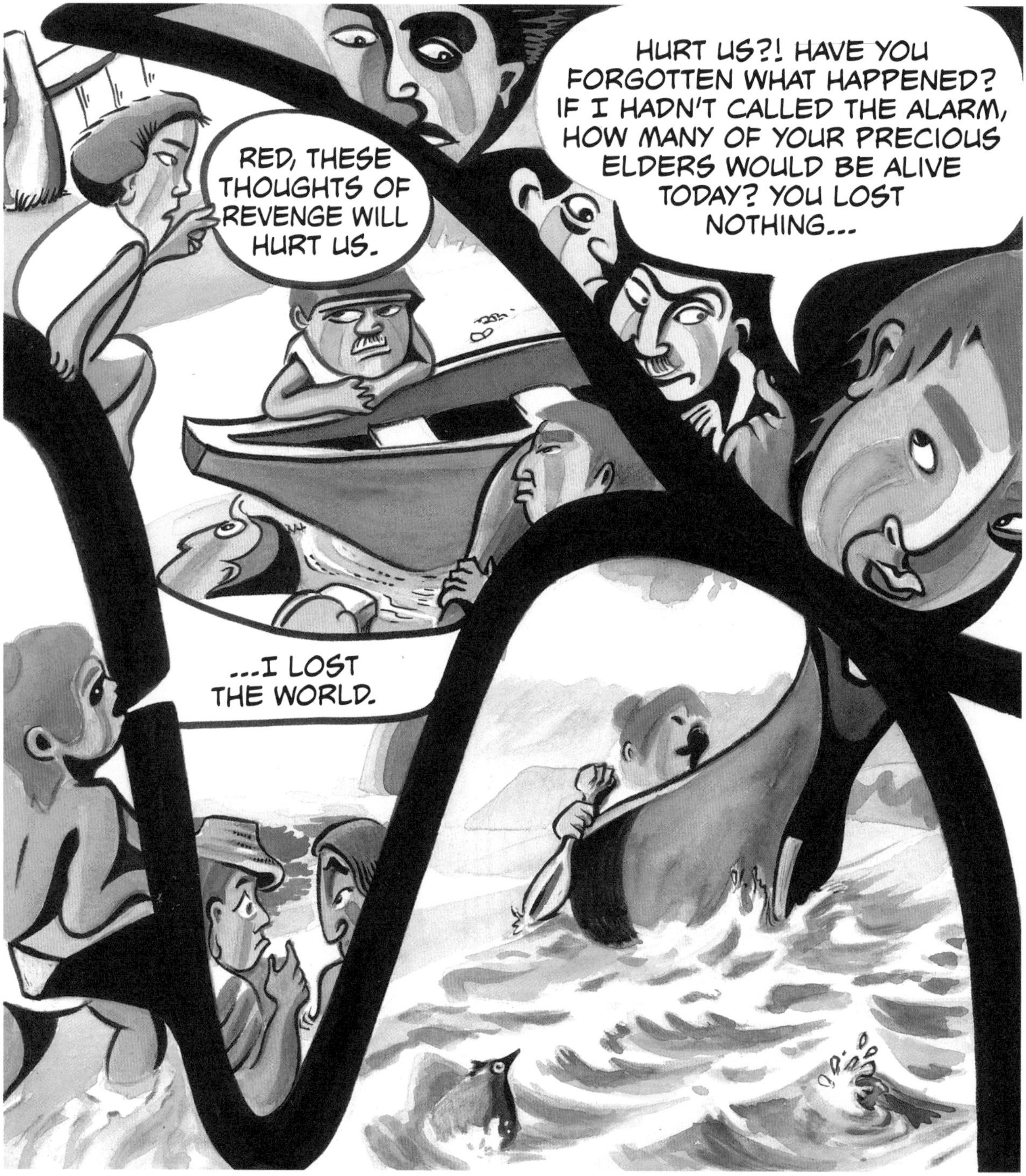
RED, THESE THOUGHTS OF REVENGE WILL HURT US.
HURT US?! HAVE YOU FORGOTTEN WHAT HAPPENED? IF I HADN'T CALLED THE ALARM, HOW MANY OF YOUR PRECIOUS ELDERS WOULD BE ALIVE TODAY? YOU LOST NOTHING...
...I LOST THE WORLD.

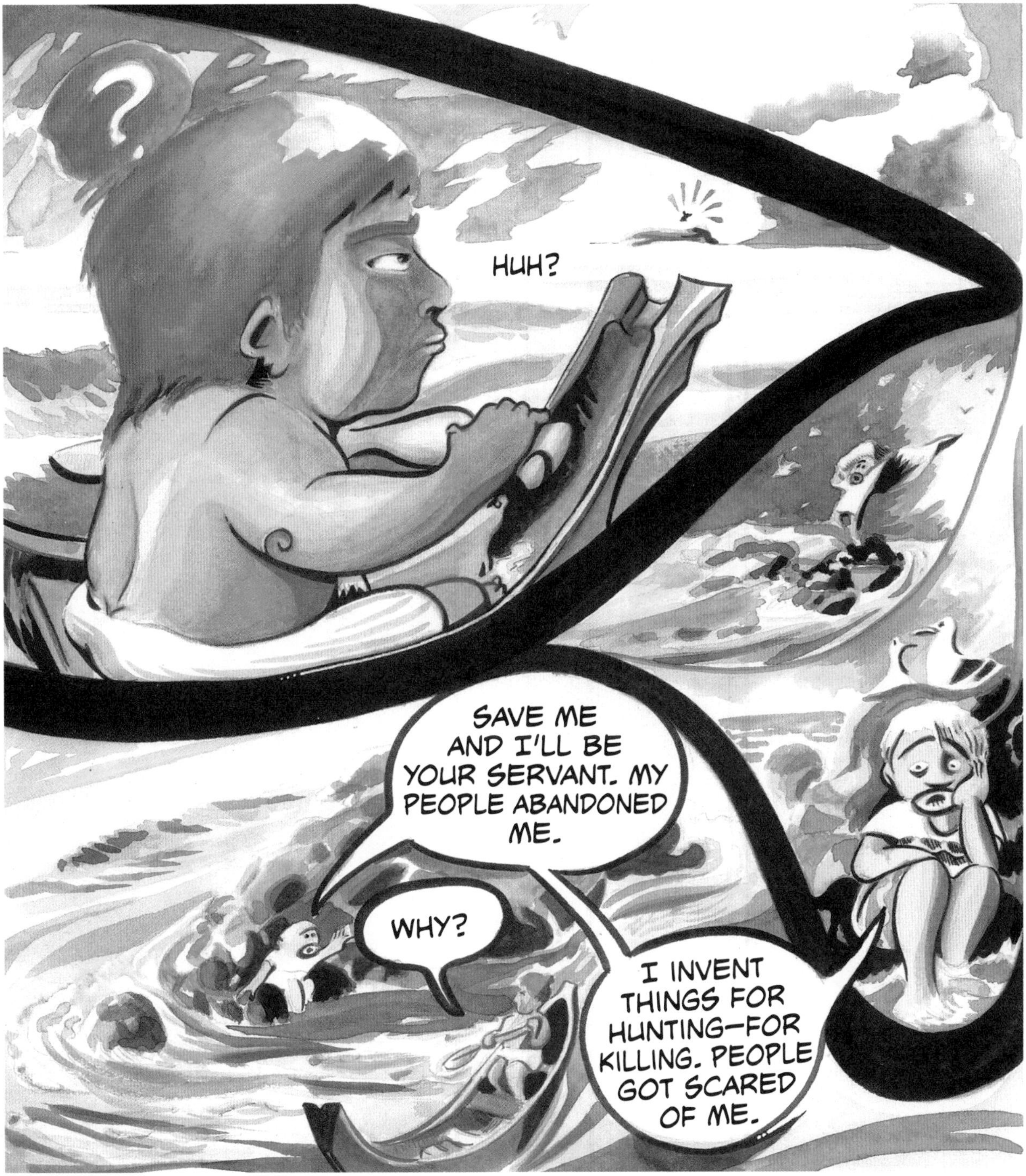
?
HUH?
SAVE ME AND I'LL BE YOUR SERVANT. MY PEOPLE ABANDONED ME.
WHY?
I INVENT THINGS FOR HUNTING—FOR KILLING. PEOPLE GOT SCARED OF ME.

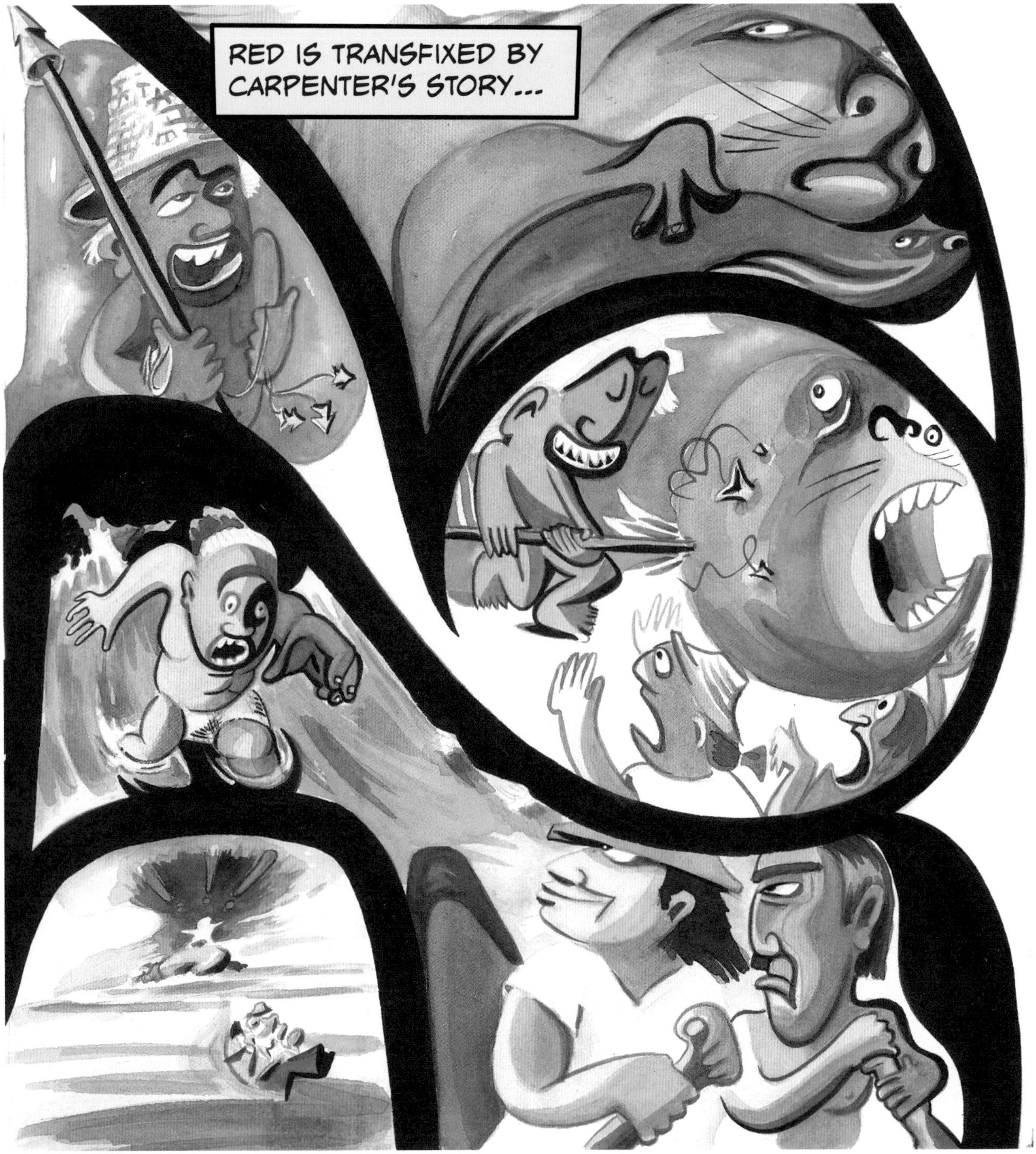
RED IS TRANSFIXED BY
CARPENTER'S STORY...

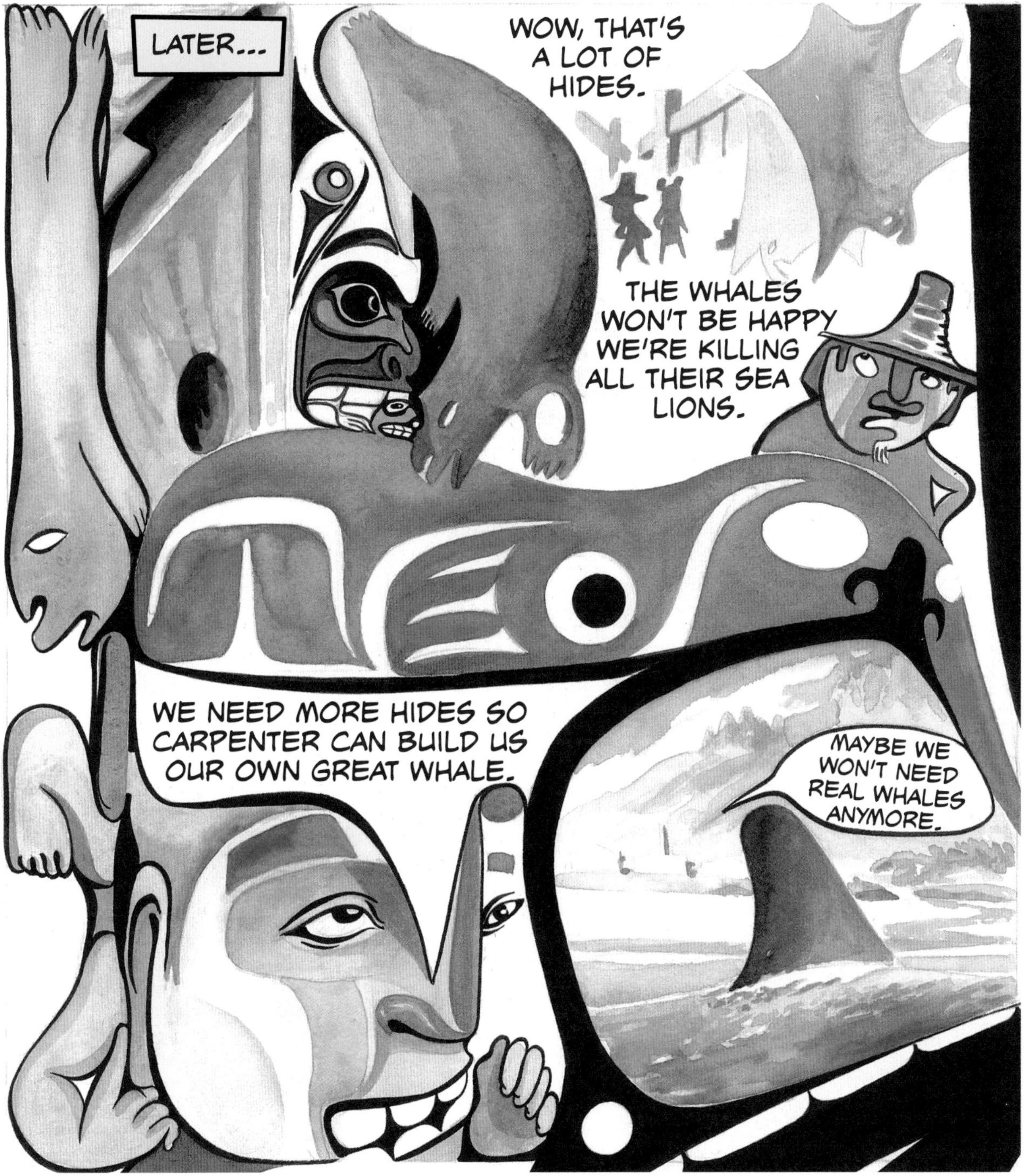
LATER...
WOW, THAT'S A LOT OF HIDES.
THE WHALES WON'T BE HAPPY WE'RE KILLING ALL THEIR SEA LIONS.
WE NEED MORE HIDES SO CARPENTER CAN BUILD US OUR OWN GREAT WHALE.
MAYBE WE WON'T NEED REAL WHALES ANYMORE.

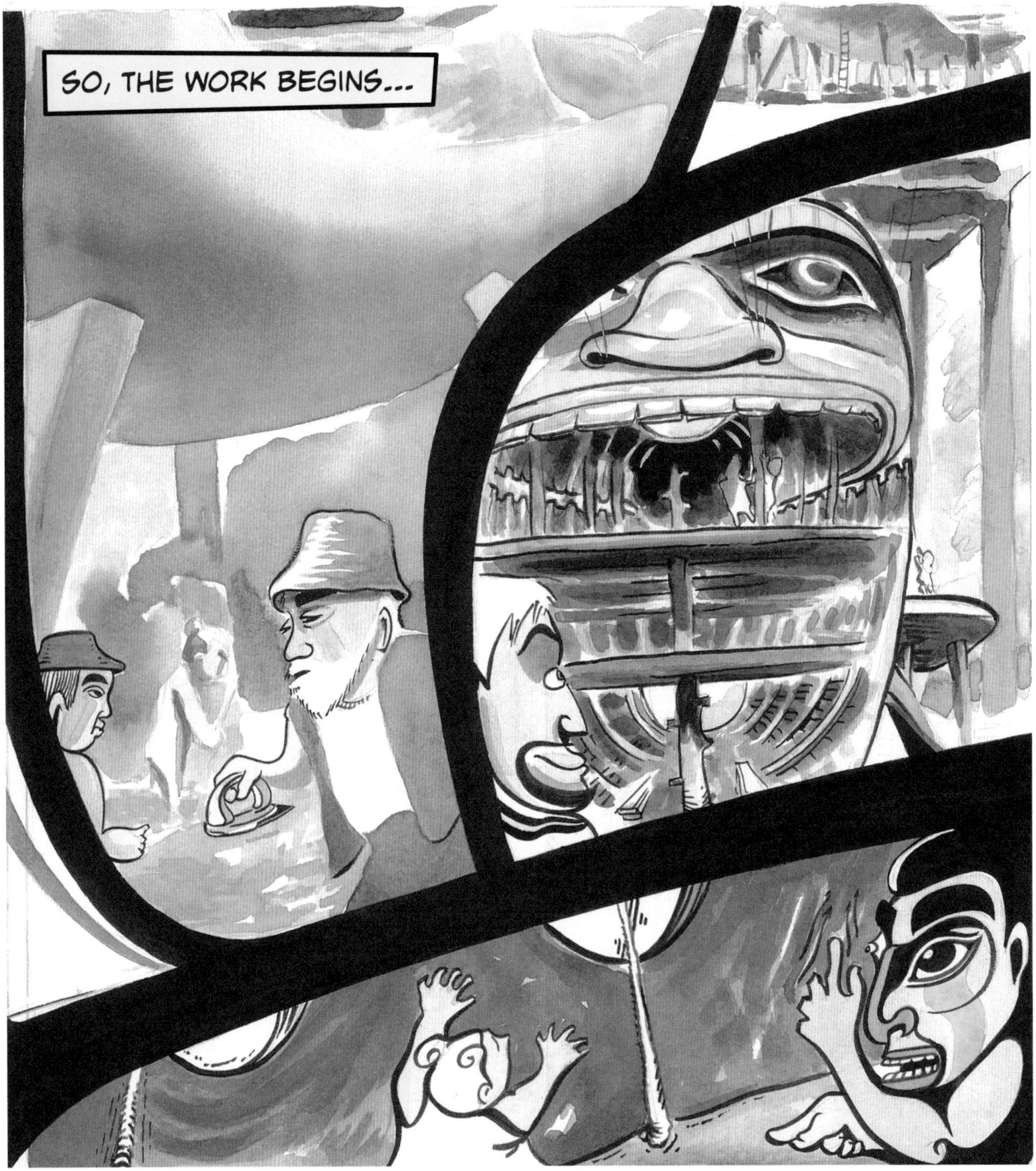
SO, THE WORK BEGINS...

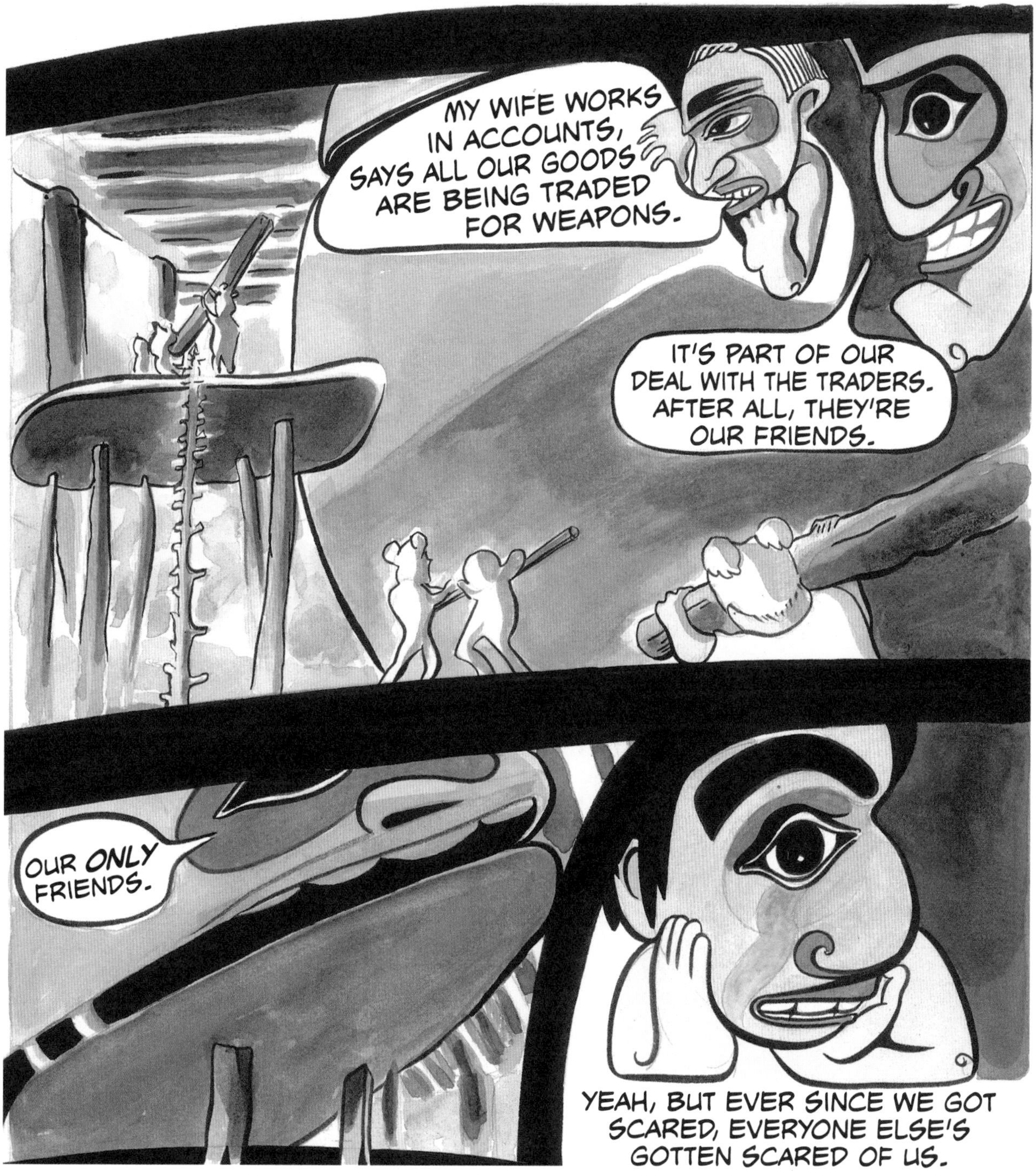
MY WIFE WORKS IN ACCOUNTS, SAYS ALL OUR GOODS ARE BEING TRADED FOR WEAPONS.
IT'S PART OF OUR DEAL WITH THE TRADERS. AFTER ALL, THEY'RE OUR FRIENDS.
OUR ONLY FRIENDS.
YEAH, BUT EVER SINCE WE GOT SCARED, EVERYONE ELSE'S GOTTEN SCARED OF US.

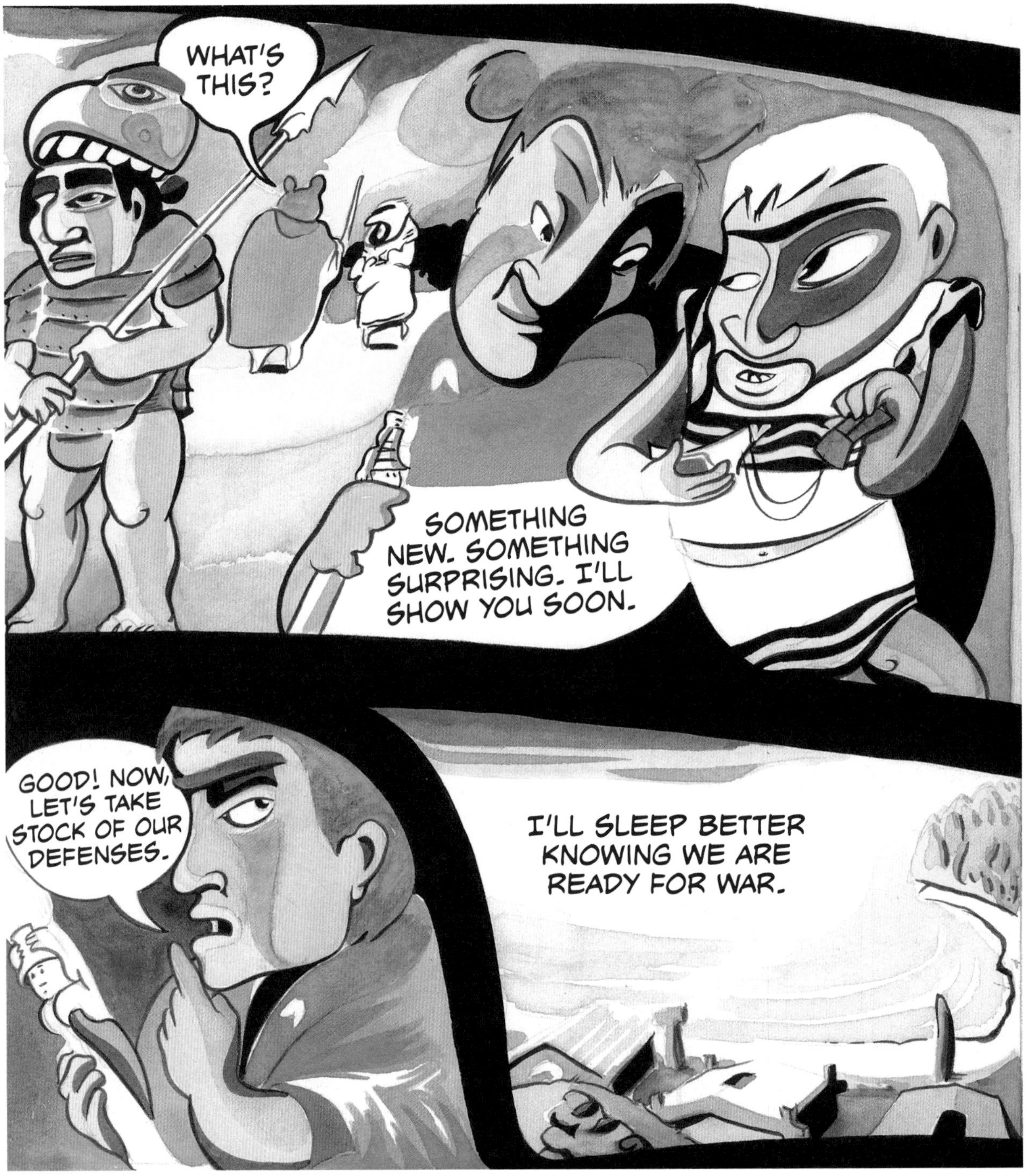
WHAT'S THIS?
SOMETHING NEW. SOMETHING SURPRISING. I'LL SHOW YOU SOON.
GOOD! NOW, LET'S TAKE STOCK OF OUR DEFENSES.
I'LL SLEEP BETTER KNOWING WE ARE READY FOR WAR.

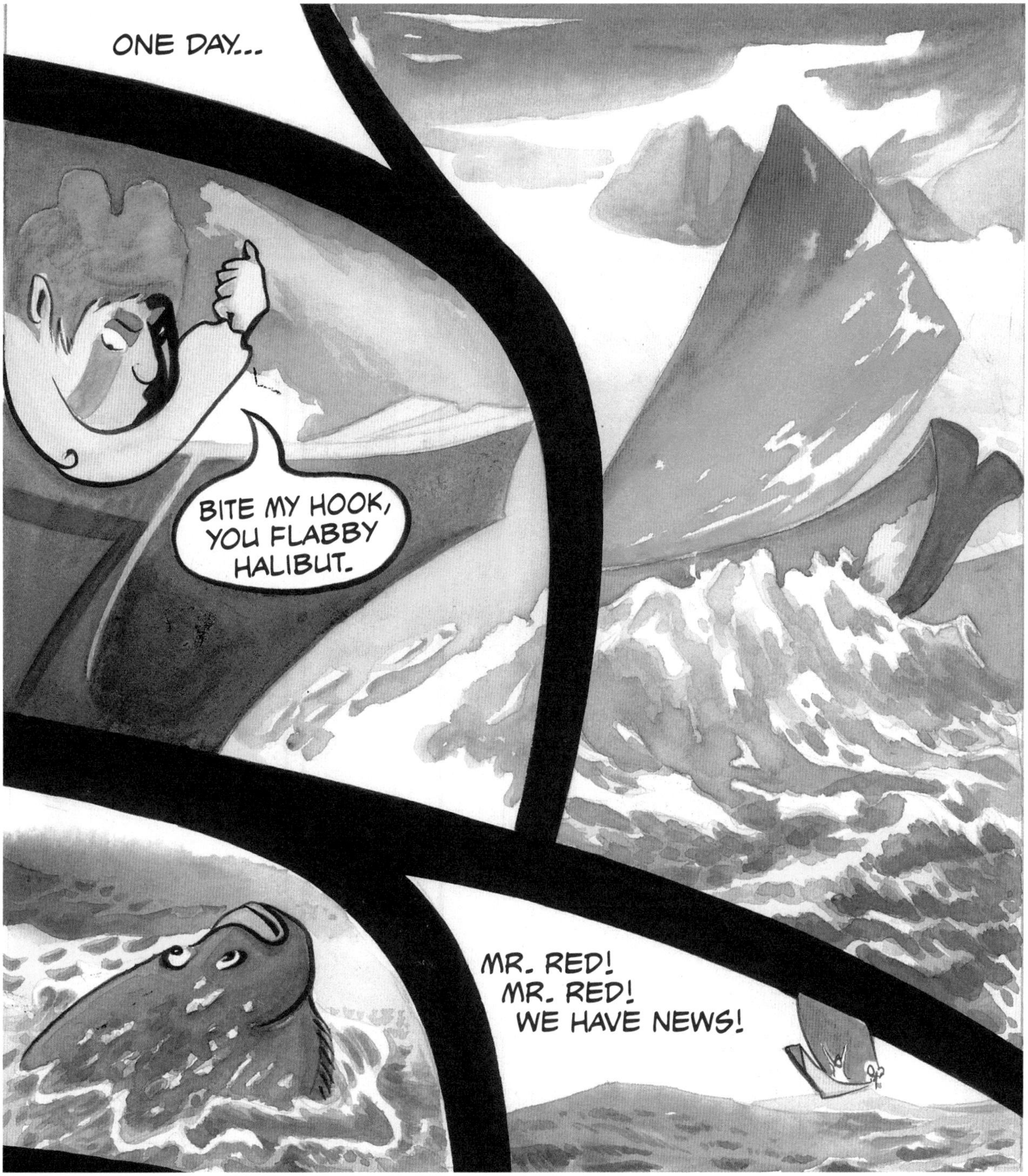
ONE DAY...
BITE MY HOOK, YOU FLABBY HALIBUT.
MR. RED! MR. RED! WE HAVE NEWS!

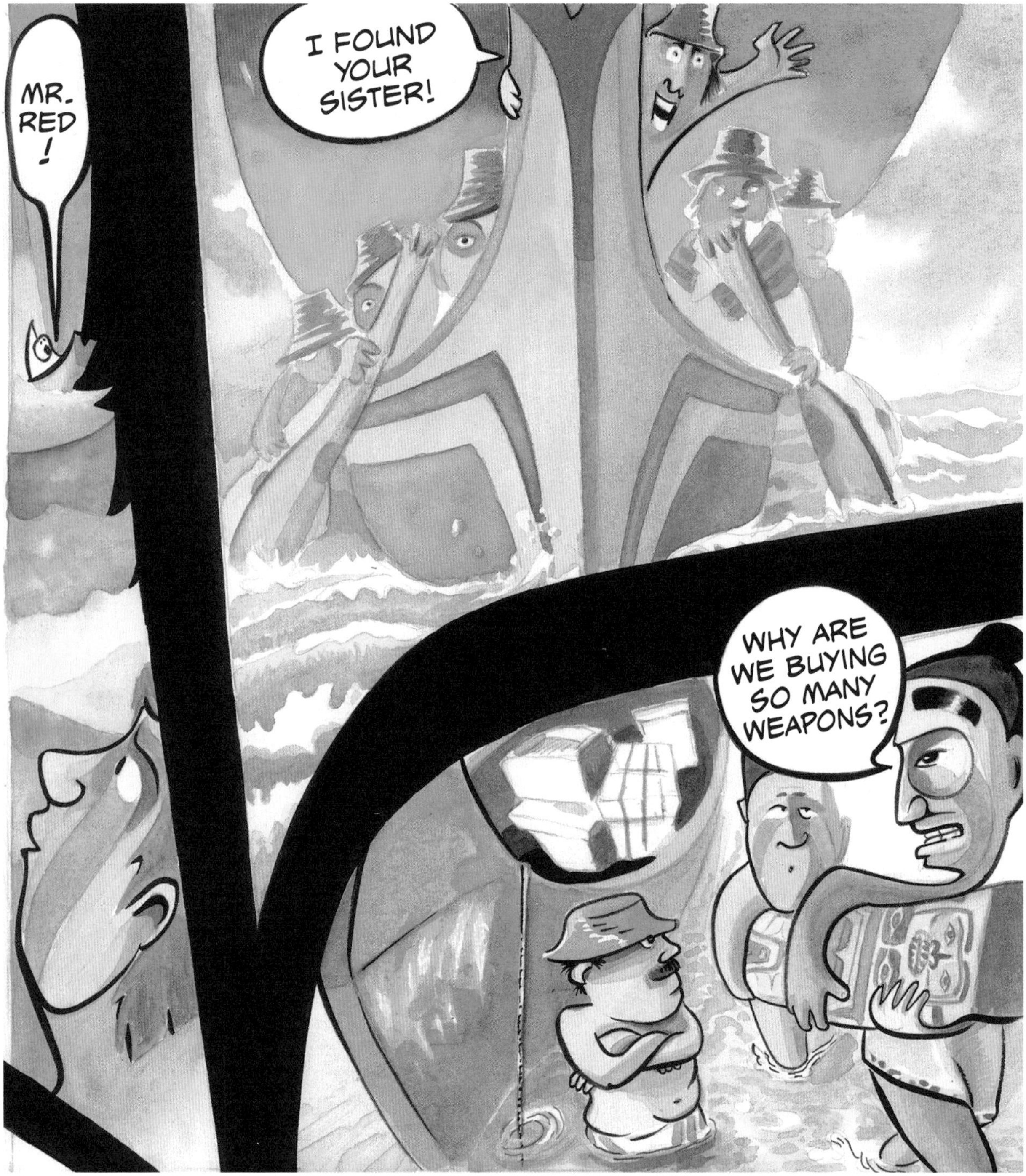
I FOUND YOUR SISTER!
MR. RED!
WHY ARE WE BUYING SO MANY WEAPONS?

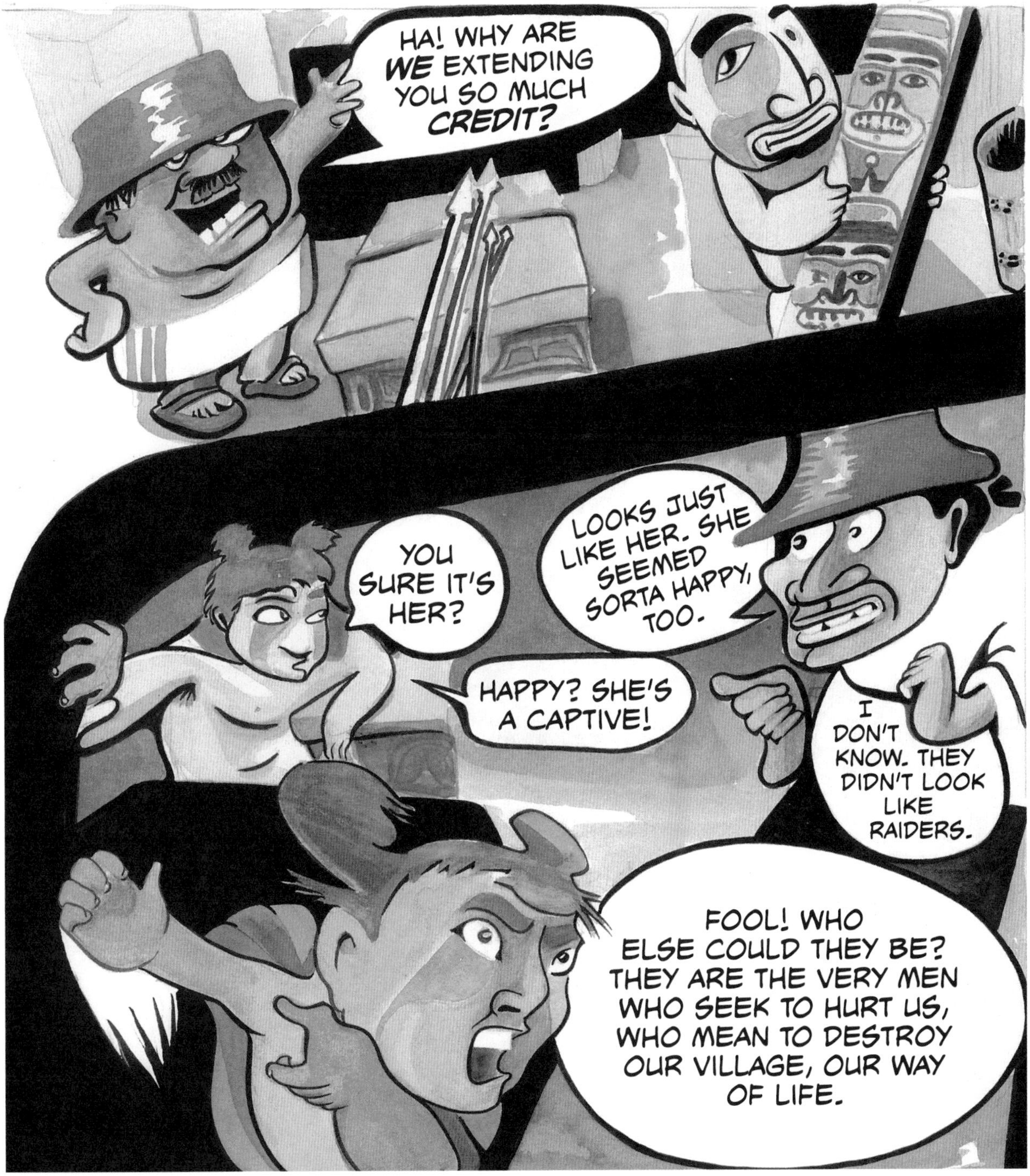
HA! WHY ARE WE EXTENDING YOU SO MUCH CREDIT?
YOU SURE IT'S HER?
LOOKS JUST LIKE HER. SHE SEEMED SORTA HAPPY, TOO.
HAPPY? SHE'S A CAPTIVE!
I DON'T KNOW. THEY DIDN'T LOOK LIKE RAIDERS.
FOOL! WHO ELSE COULD THEY BE? THEY ARE THE VERY MEN WHO SEEK TO HURT US, WHO MEAN TO DESTROY OUR VILLAGE, OUR WAY OF LIFE.

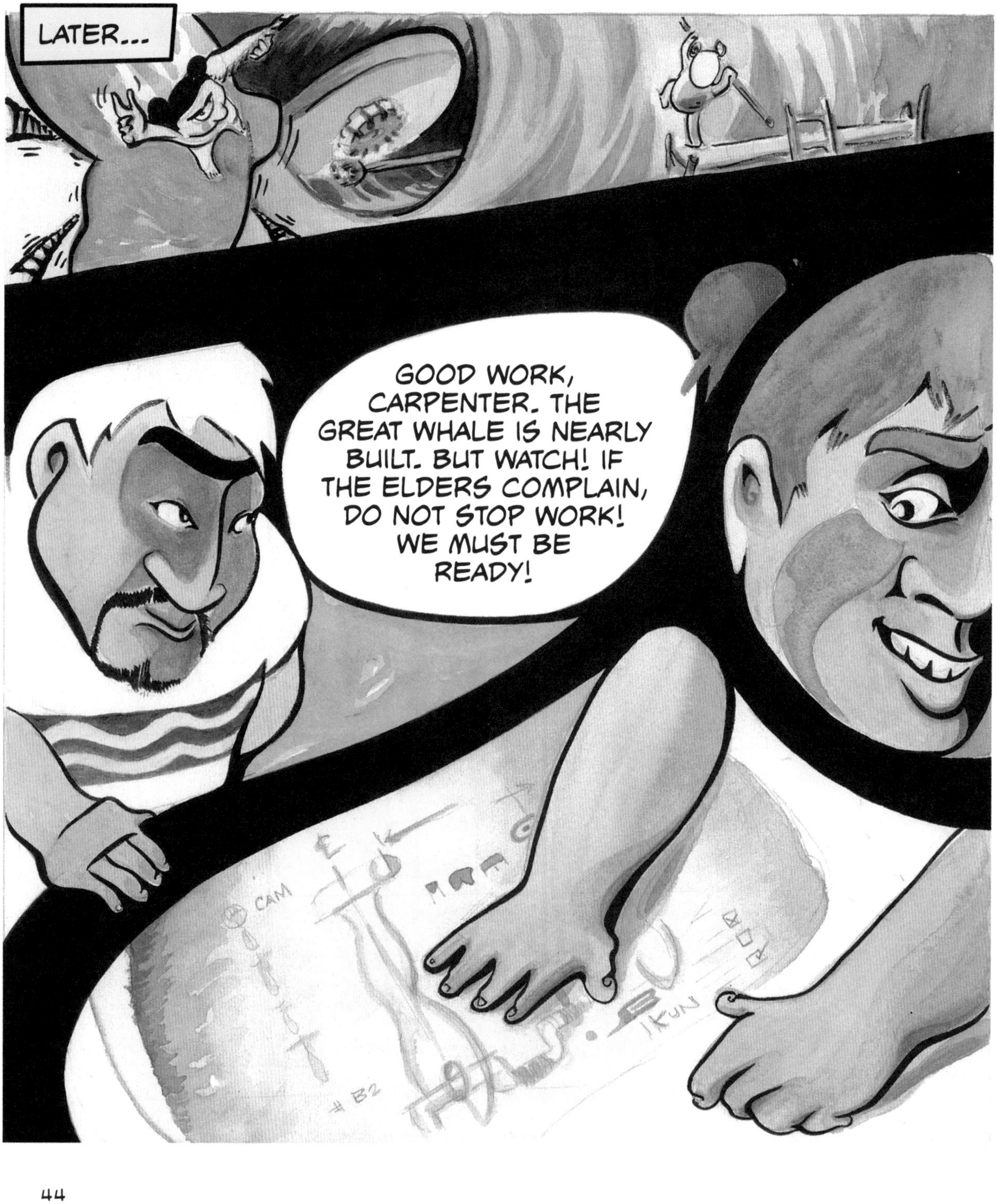
LATER...
GOOD WORK, CARPENTER. THE GREAT WHALE IS NEARLY BUILT. BUT WATCH! IF THE ELDERS COMPLAIN, DO NOT STOP WORK! WE MUST BE READY!

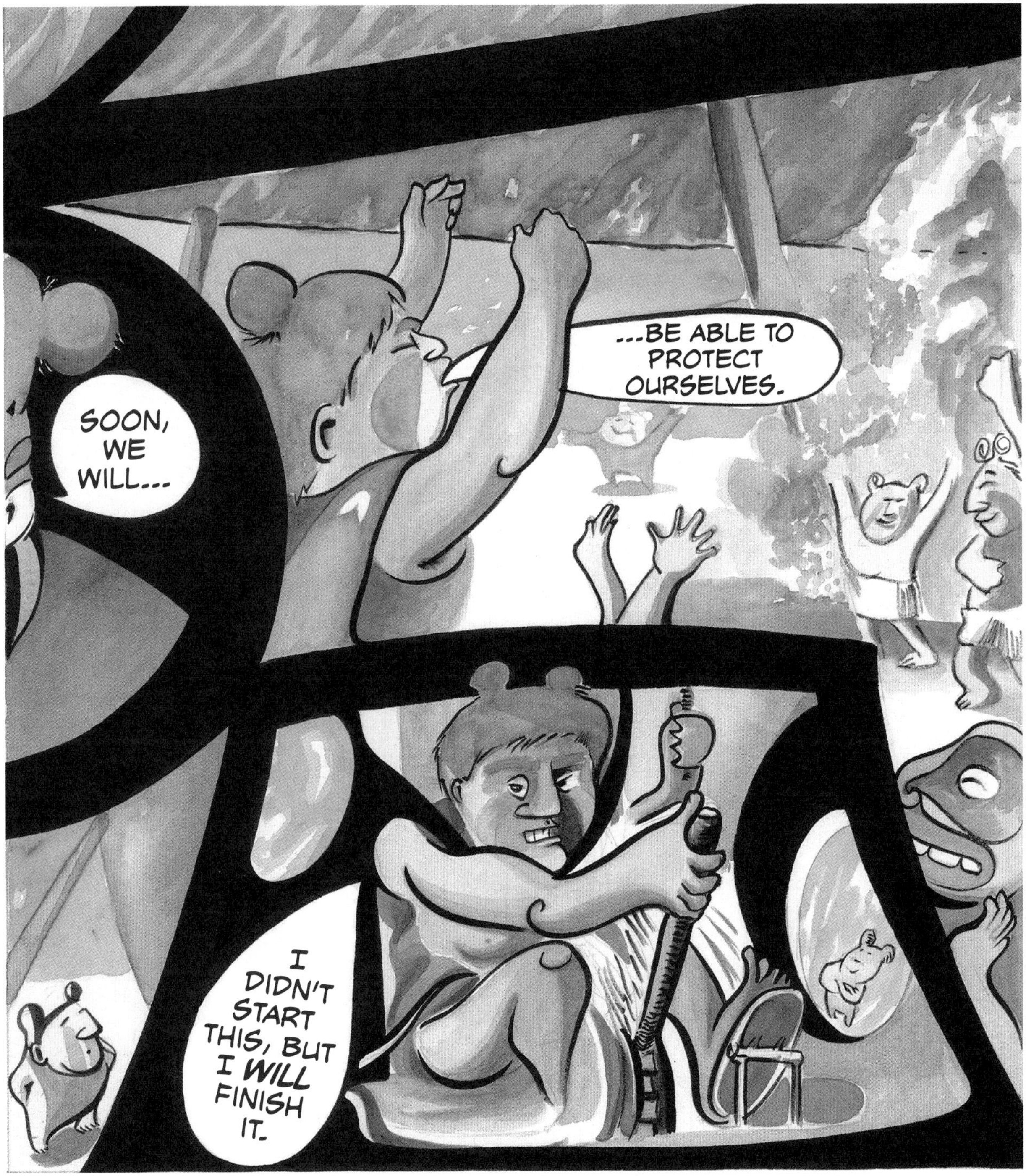
SOON, WE WILL...
...BE ABLE TO PROTECT OURSELVES.
I DIDN'T START THIS, BUT I WILL FINISH IT.

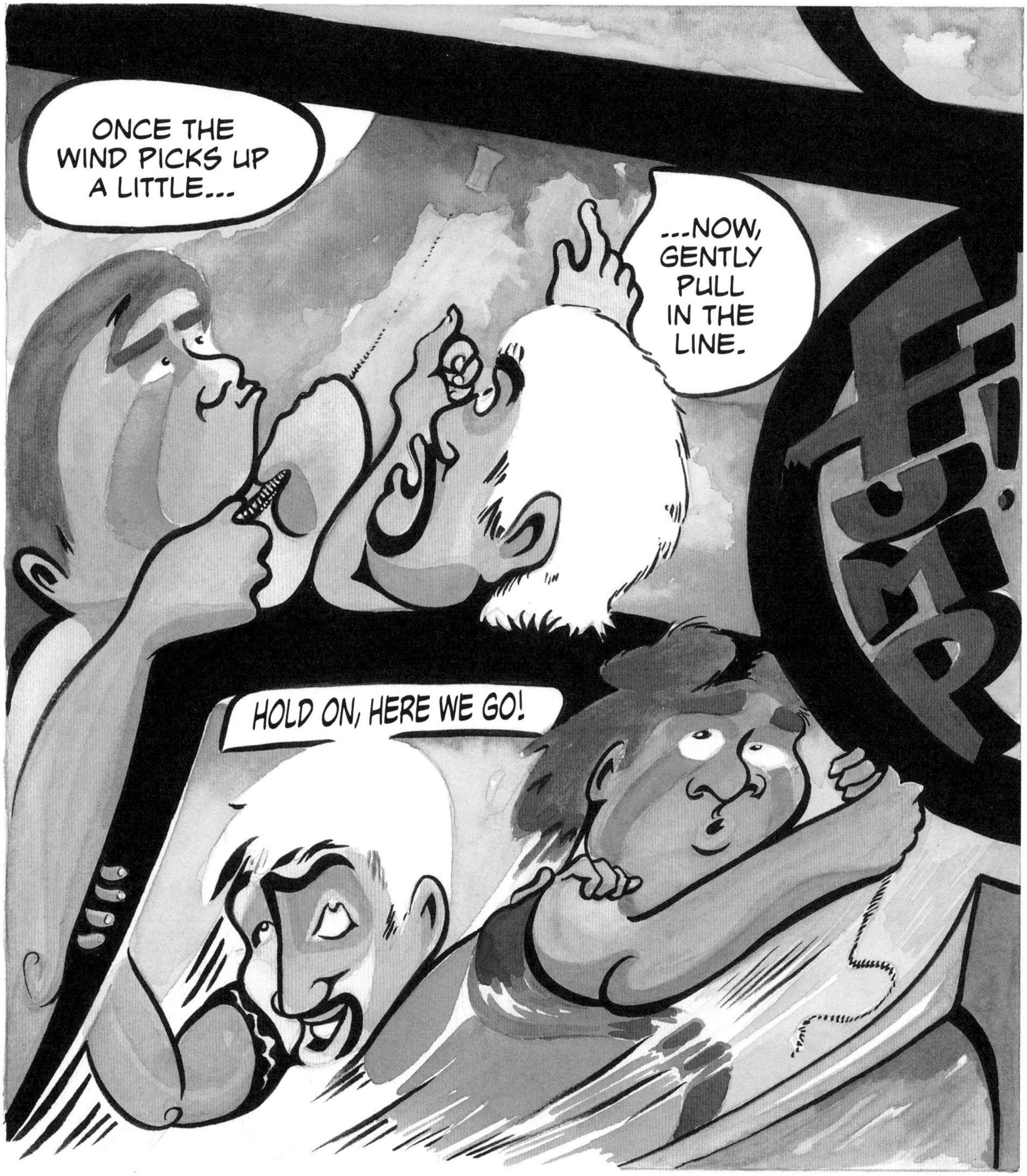
ONCE THE WIND PICKS UP A LITTLE...
...NOW, GENTLY PULL IN THE LINE.
FUMP!
HOLD ON, HERE WE GO!

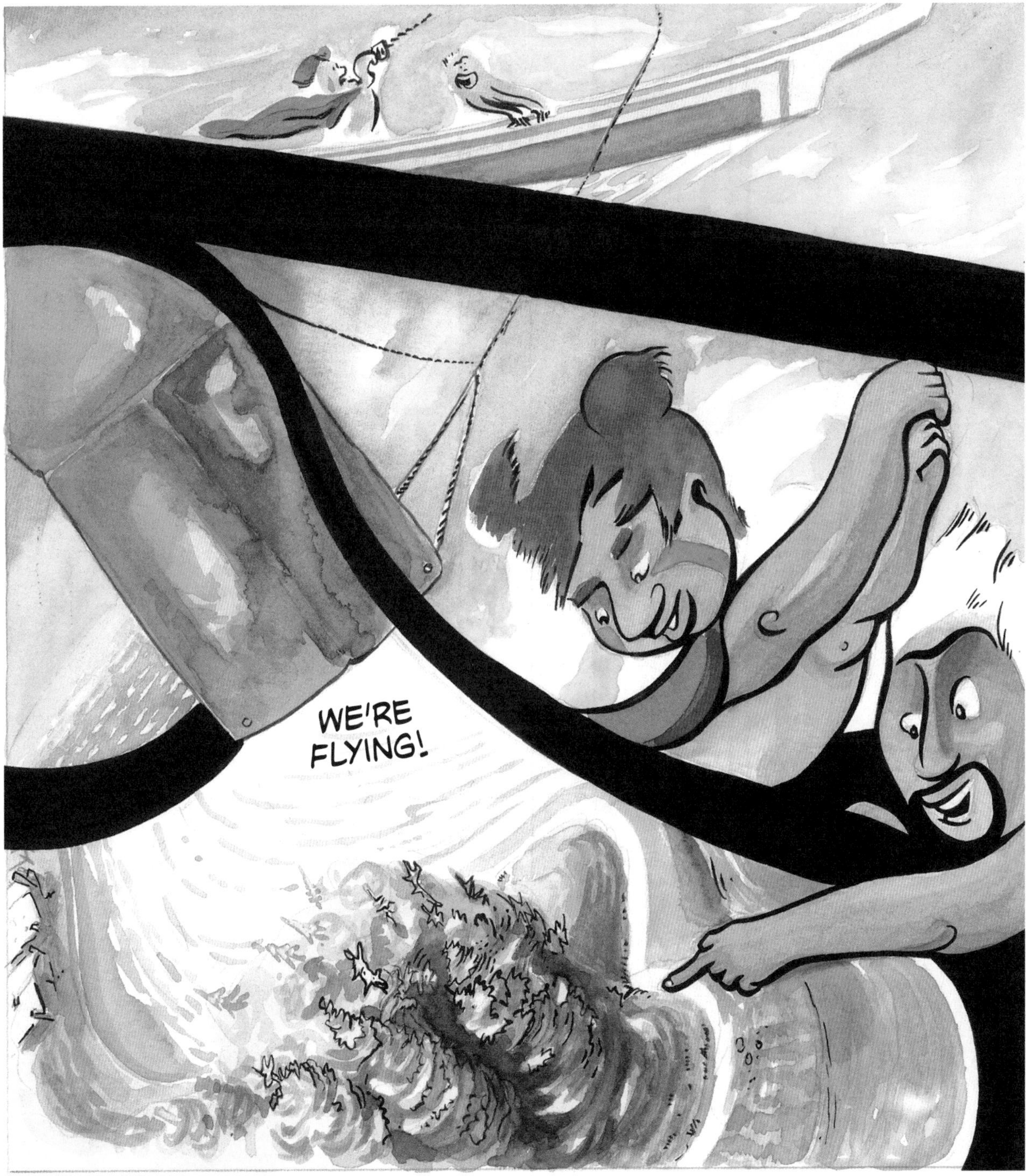
WE'RE FLYING!

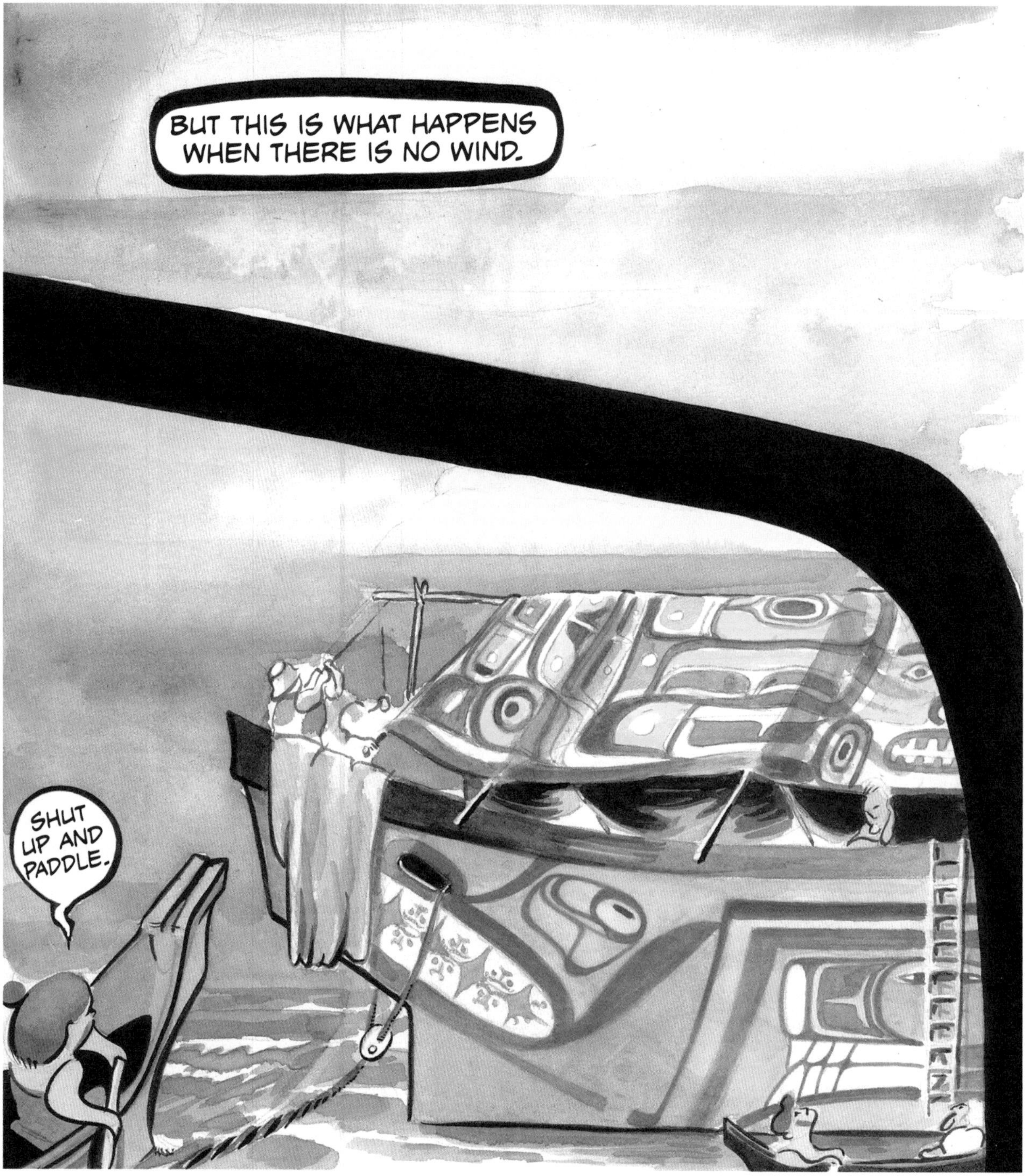
BUT THIS IS WHAT HAPPENS WHEN THERE IS NO WIND.
SHUT UP AND PADDLE.

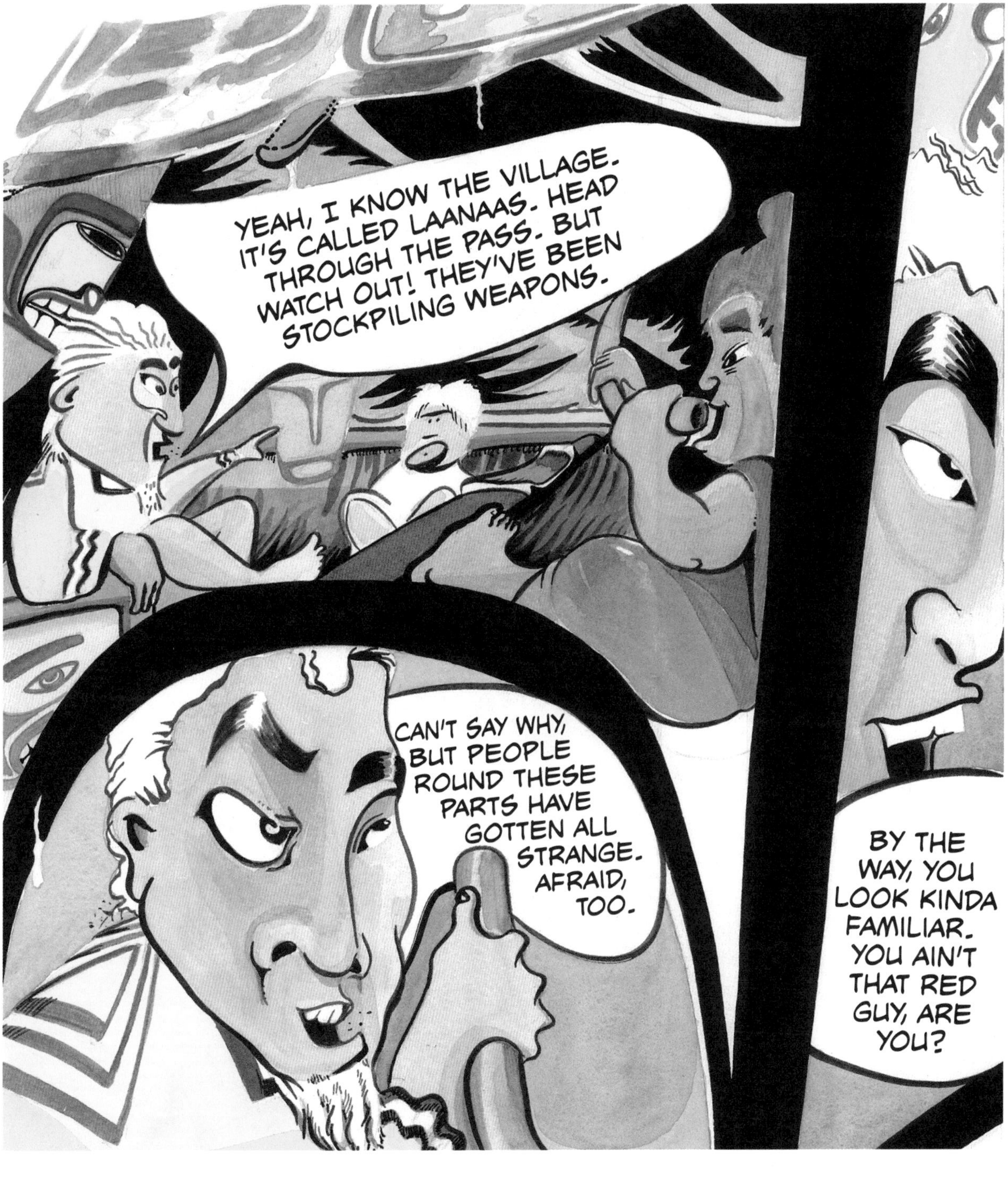
YEAH, I KNOW THE VILLAGE. IT'S CALLED LAANAAS. HEAD THROUGH THE PASS. BUT WATCH OUT! THEY'VE BEEN STOCKPILING WEAPONS.
CAN'T SAY WHY, BUT PEOPLE ROUND THESE PARTS HAVE GOTTEN ALL STRANGE. AFRAID, TOO.
BY THE WAY, YOU LOOK KINDA FAMILIAR. YOU AIN'T THAT RED GUY, ARE YOU?

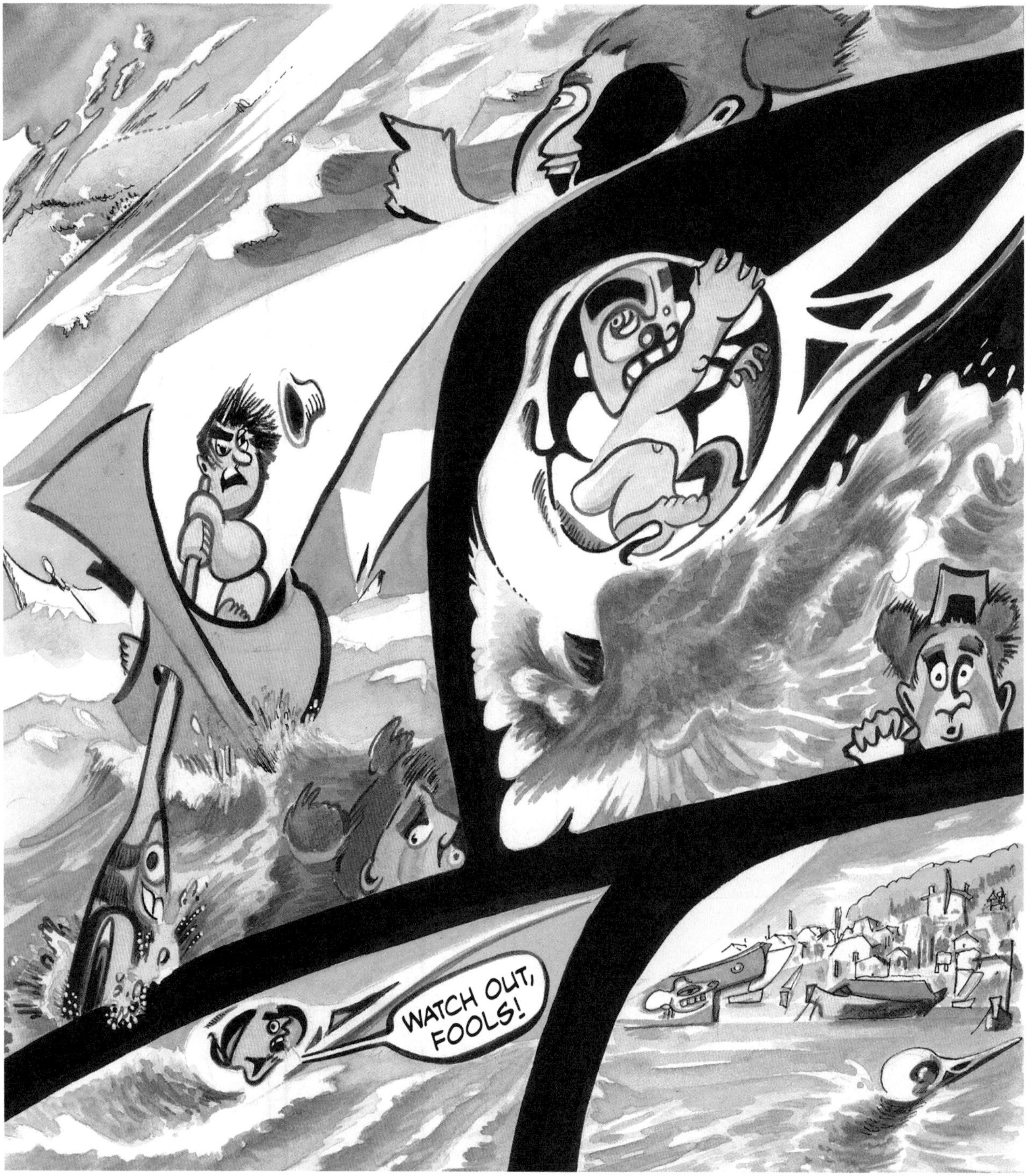
WATCH OUT, FOOLS!

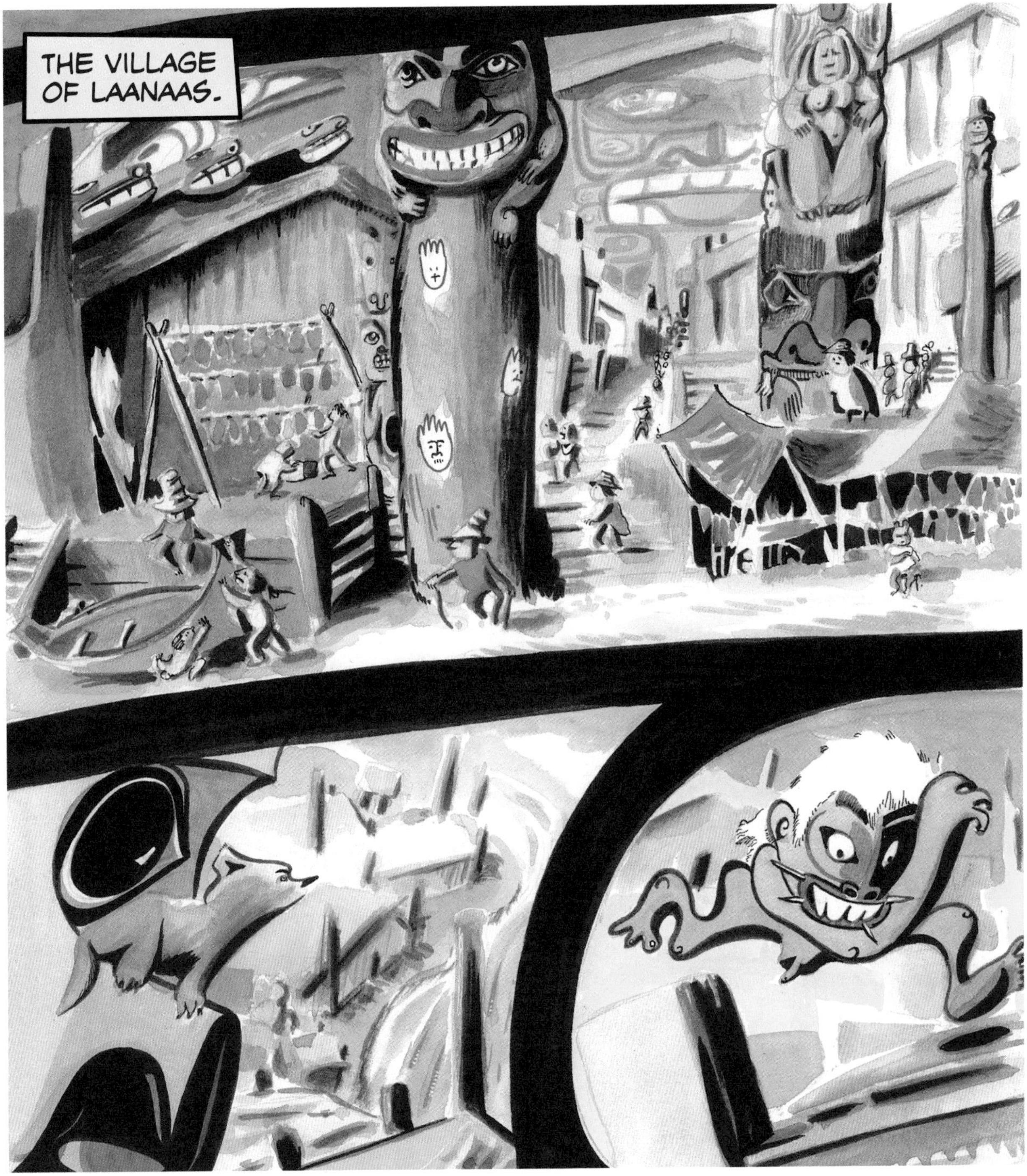
THE VILLAGE OF LAANAAS.

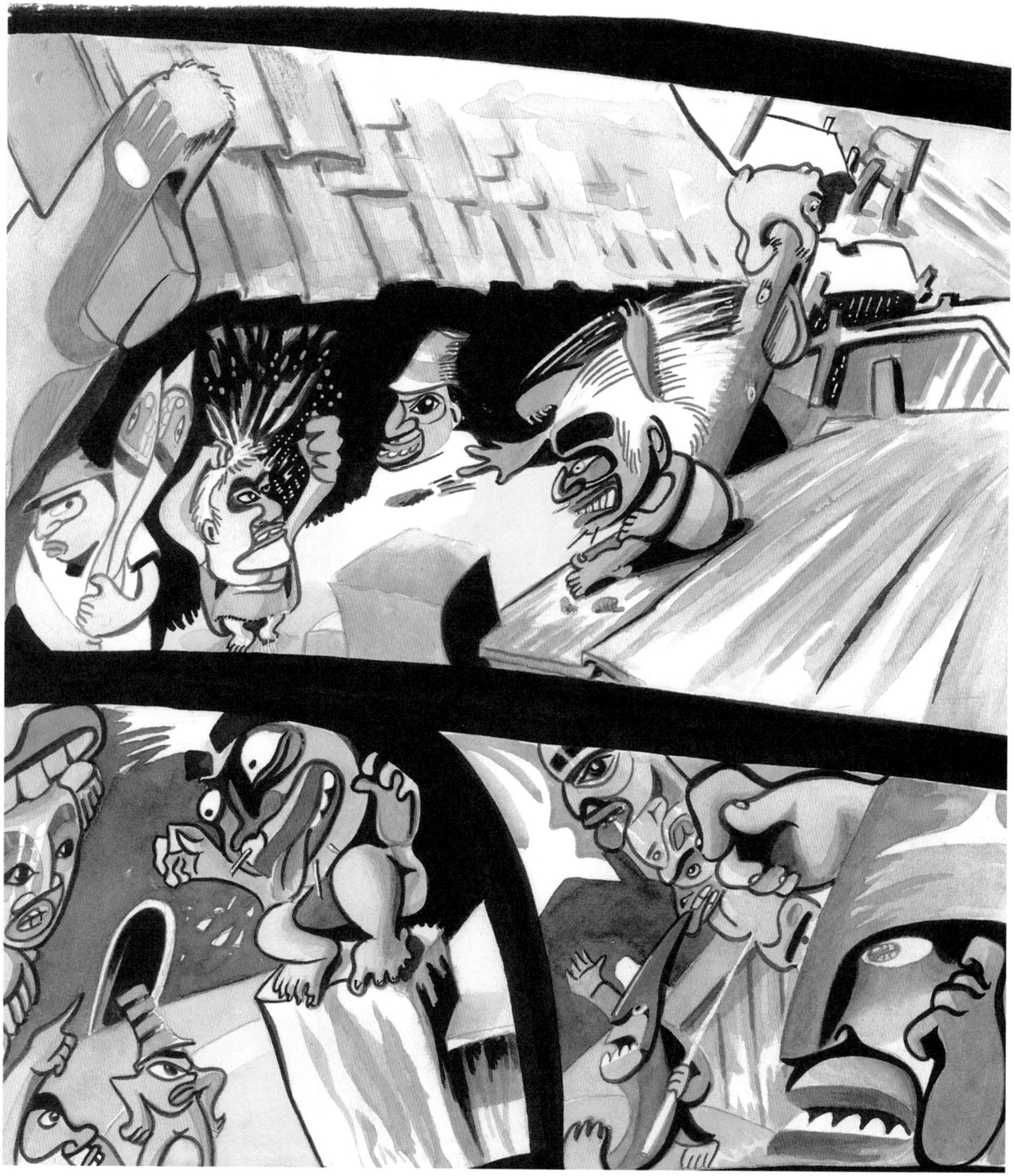

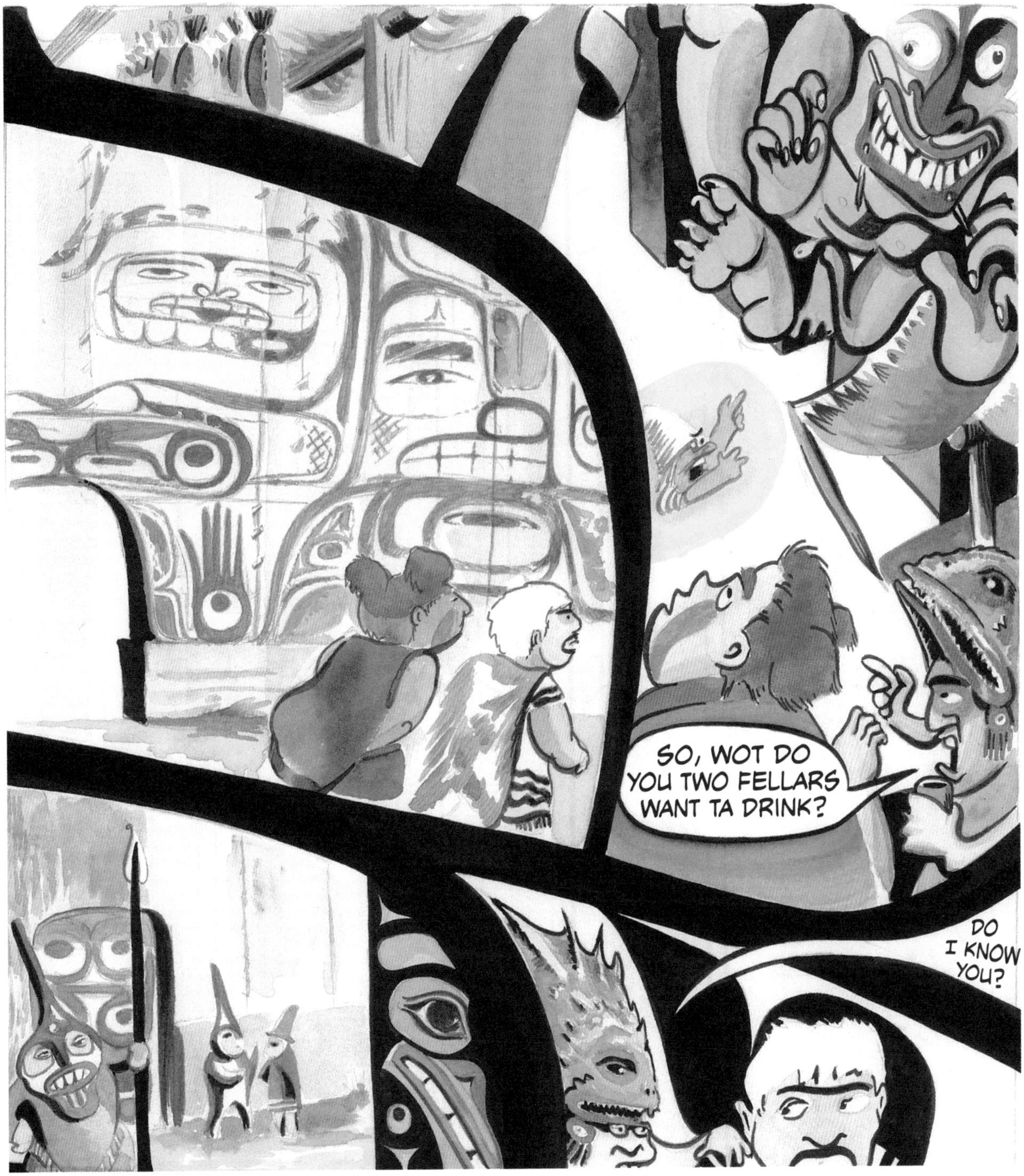
SO, WOT DO YOU TWO FELLARS WANT TA DRINK?
DO I KNOW YOU?

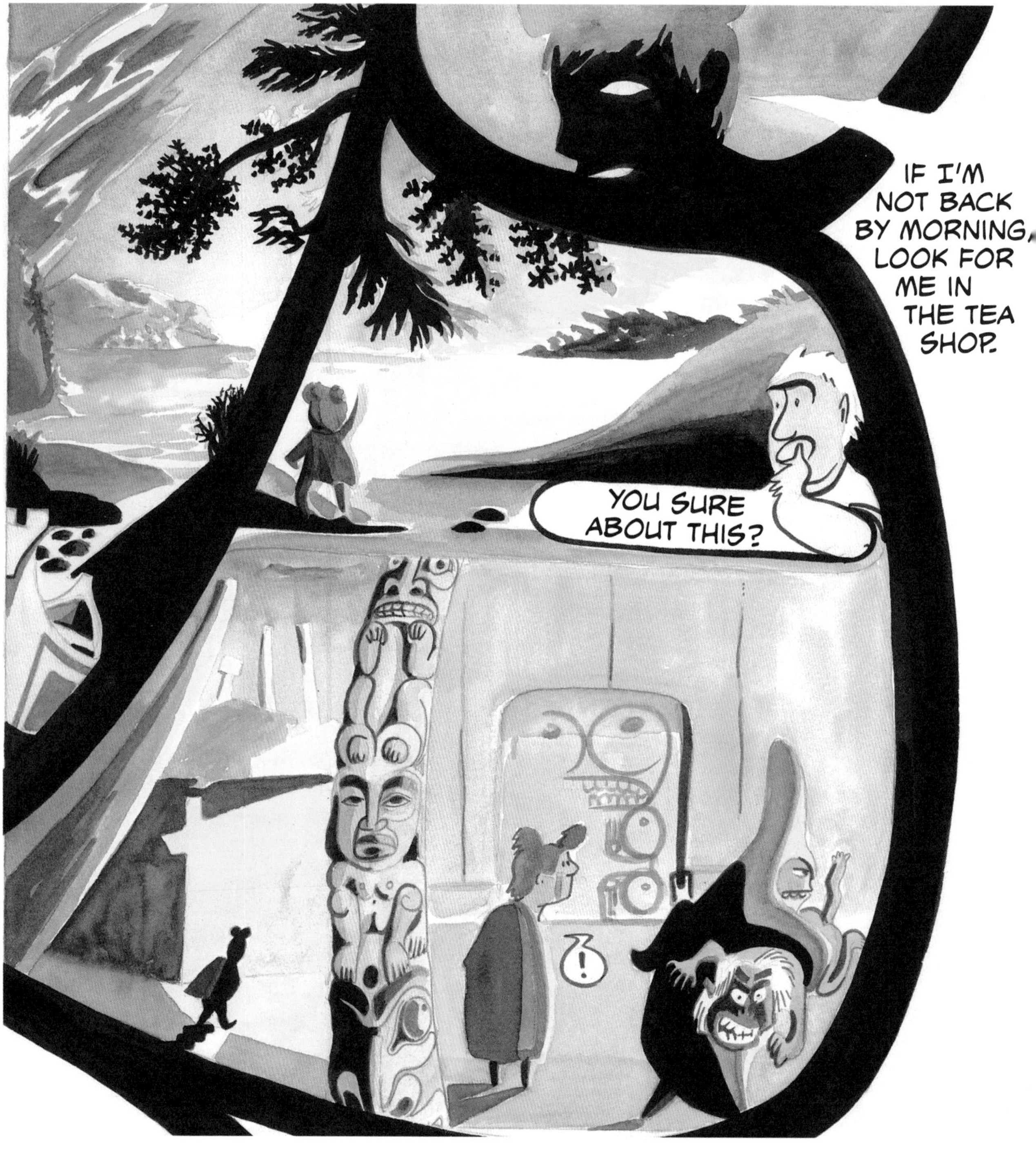
IF I'M NOT BACK BY MORNING, LOOK FOR ME IN THE TEA SHOP.
YOU SURE ABOUT THIS?
!

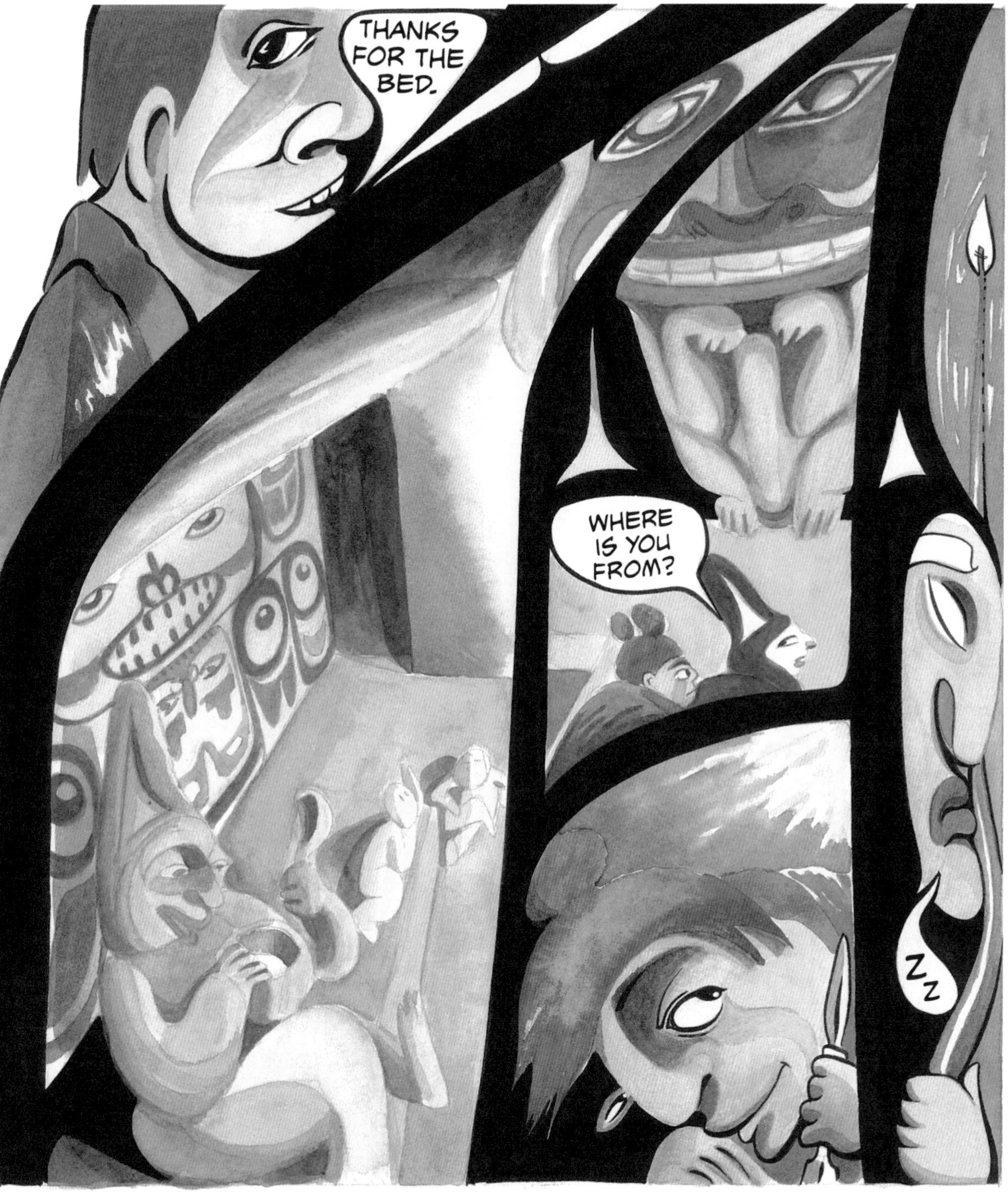
THANKS FOR THE BED.
WHERE IS YOU FROM?
ZZ

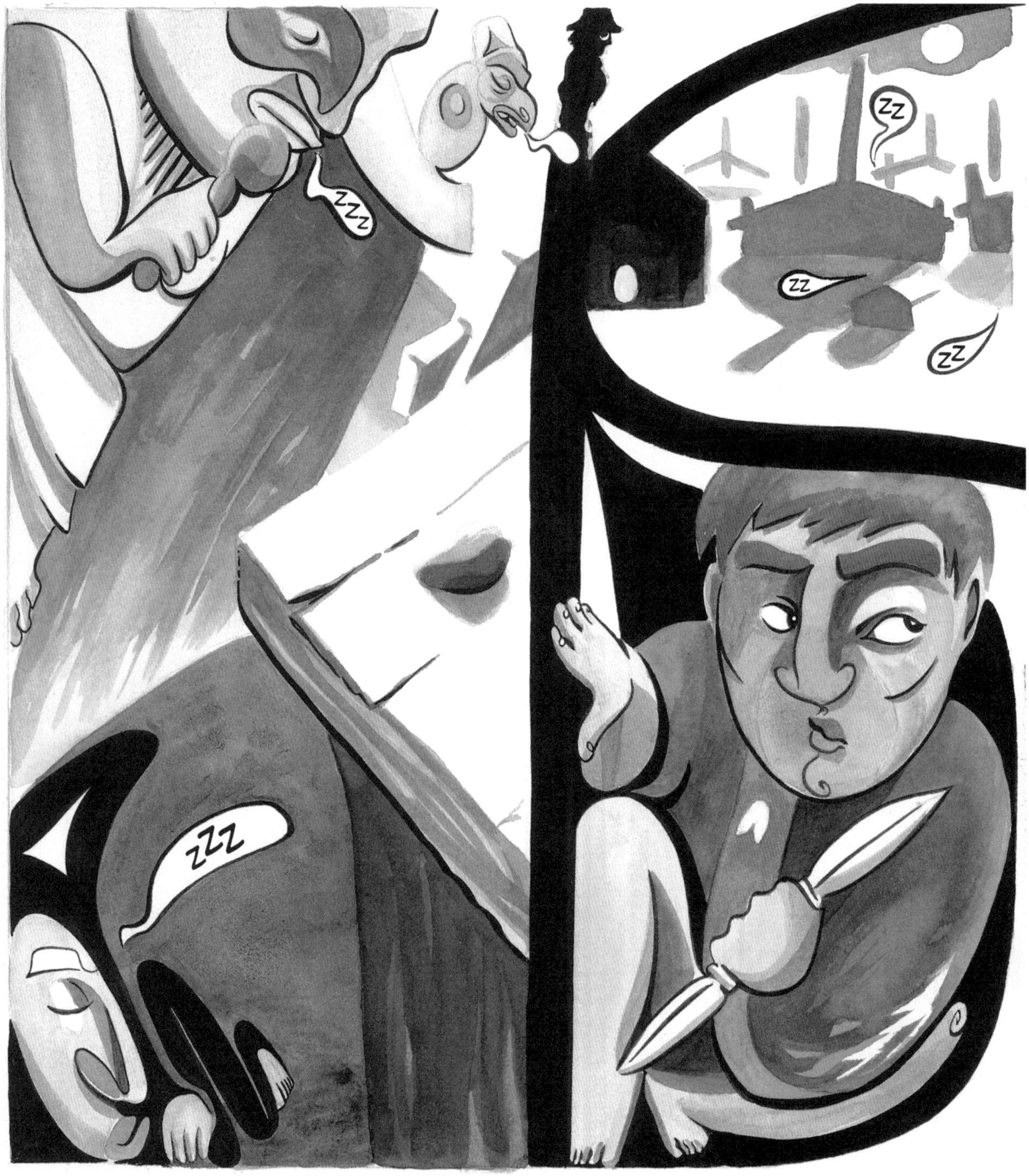
ZZZ
ZZ
ZZ
ZZ
ZZZ

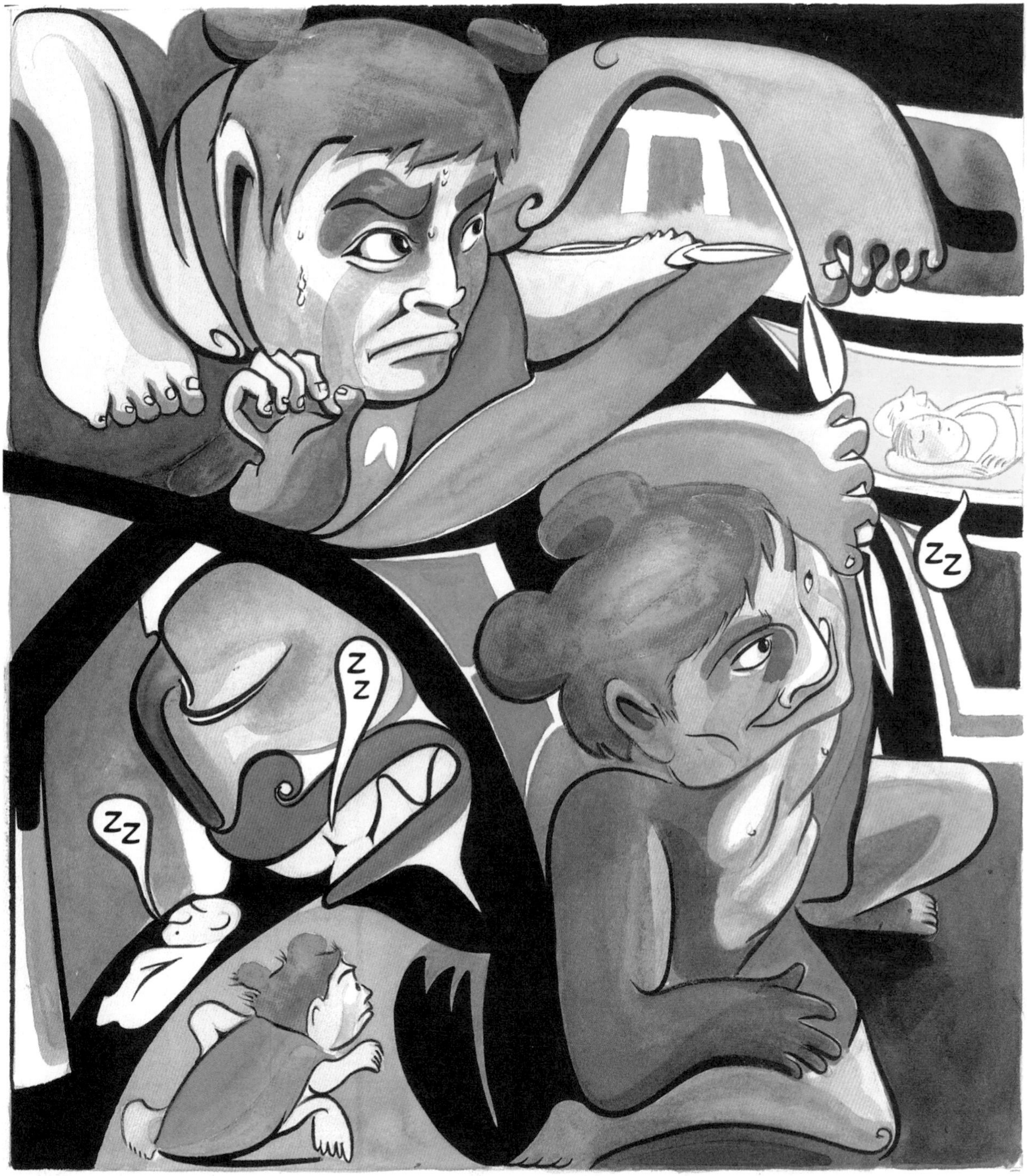
ZZ
ZZ
ZZ

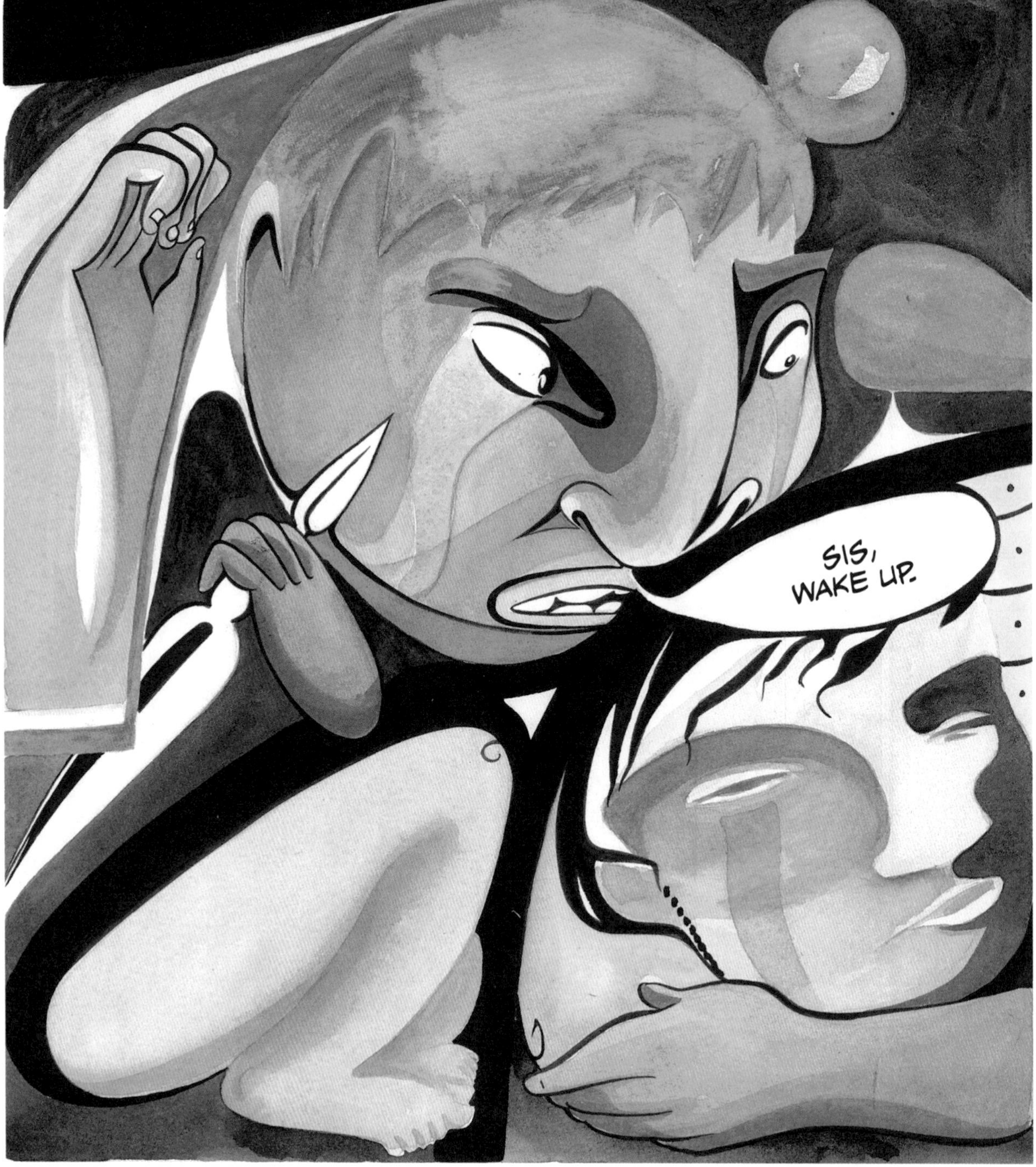
SIS, WAKE UP.

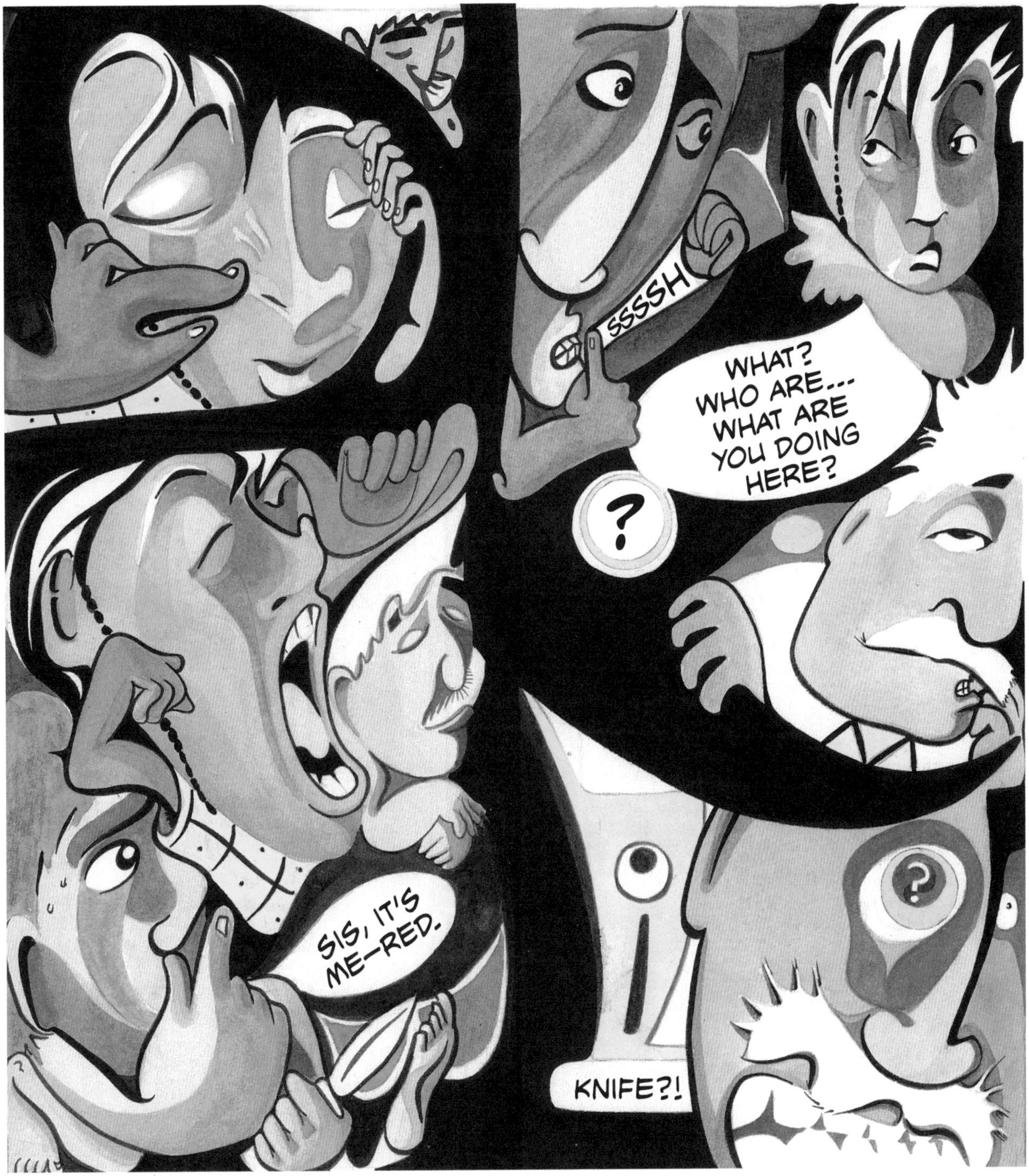
SSSSH
WHAT? WHO ARE... WHAT ARE YOU DOING HERE?
?
SIS, IT'S ME—RED.
KNIFE?!

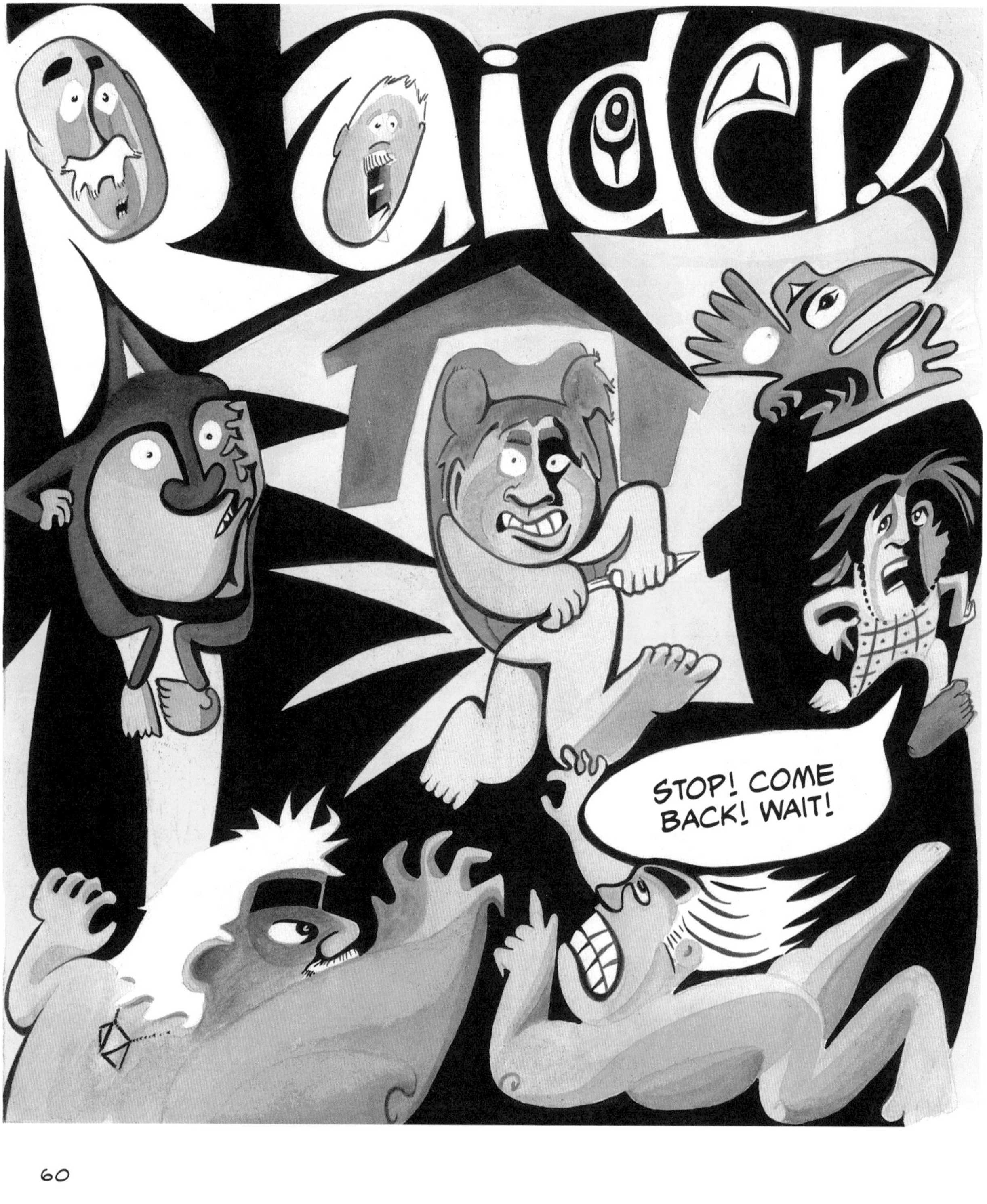
STOP! COME BACK! WAIT!

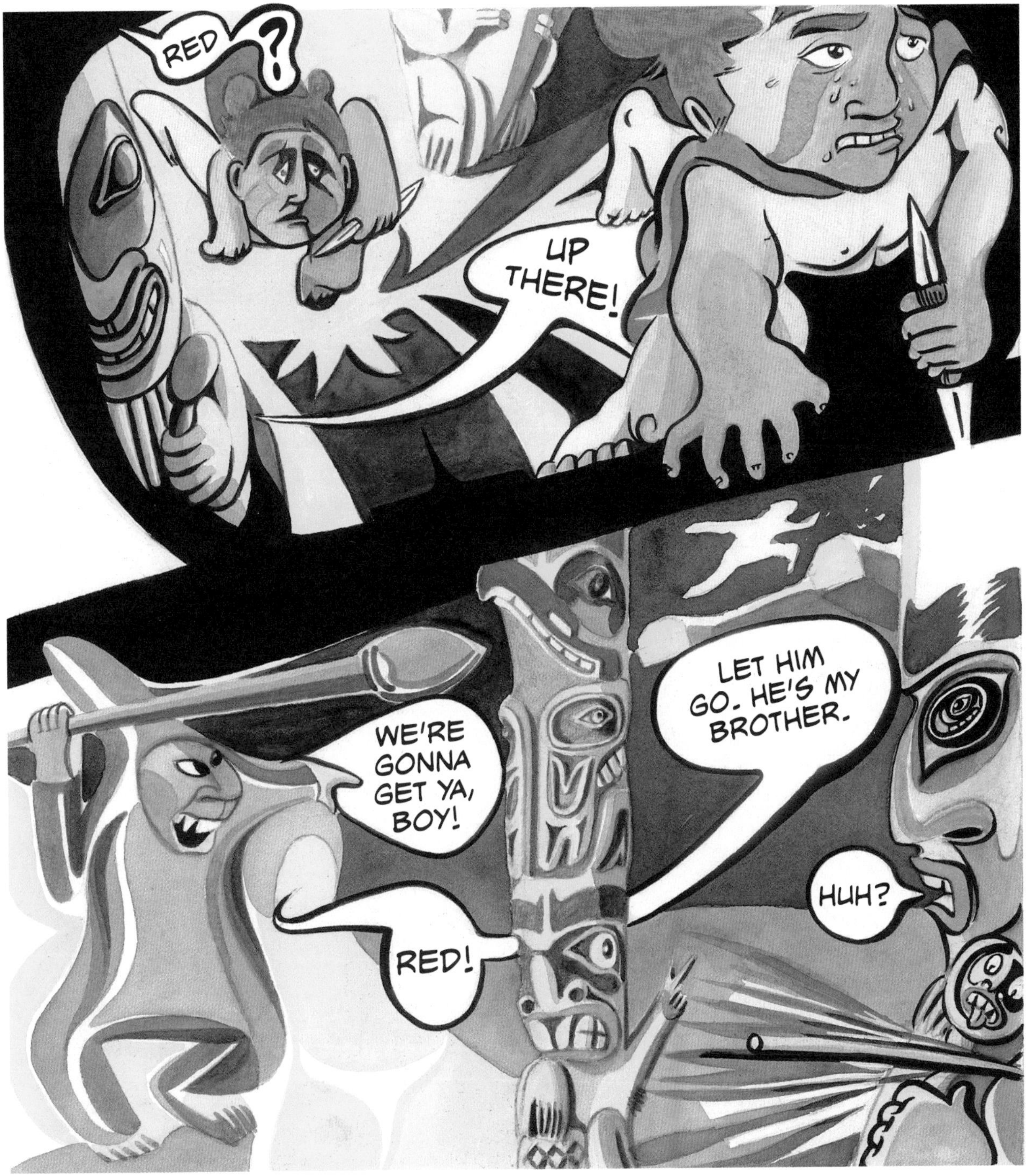
RED?
UP THERE!
WE'RE GONNA GET YA, BOY!
RED!
LET HIM GO. HE'S MY BROTHER.
HUH?

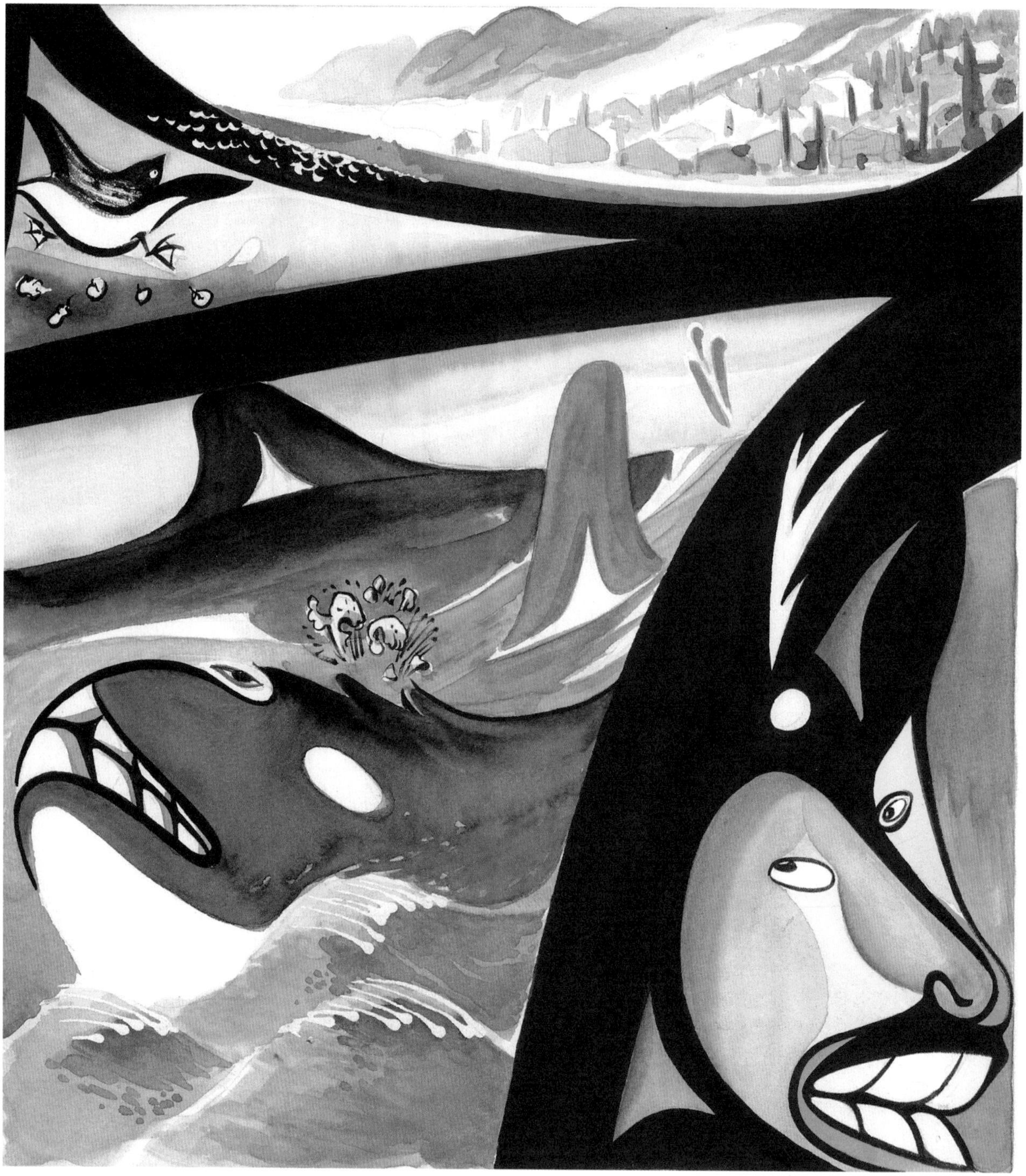

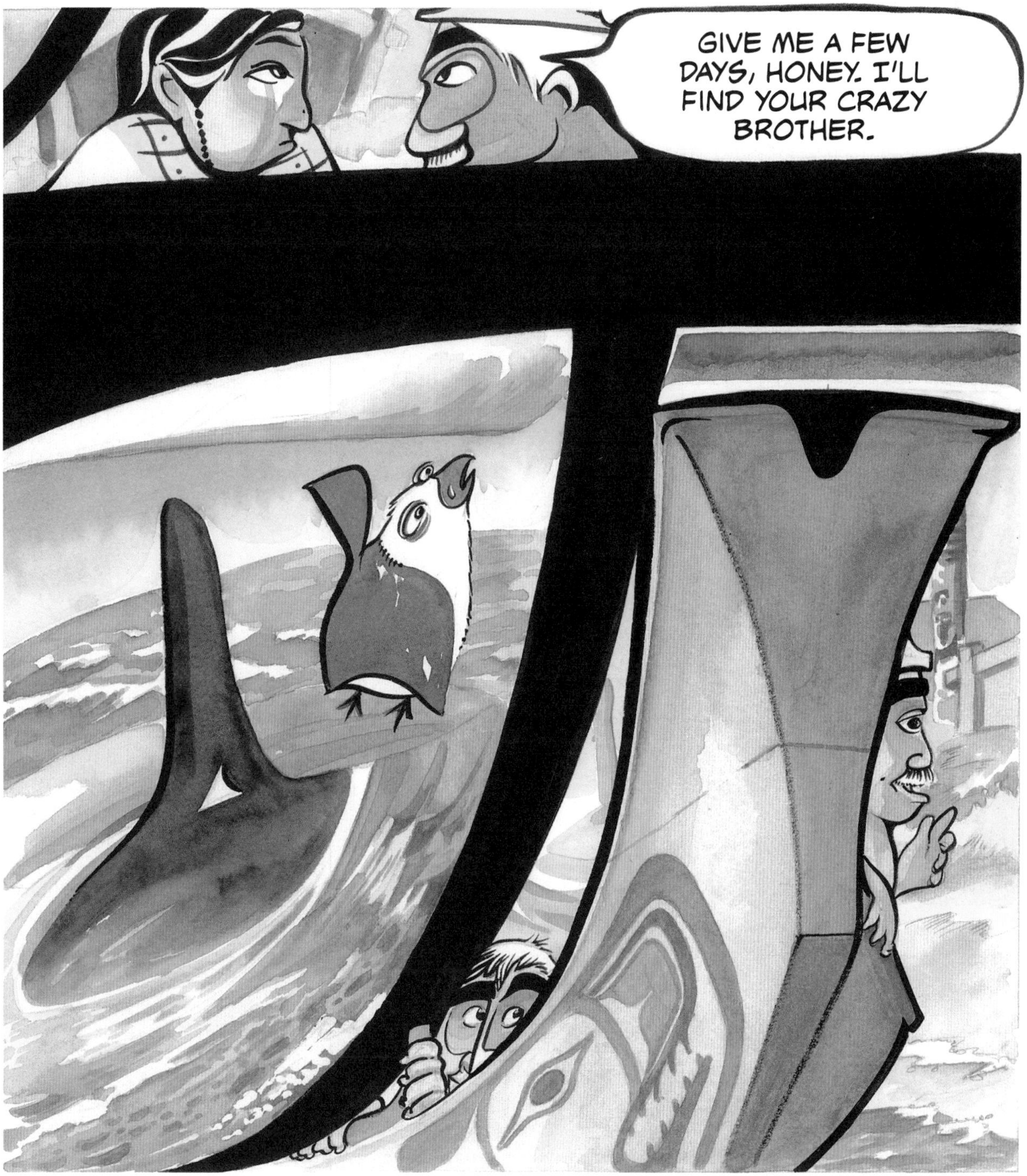
GIVE ME A FEW DAYS, HONEY. I'LL FIND YOUR CRAZY BROTHER.

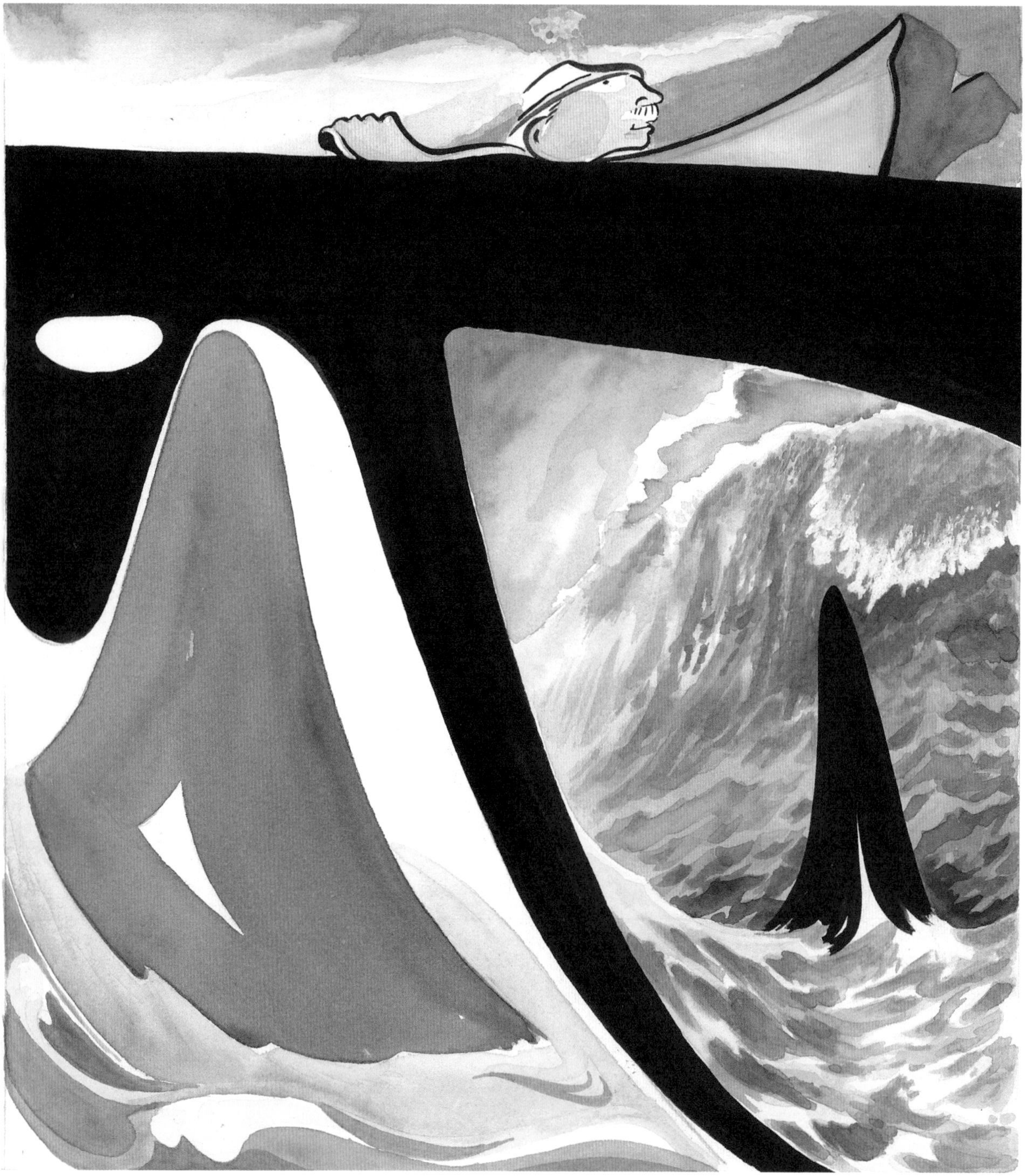

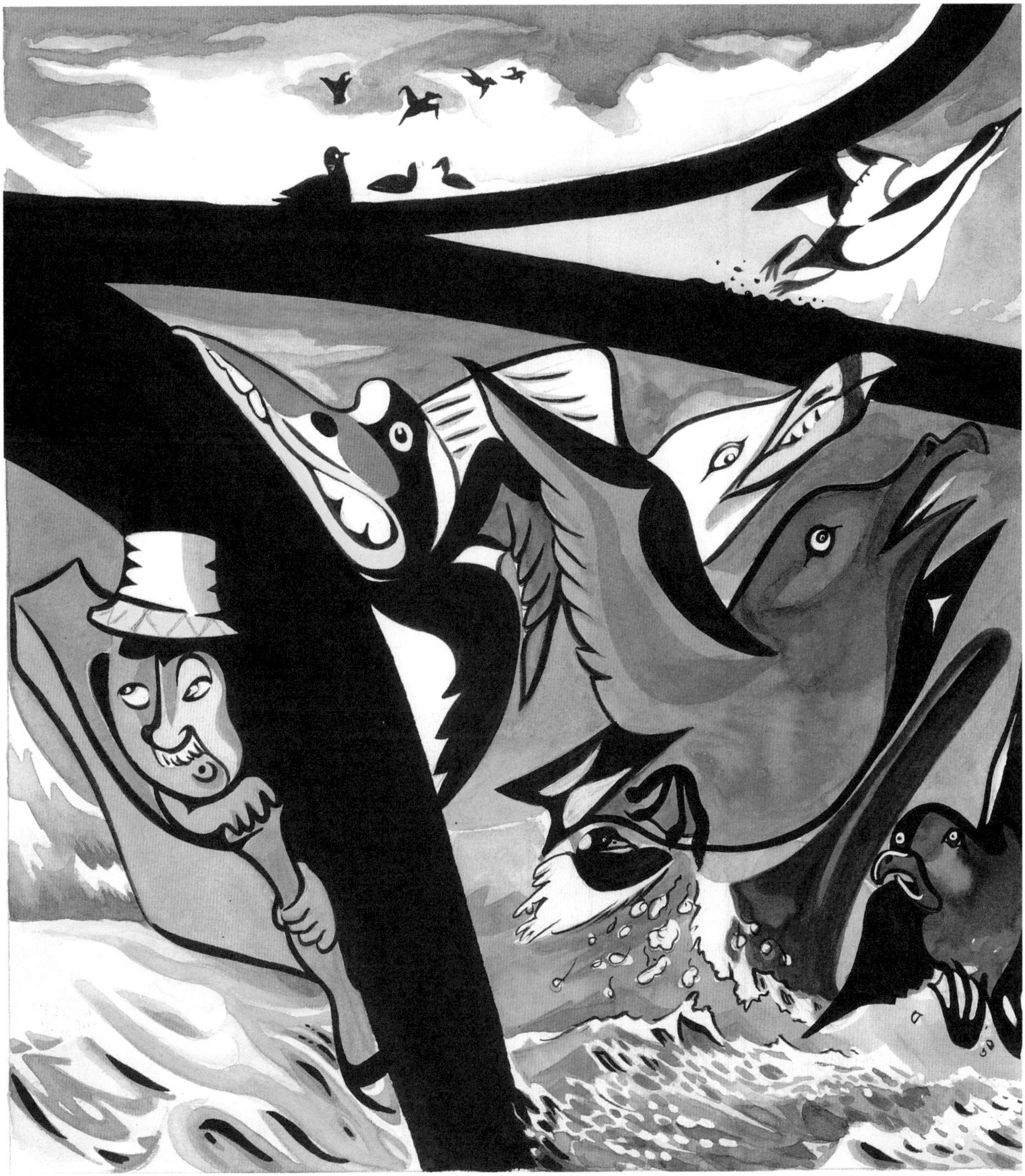

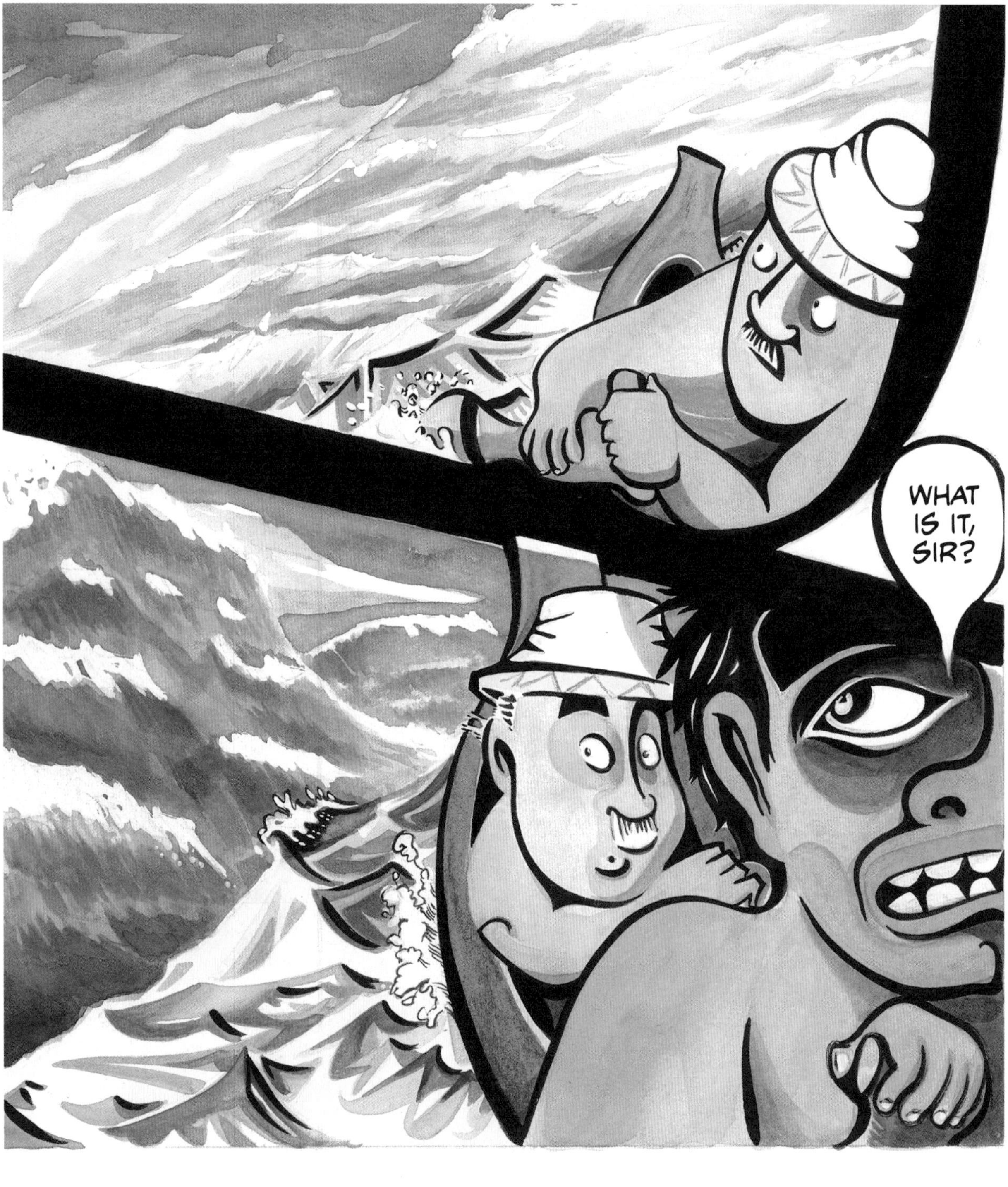
WHAT IS IT, SIR?

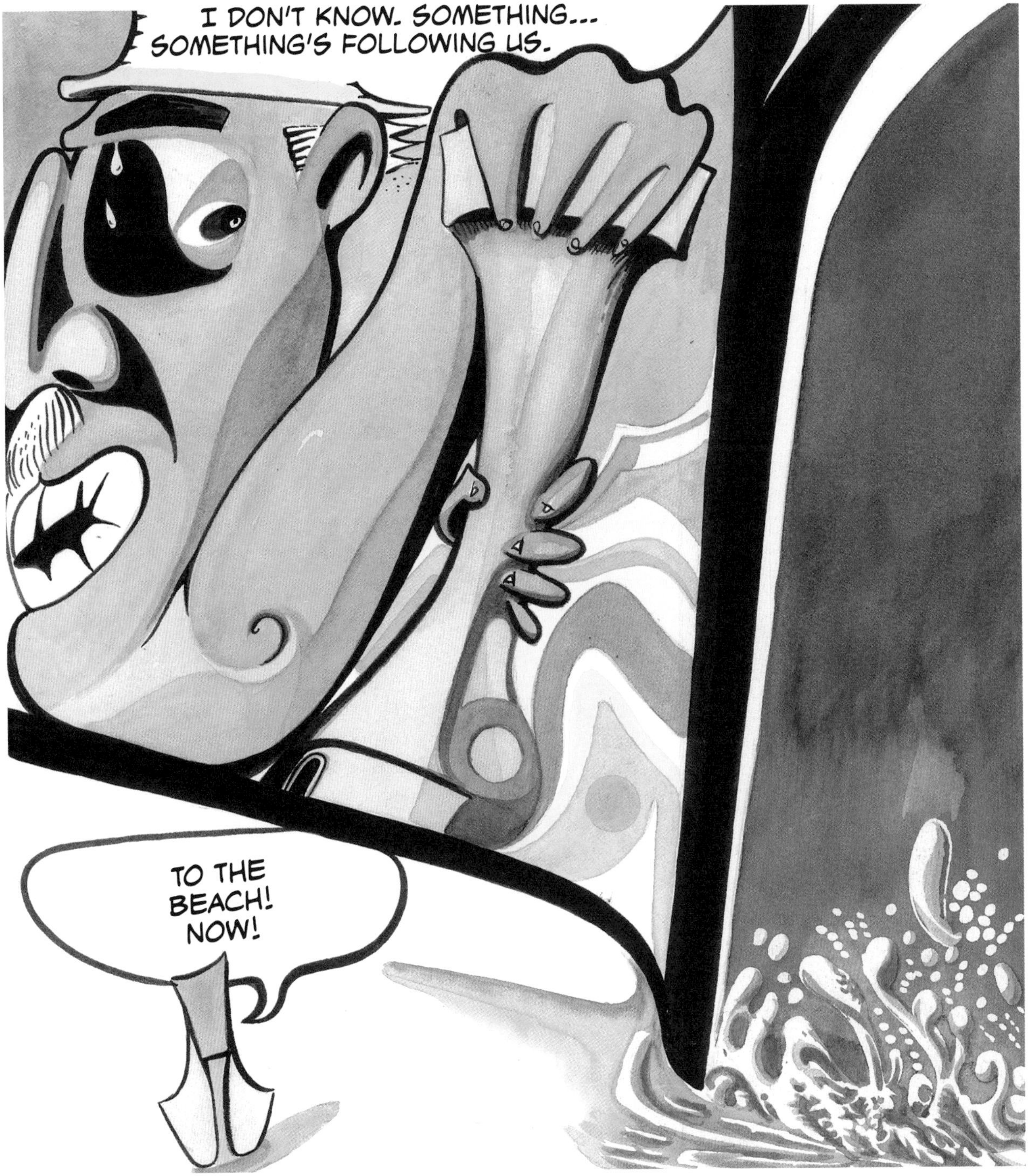
I DON'T KNOW. SOMETHING...
SOMETHING'S FOLLOWING US.
TO THE BEACH! NOW!

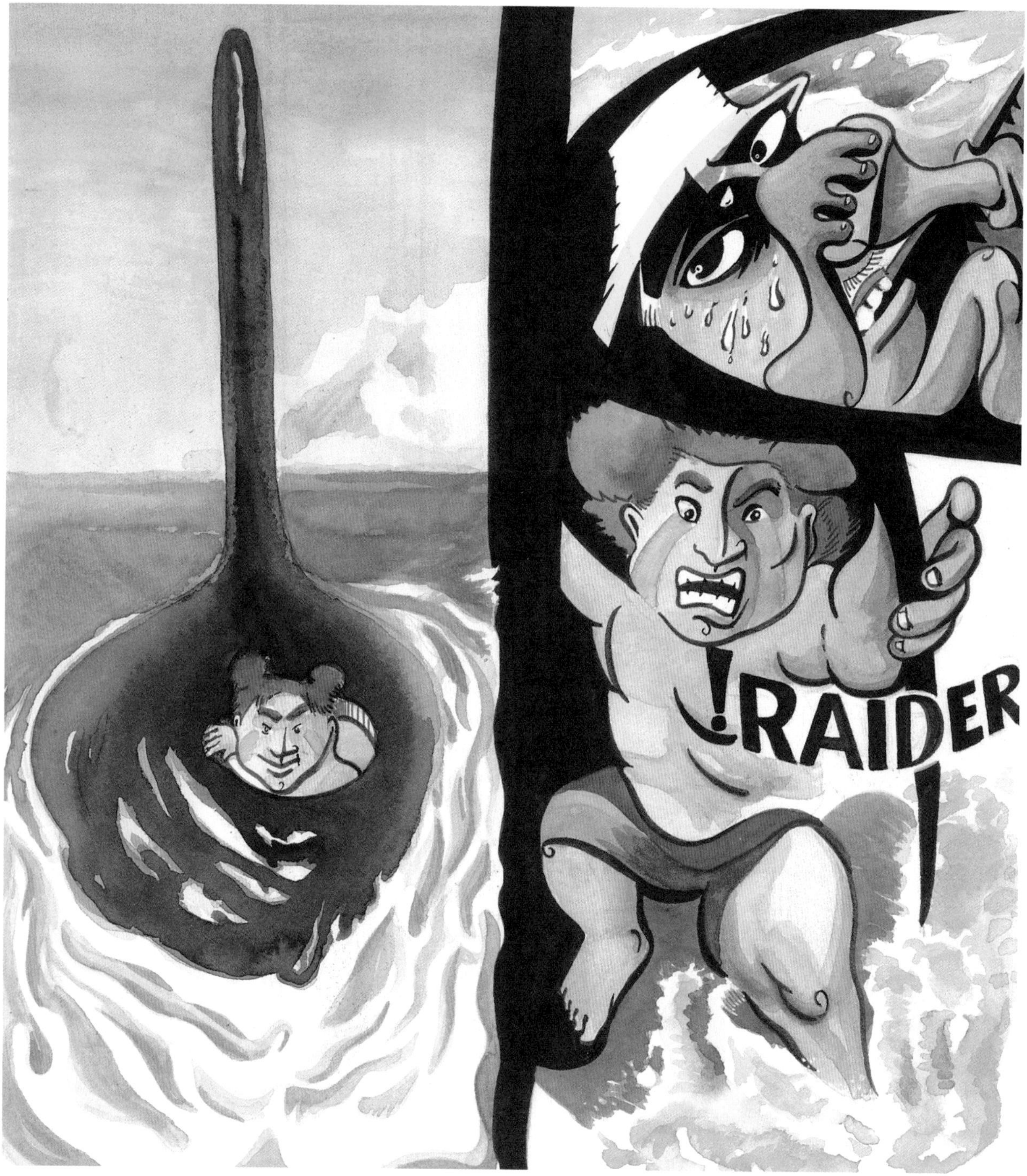
!RAIDER

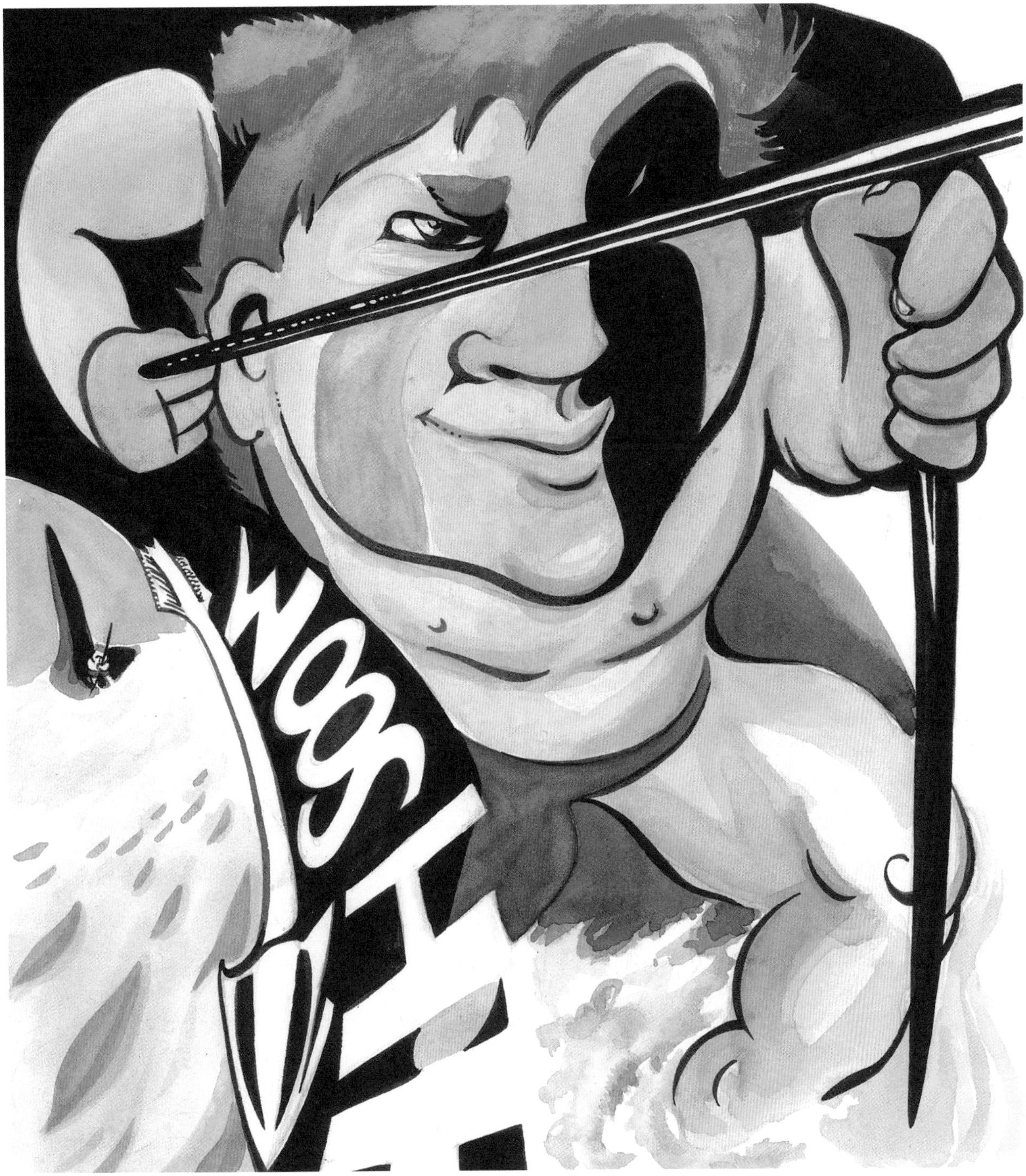
WOOSH

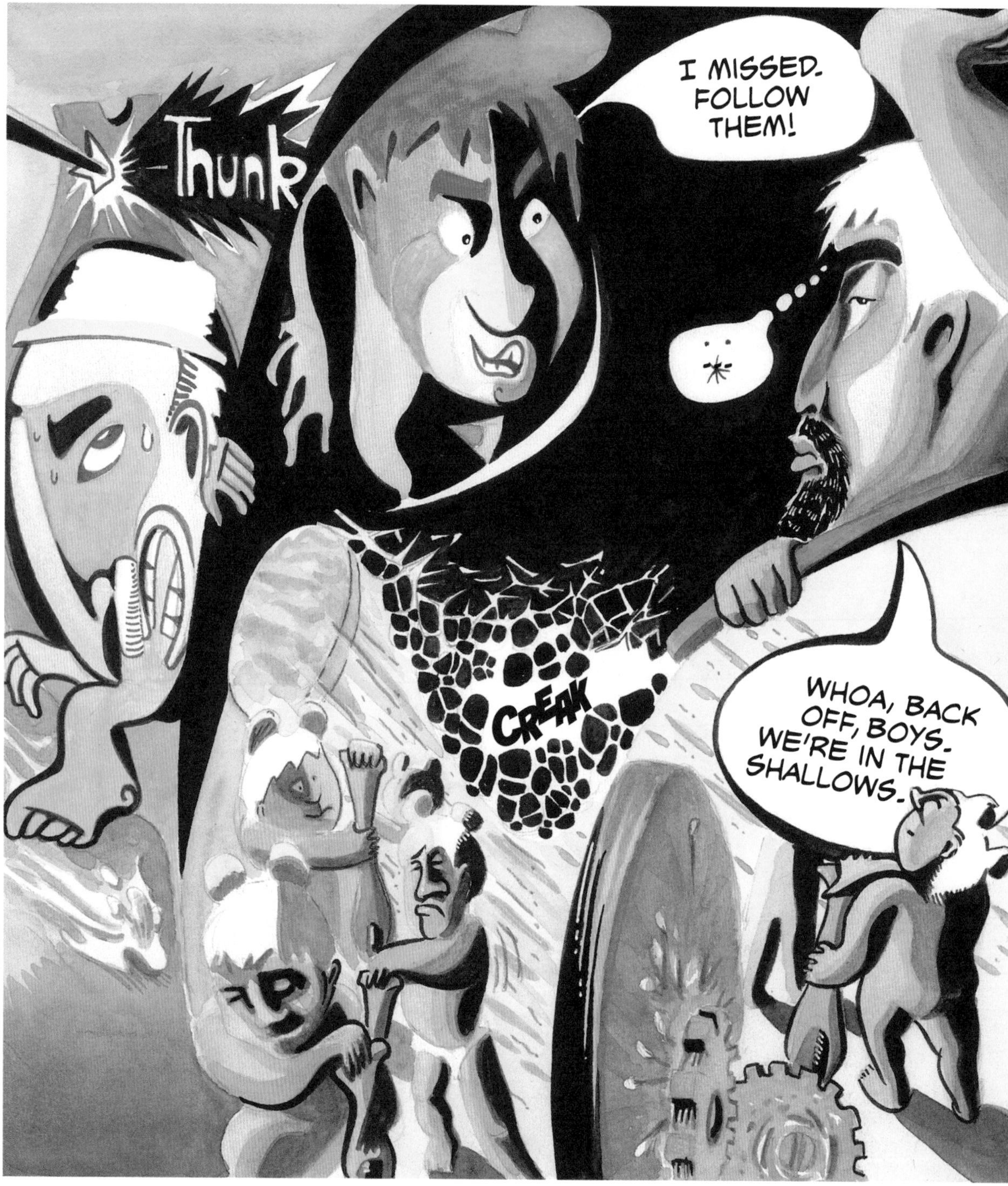
Thunk
I MISSED. FOLLOW THEM!
CREAK
WHOA, BACK OFF, BOYS. WE'RE IN THE SHALLOWS.

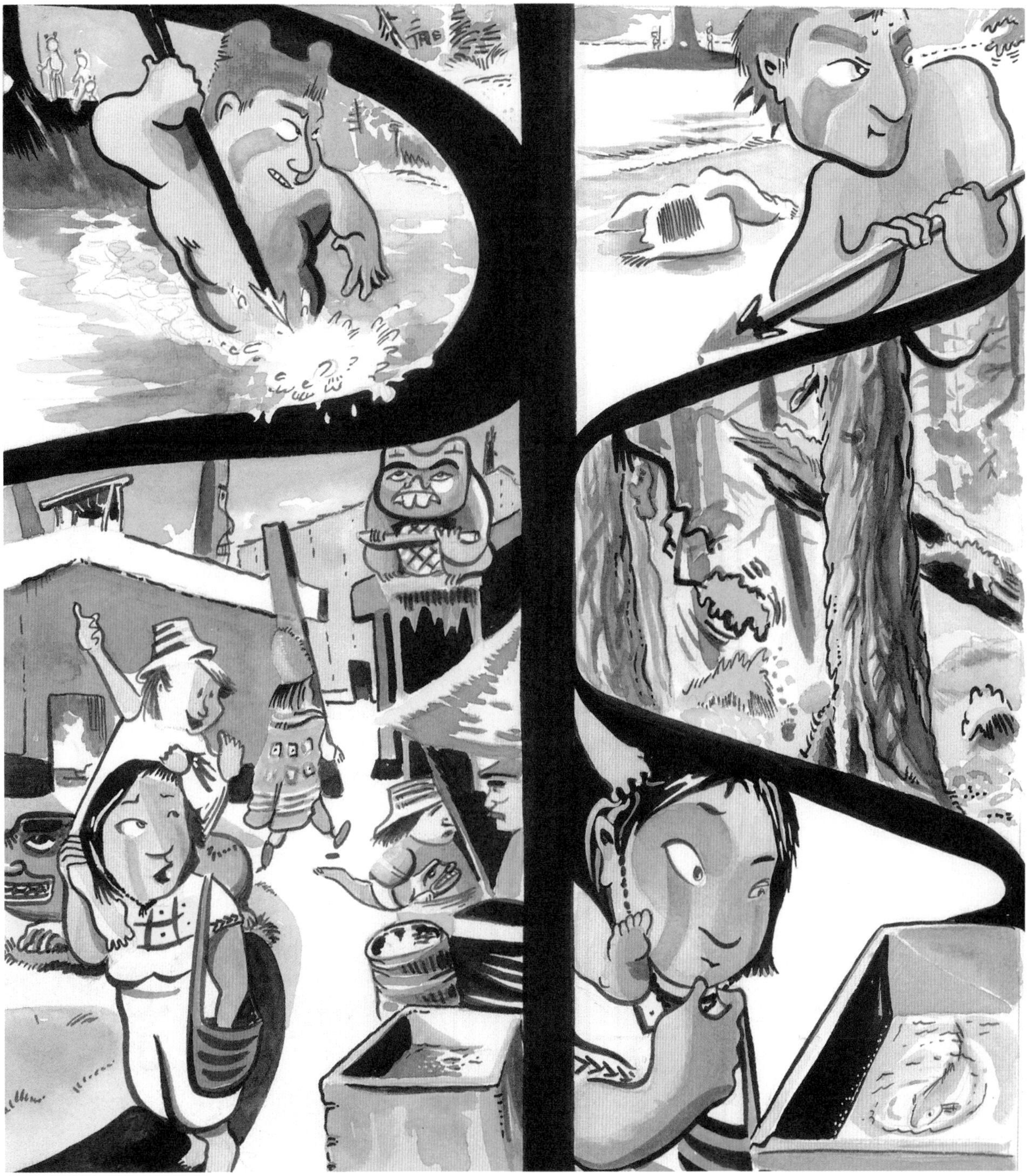

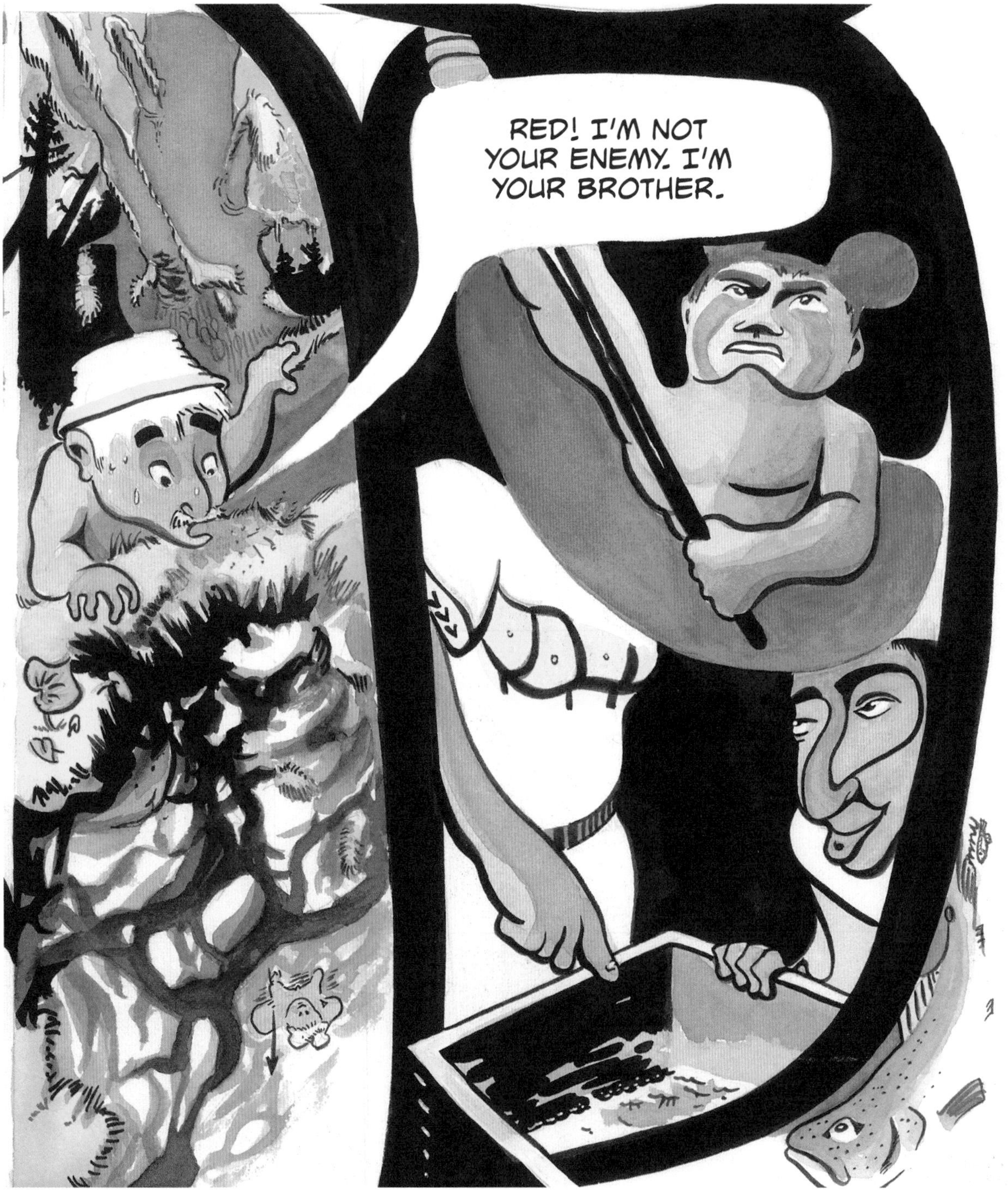
RED! I'M NOT YOUR ENEMY. I'M YOUR BROTHER.

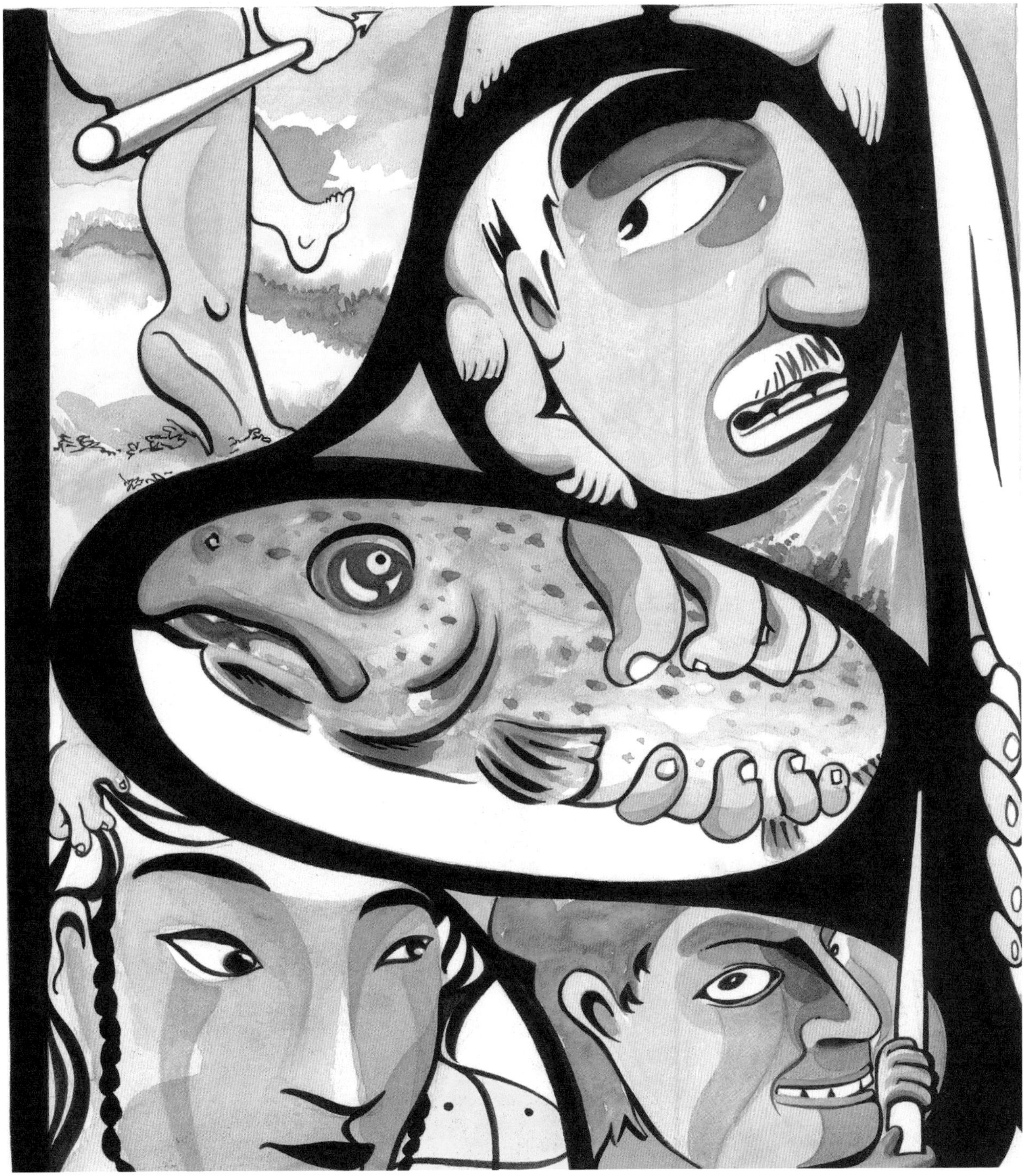

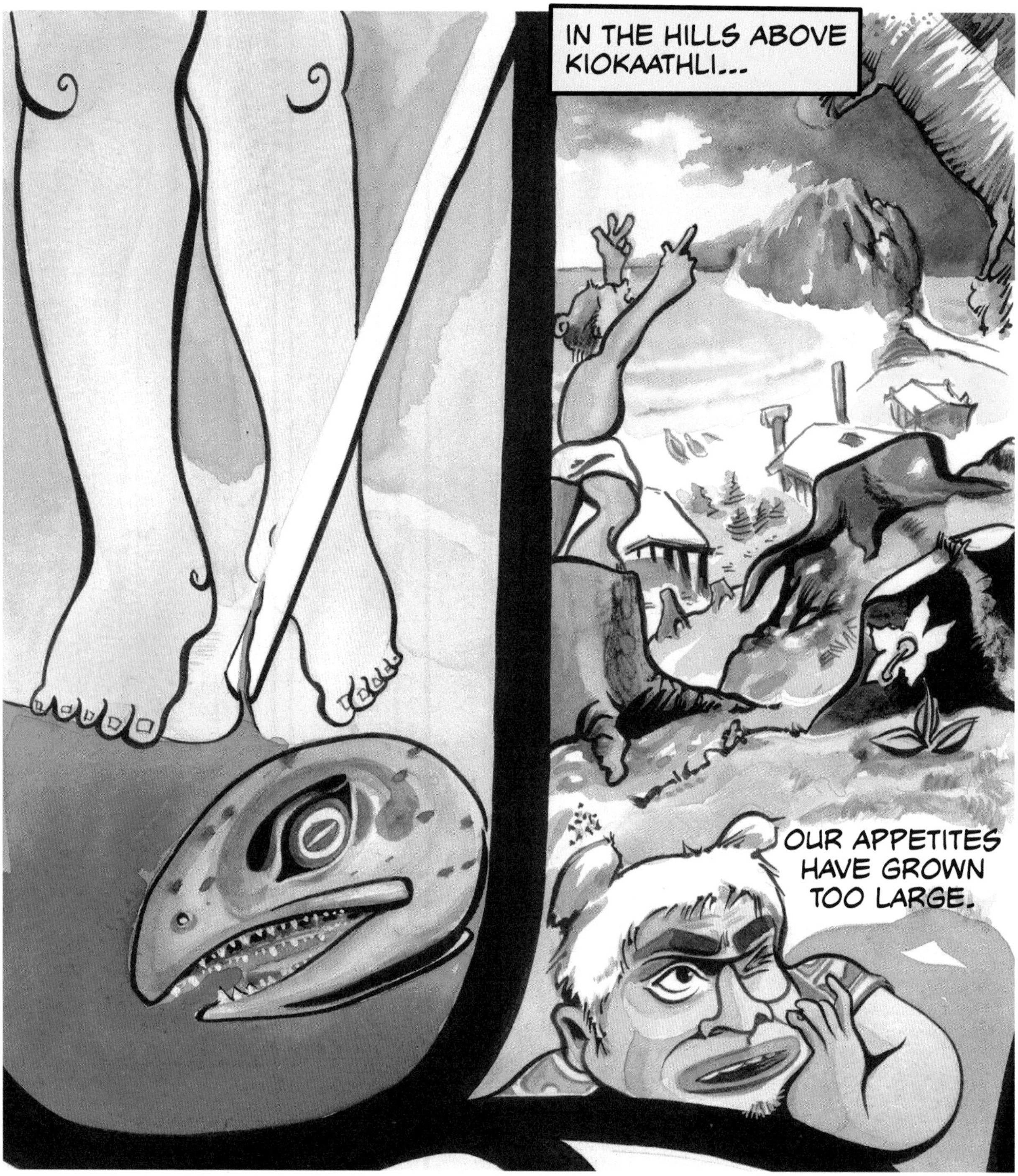
IN THE HILLS ABOVE KIOKAATHLI...
OUR APPETITES HAVE GROWN TOO LARGE.

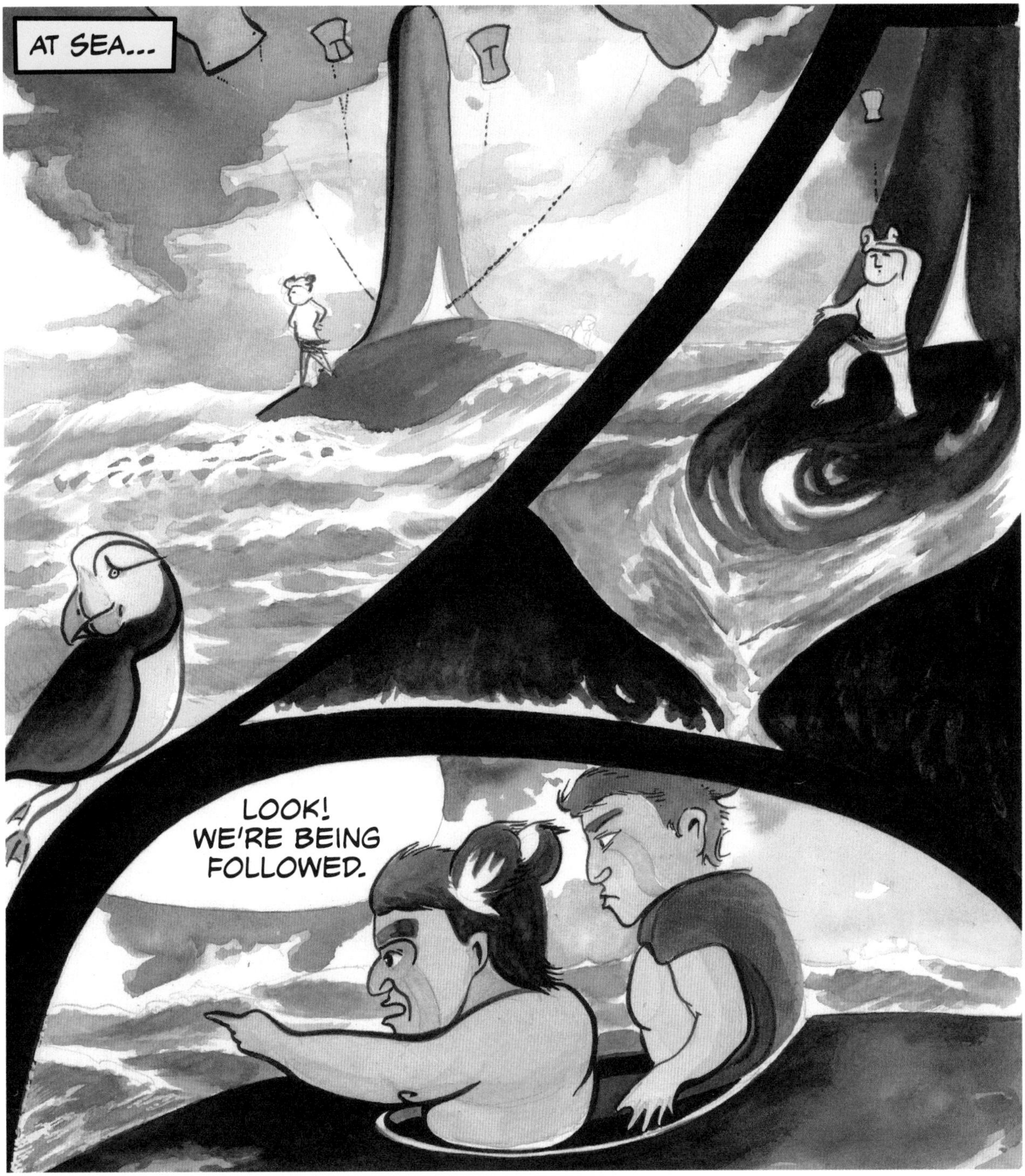
AT SEA...
LOOK! WE'RE BEING FOLLOWED.

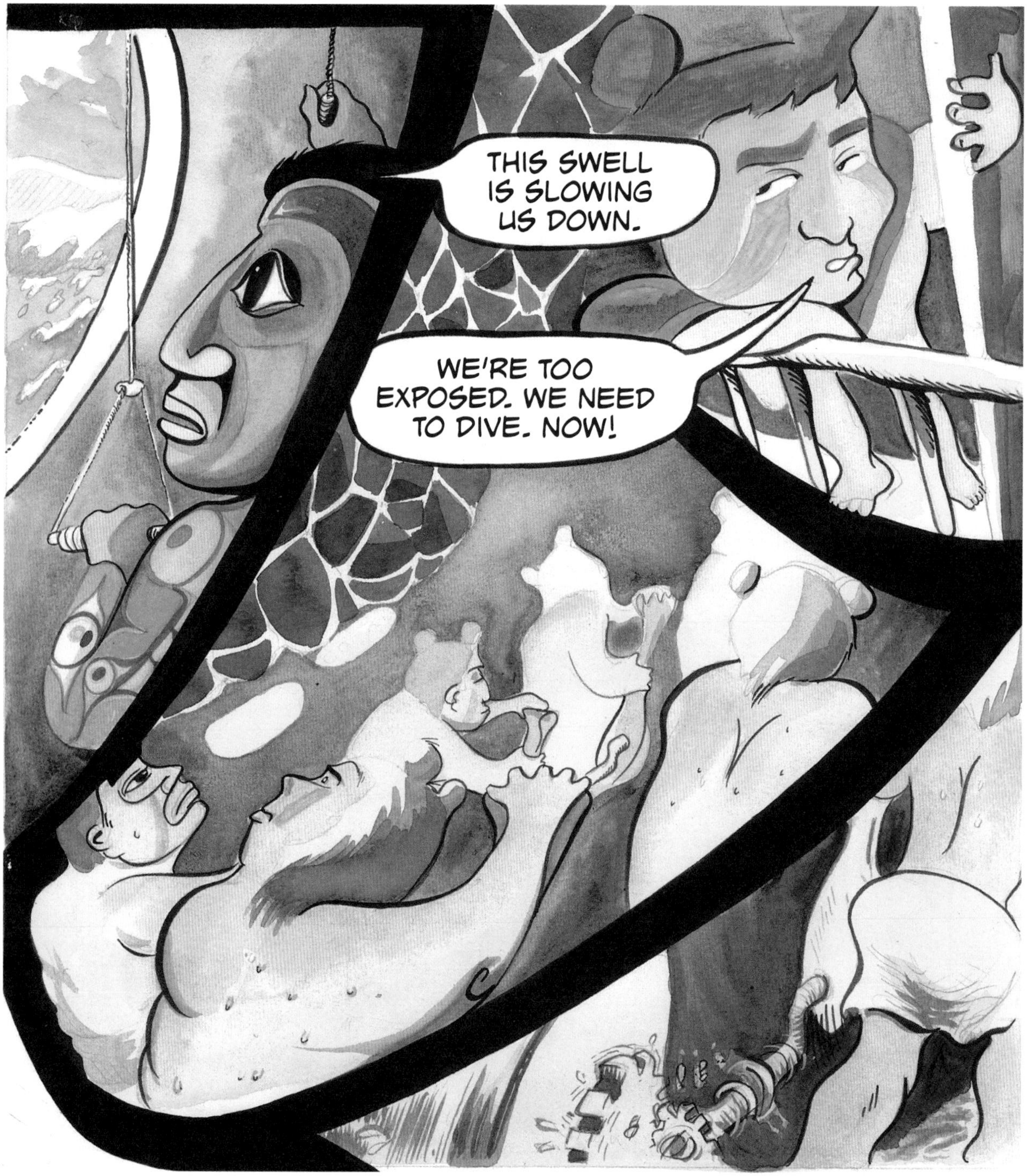
THIS SWELL IS SLOWING US DOWN.
WE'RE TOO EXPOSED. WE NEED TO DIVE. NOW!

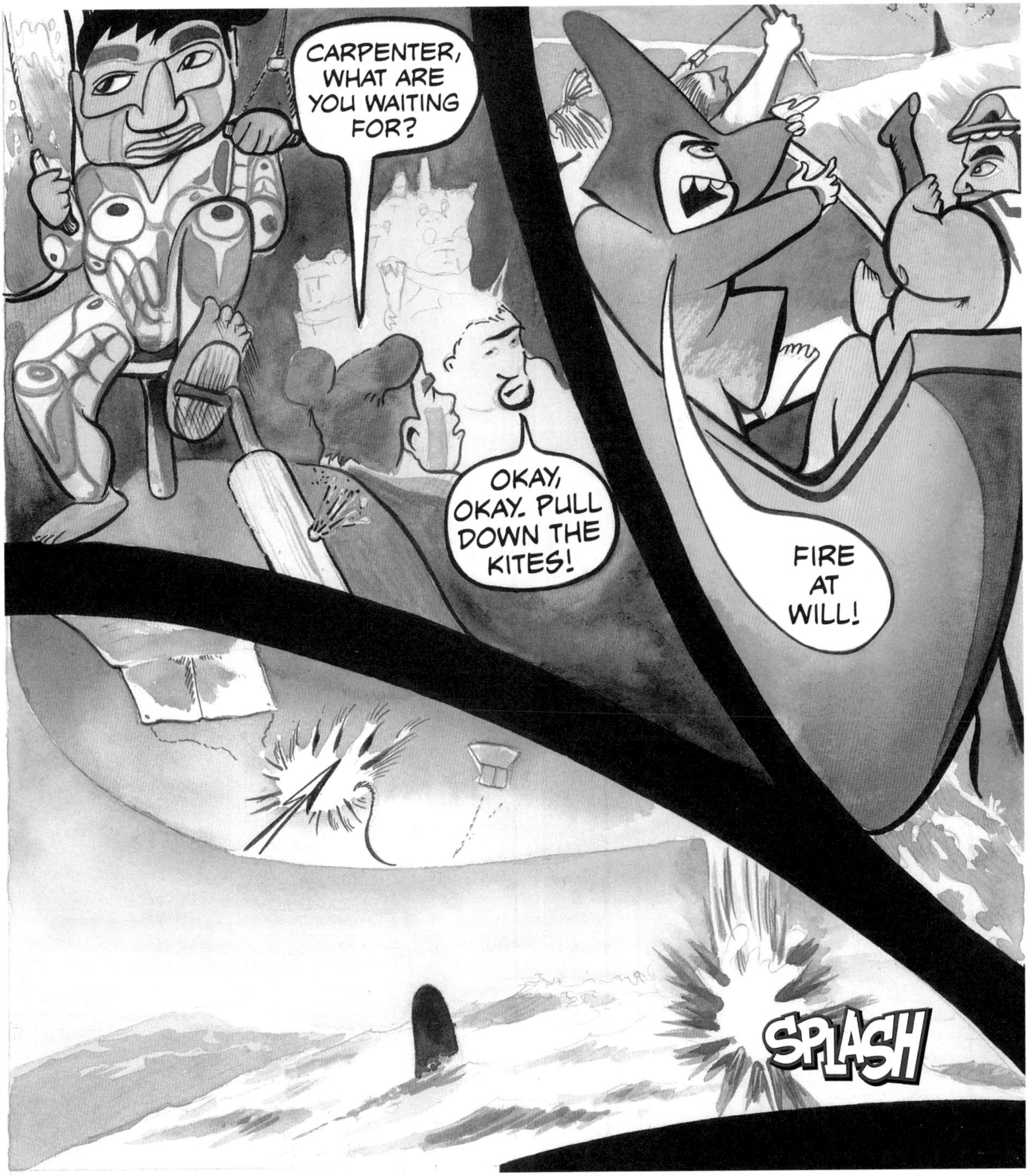
CARPENTER, WHAT ARE YOU WAITING FOR?
OKAY, OKAY. PULL DOWN THE KITES!
FIRE AT WILL!
SPLASH

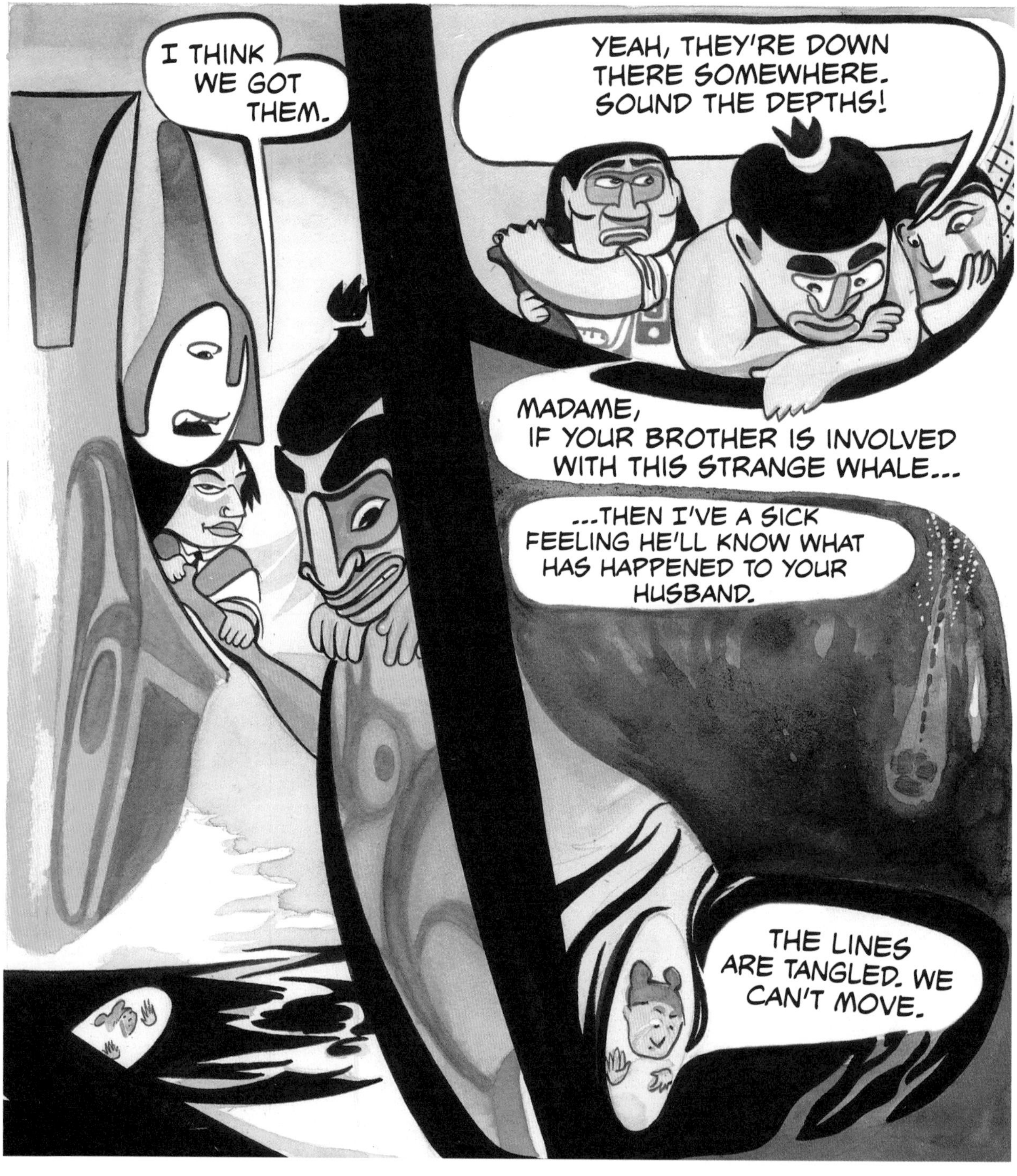
I THINK WE GOT THEM.
YEAH, THEY'RE DOWN THERE SOMEWHERE. SOUND THE DEPTHS!
MADAME, IF YOUR BROTHER IS INVOLVED WITH THIS STRANGE WHALE...
...THEN I'VE A SICK FEELING HE'LL KNOW WHAT HAS HAPPENED TO YOUR HUSBAND.
THE LINES ARE TANGLED. WE CAN'T MOVE.

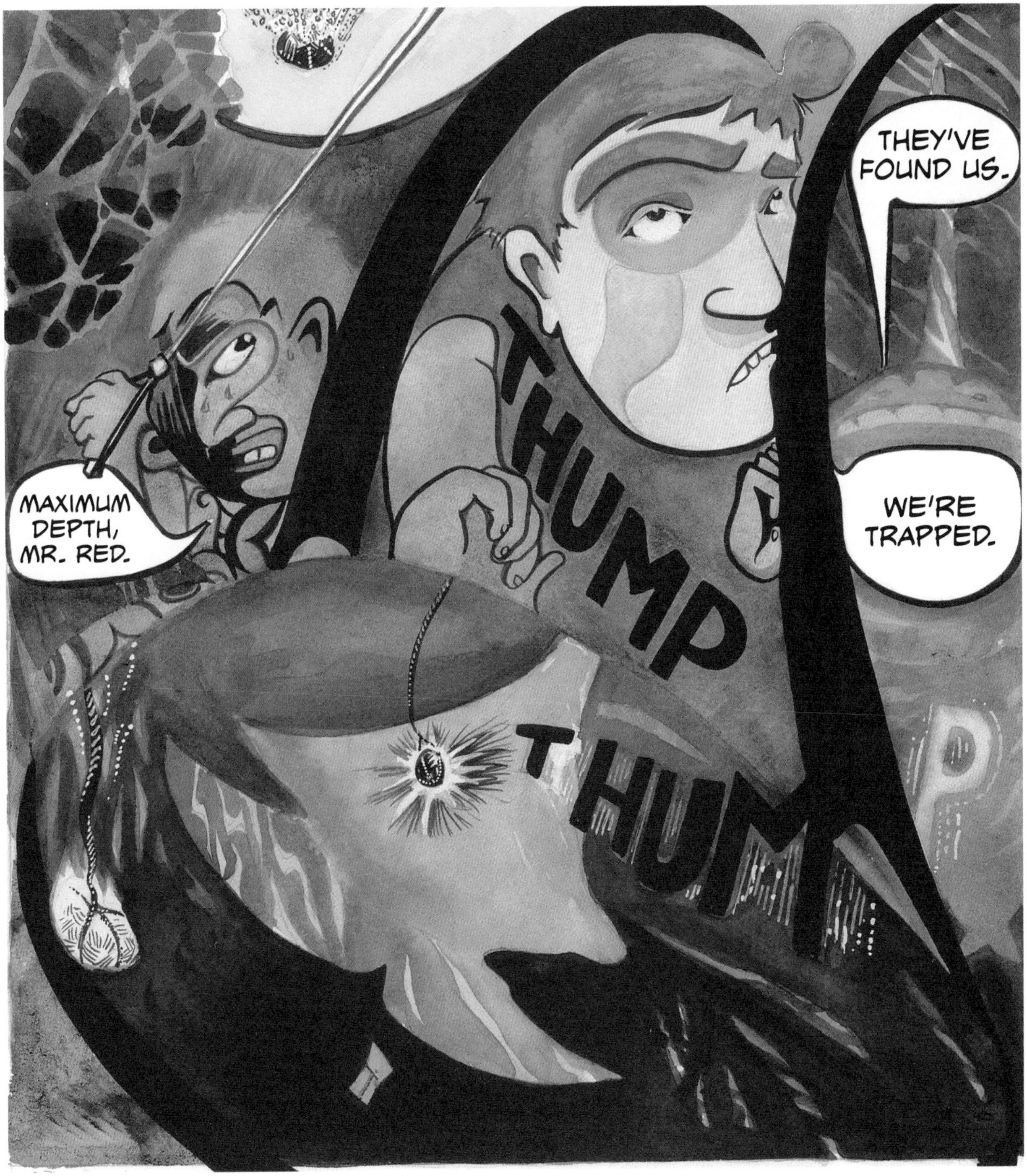
THEY'VE FOUND US.
MAXIMUM DEPTH, MR. RED.
WE'RE TRAPPED.
THUMP
THUMP

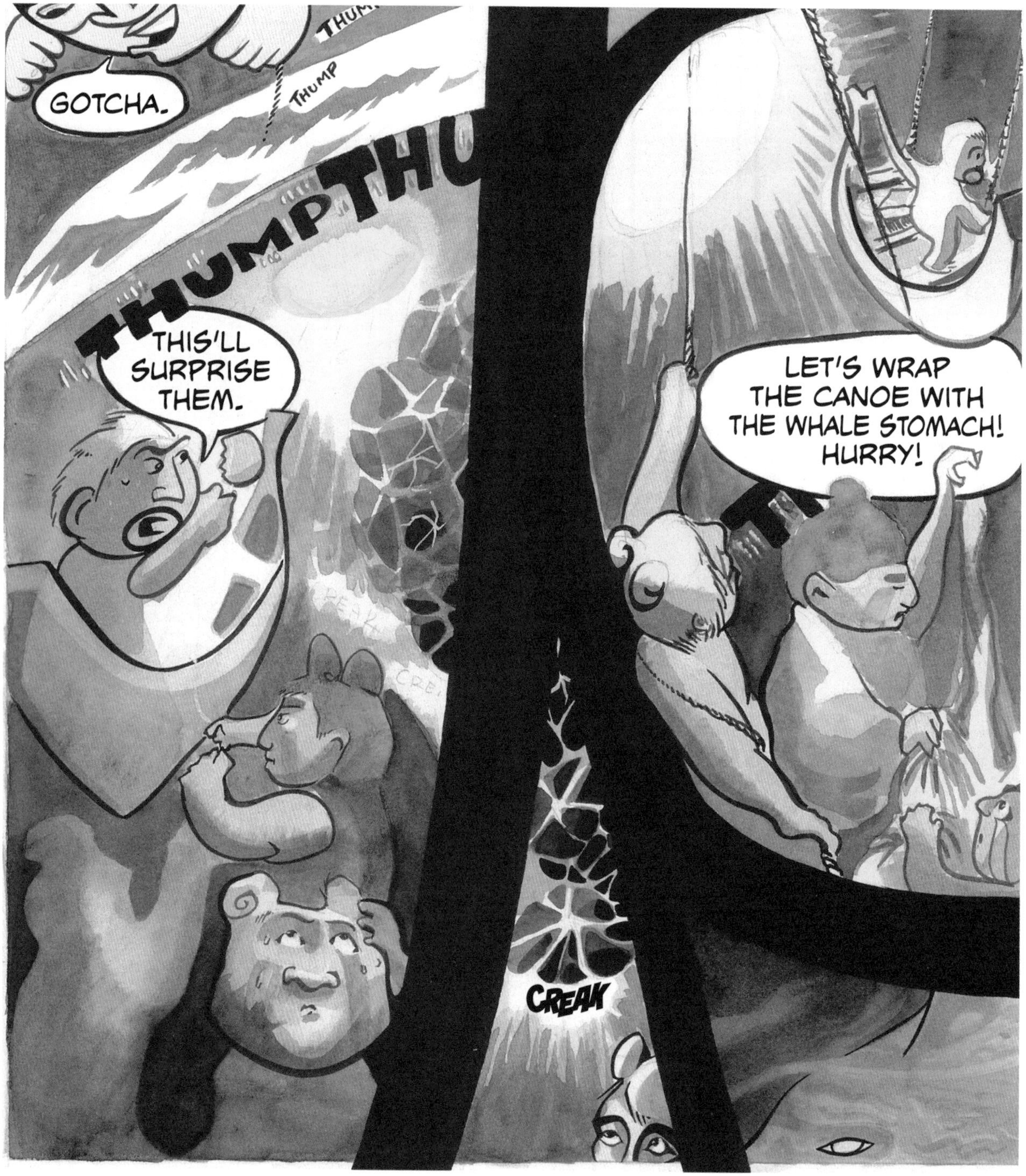
GOTCHA.
THUMP
THUMP
THIS'LL SURPRISE THEM.
LET'S WRAP THE CANOE WITH THE WHALE STOMACH! HURRY!
CREAK

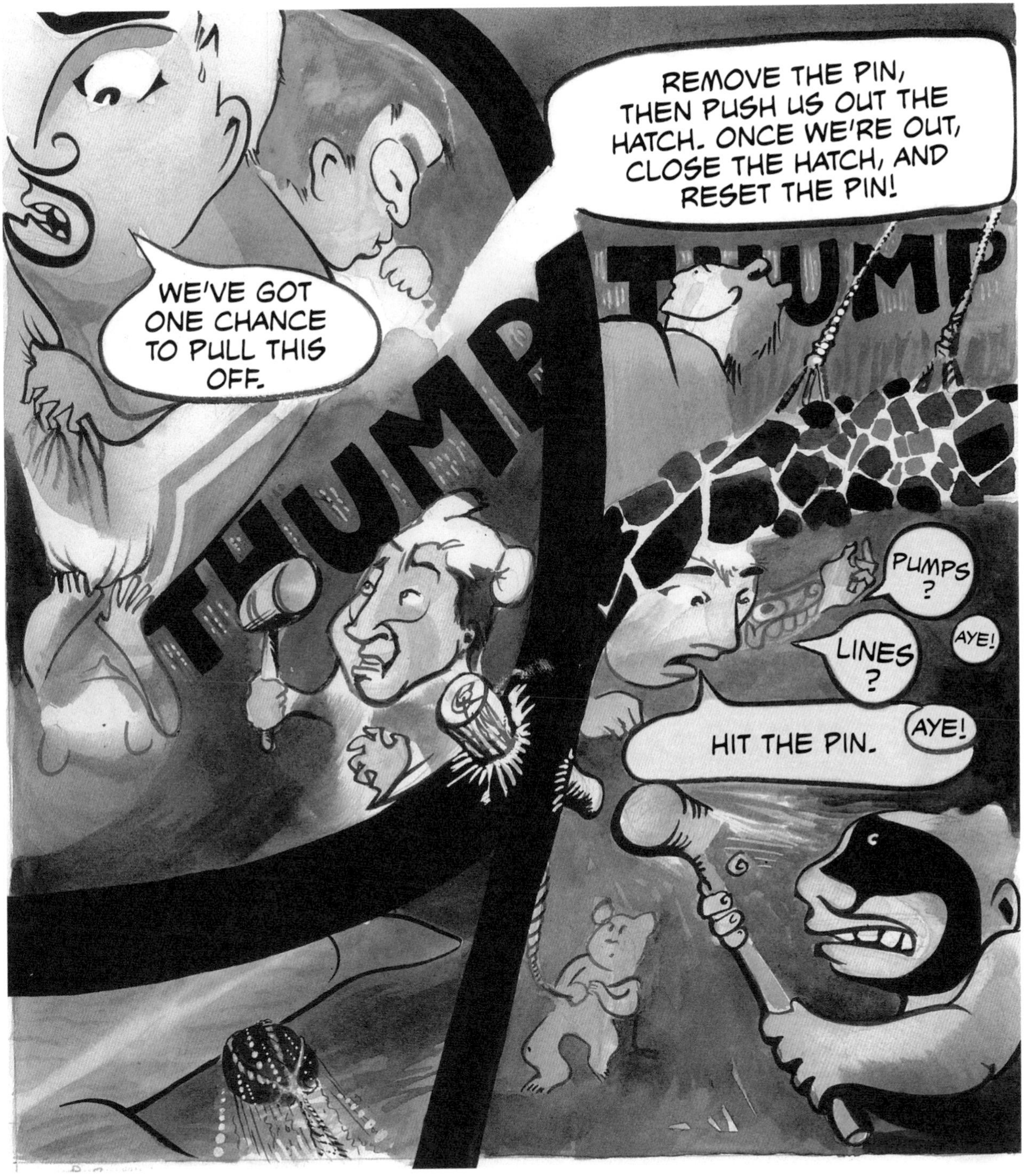
WE'VE GOT ONE CHANCE TO PULL THIS OFF.
REMOVE THE PIN, THEN PUSH US OUT THE HATCH. ONCE WE'RE OUT, CLOSE THE HATCH, AND RESET THE PIN!
THUMP
THUMP
PUMPS?
AYE!
LINES?
AYE!
HIT THE PIN.

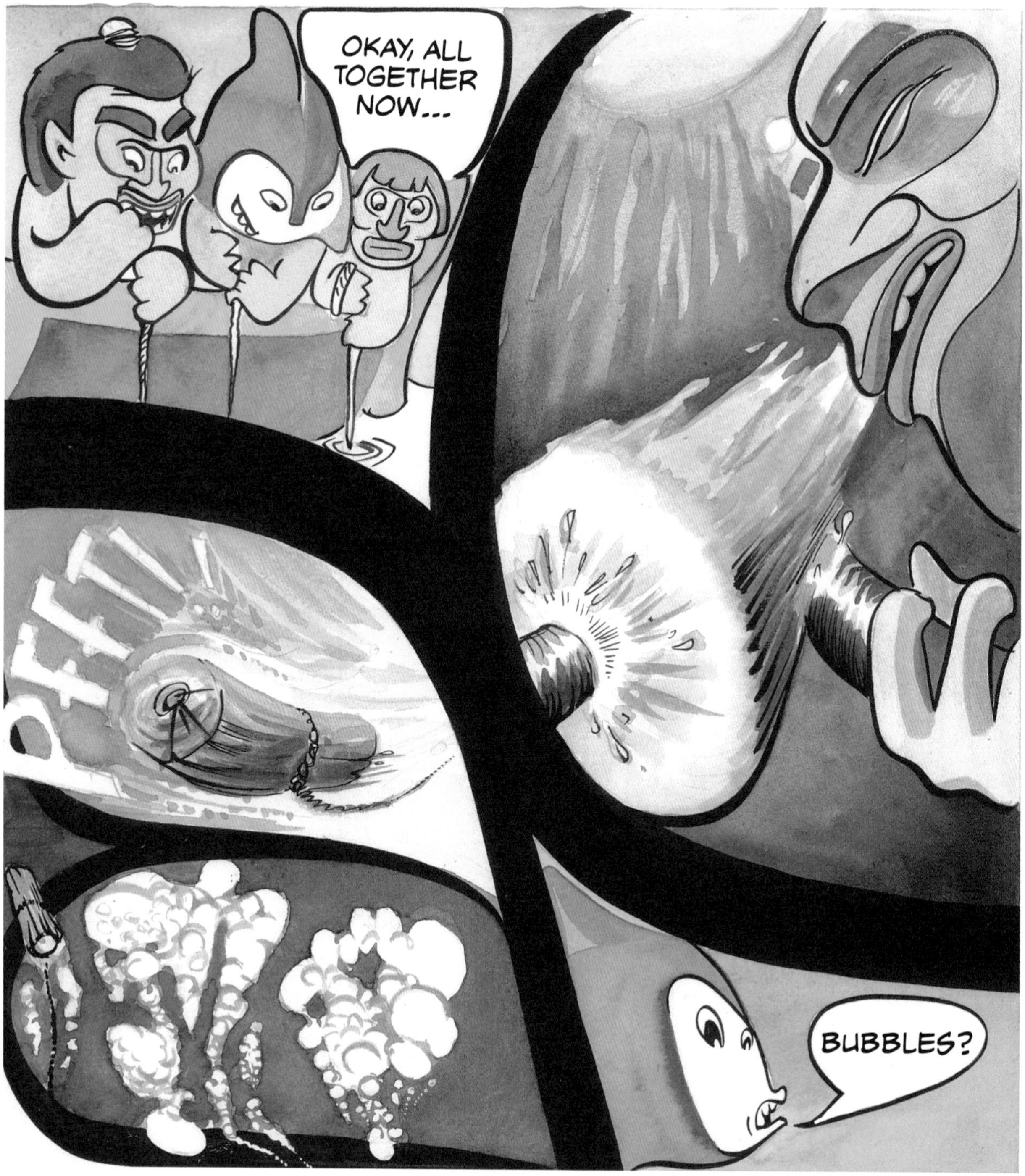
OKAY, ALL TOGETHER NOW...
BUBBLES?

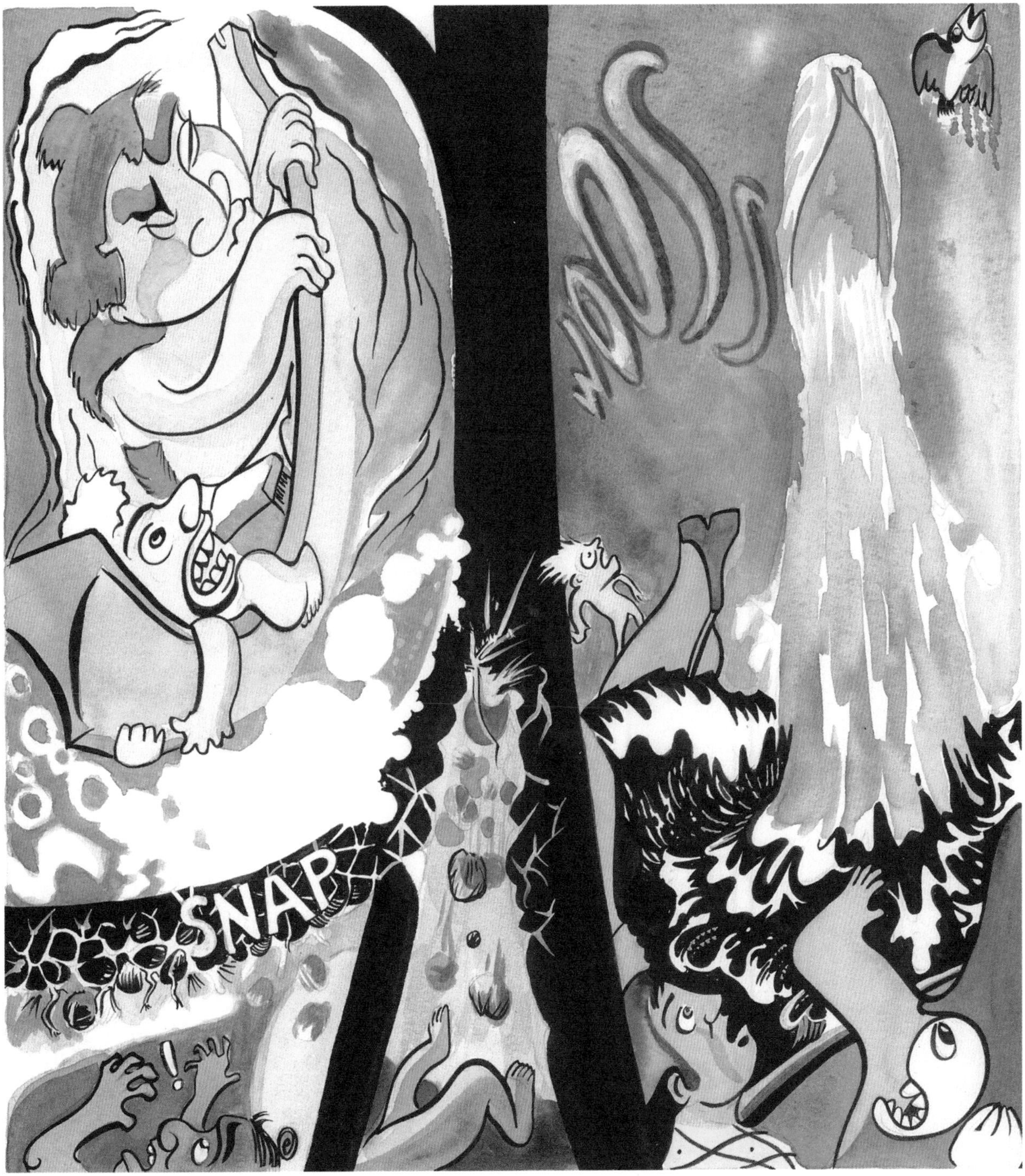
SNAP
!

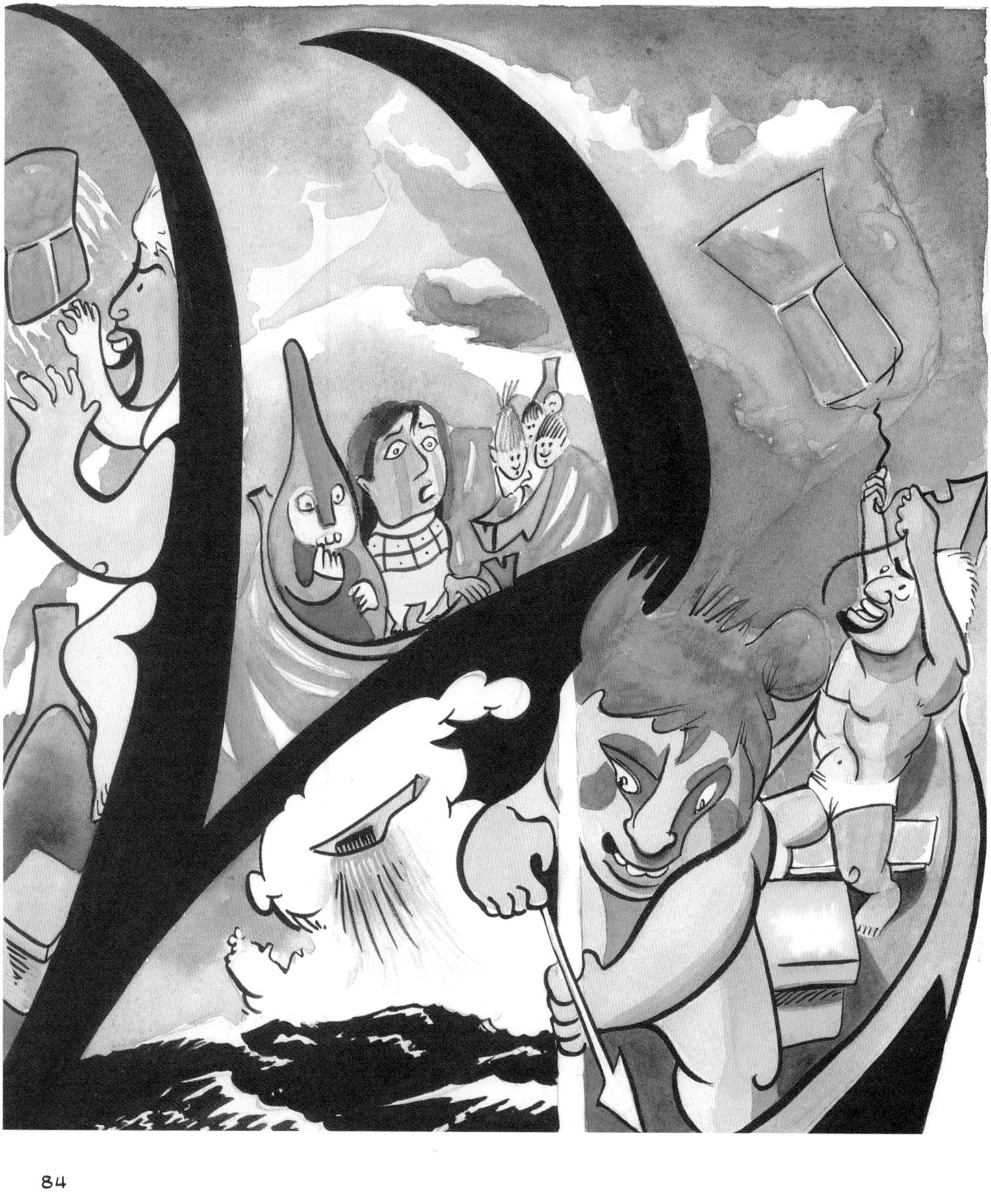

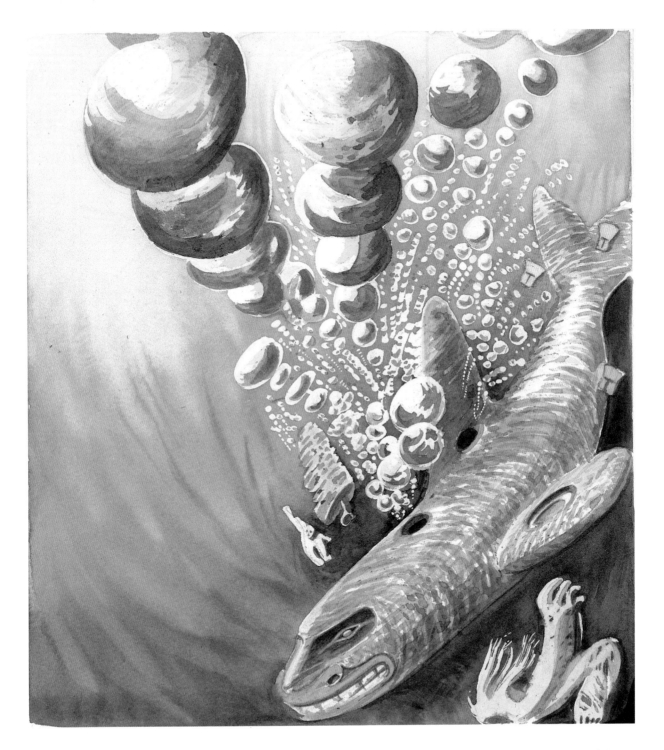

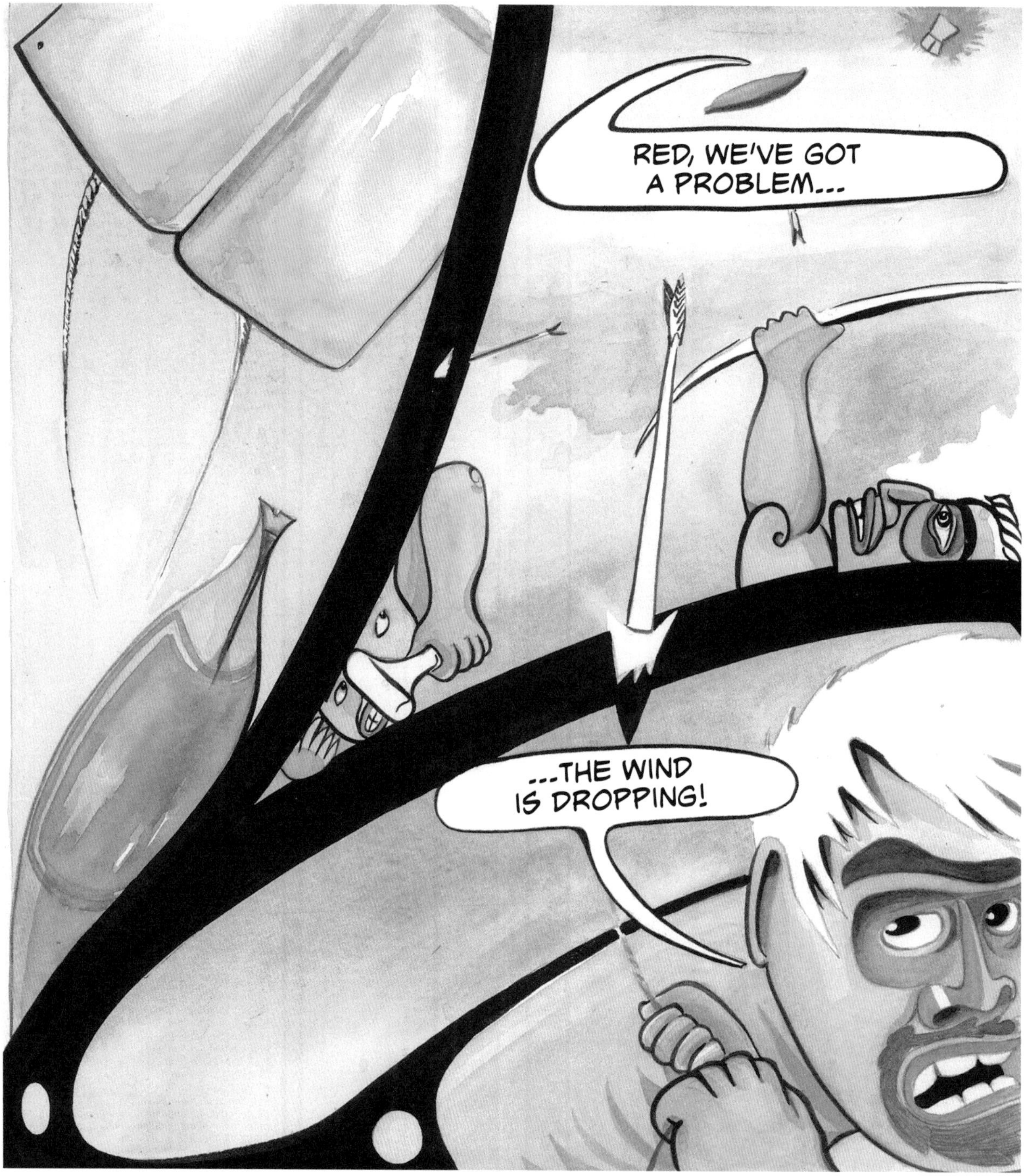
RED, WE'VE GOT A PROBLEM...
...THE WIND IS DROPPING!

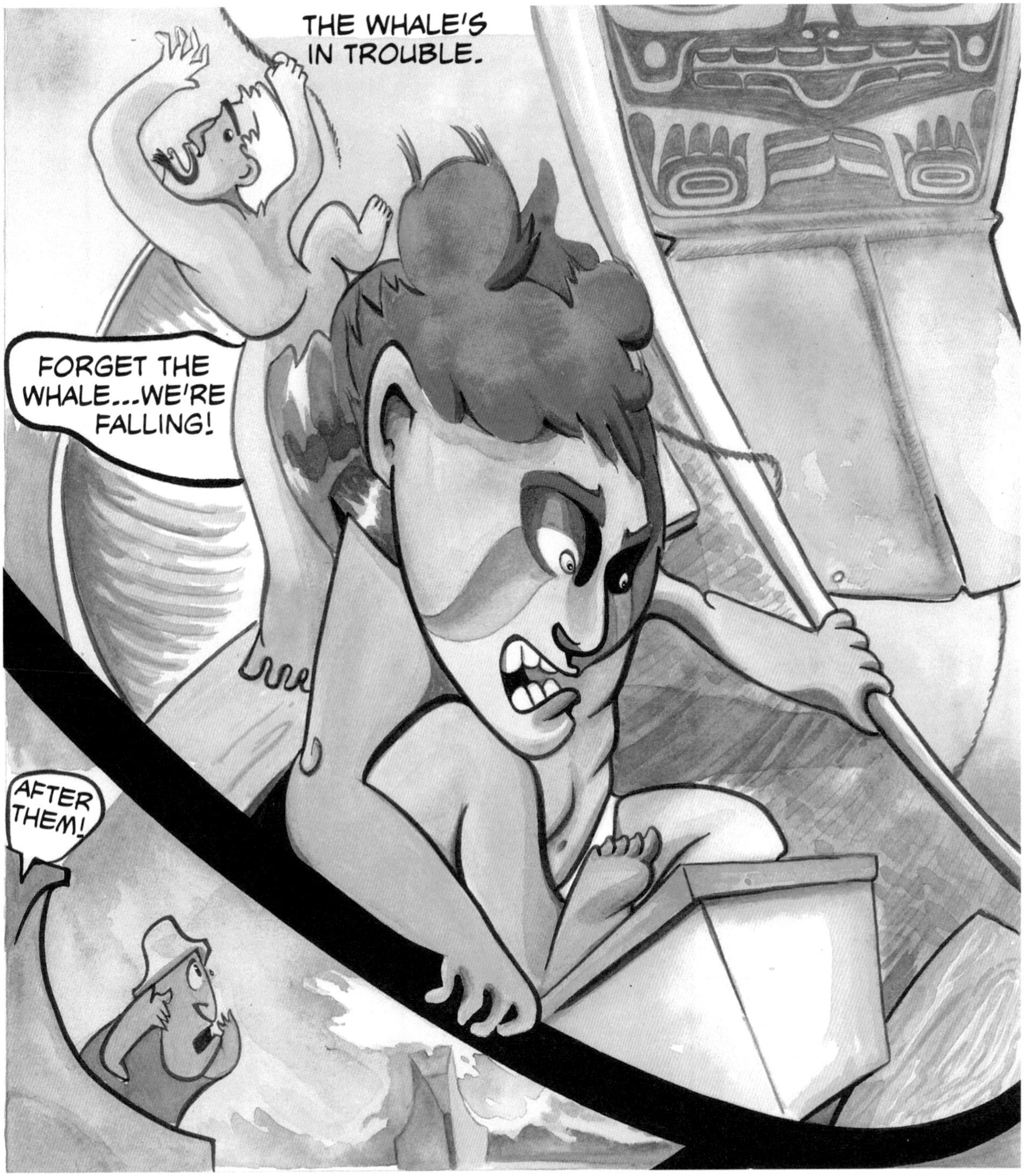
THE WHALE'S IN TROUBLE.
FORGET THE WHALE...WE'RE FALLING!
AFTER THEM!

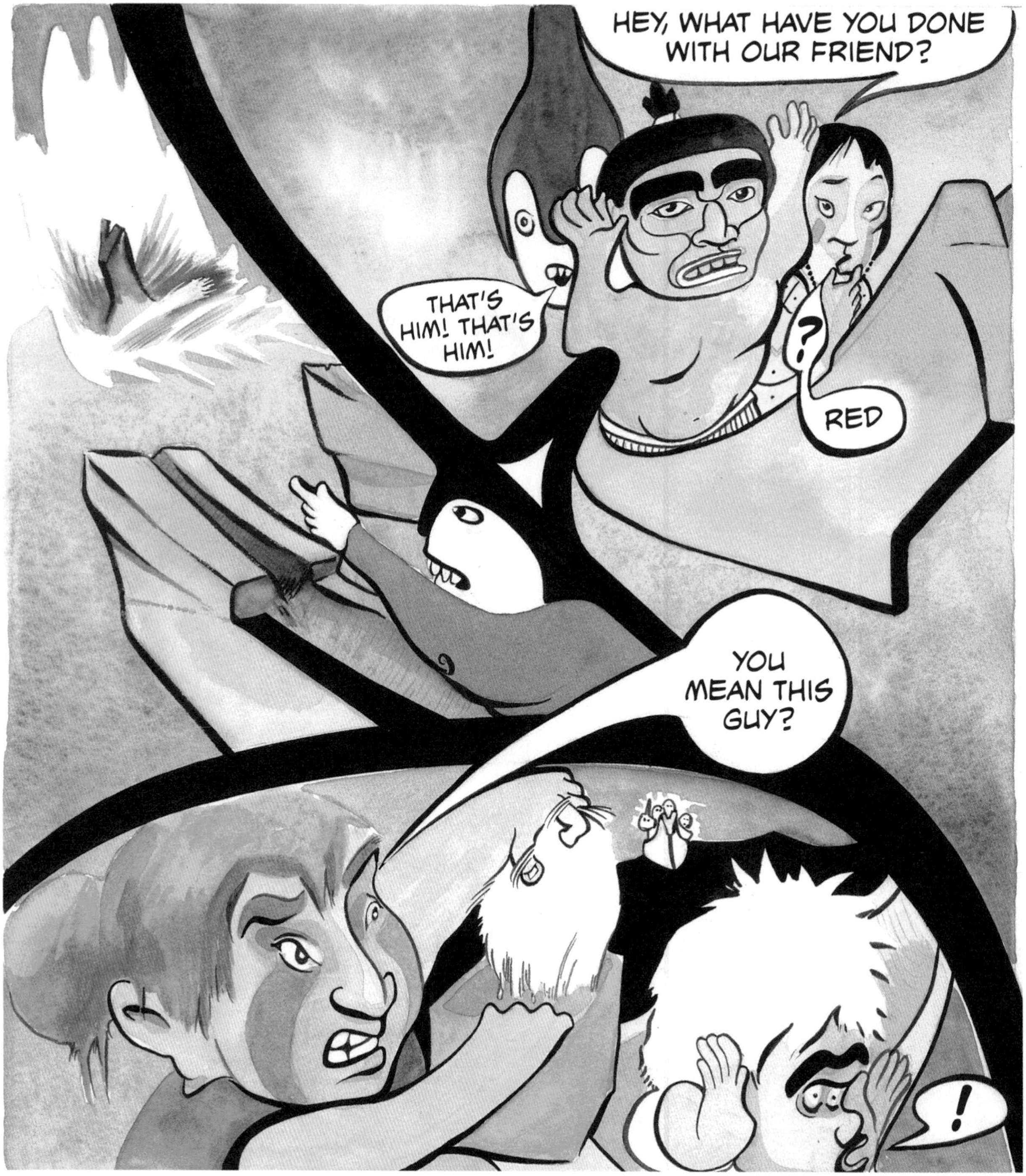
HEY, WHAT HAVE YOU DONE WITH OUR FRIEND?
THAT'S HIM! THAT'S HIM!
?
RED
YOU MEAN THIS GUY?
!

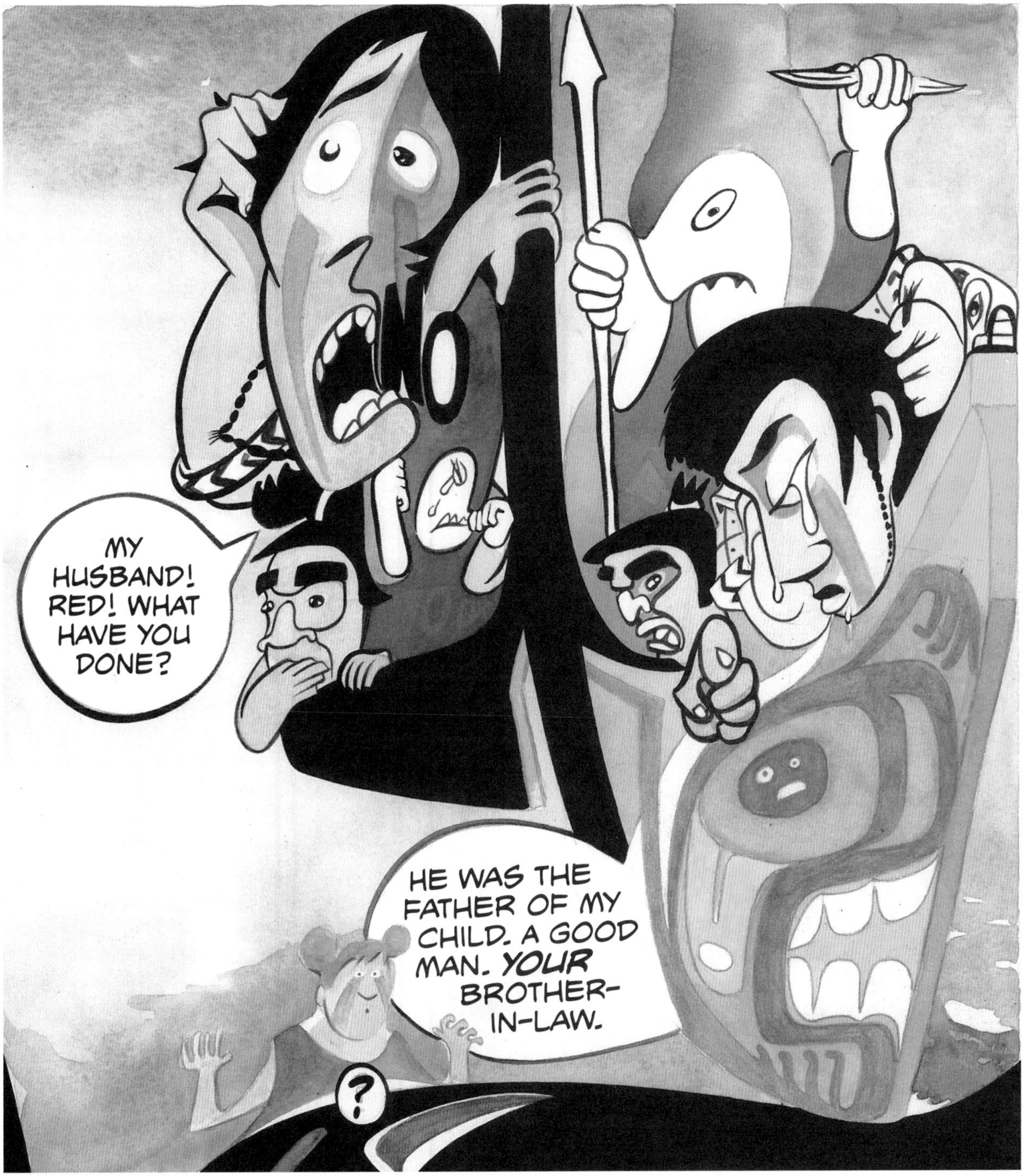
NO
MY HUSBAND! RED! WHAT HAVE YOU DONE?
HE WAS THE FATHER OF MY CHILD. A GOOD MAN. ***YOUR*** BROTHER-IN-LAW.
?

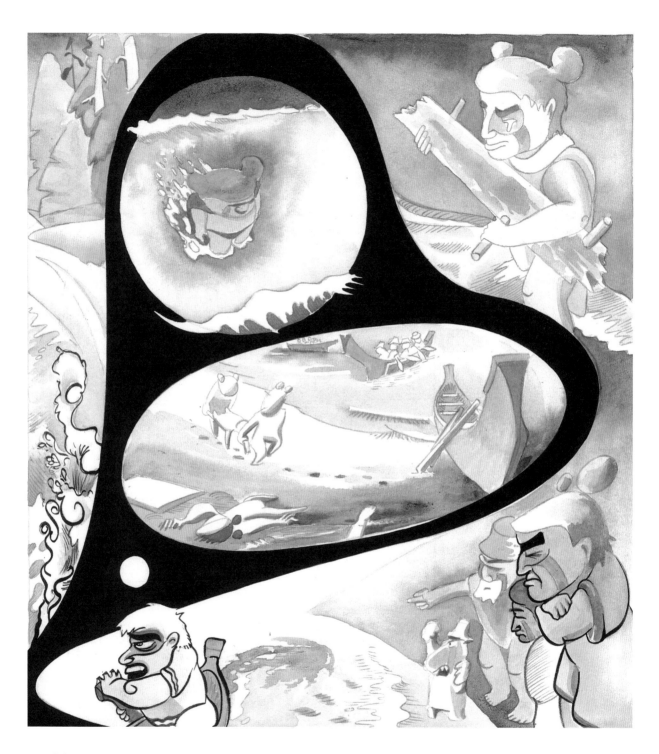

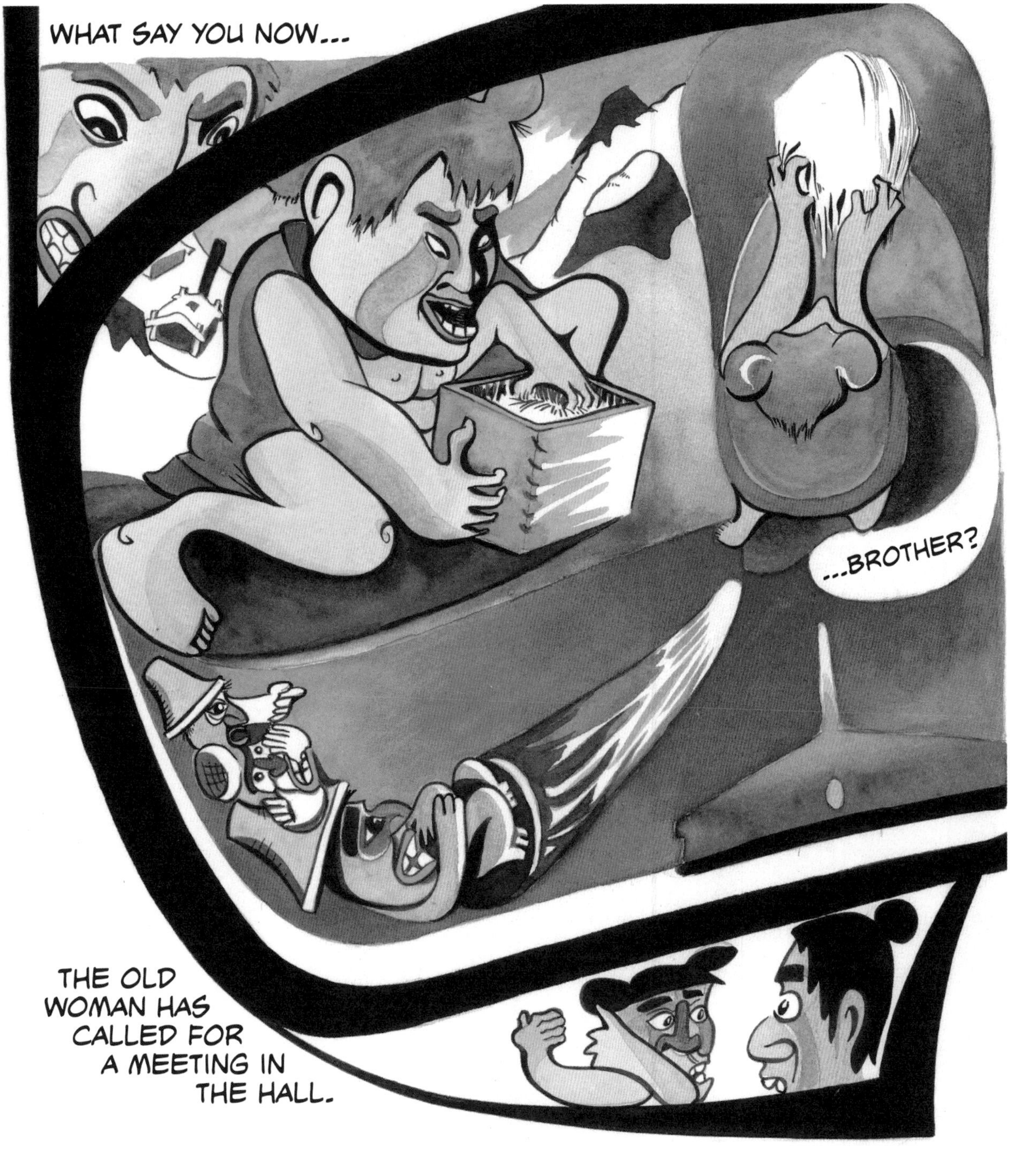
WHAT SAY YOU NOW...
...BROTHER?
THE OLD WOMAN HAS CALLED FOR A MEETING IN THE HALL.

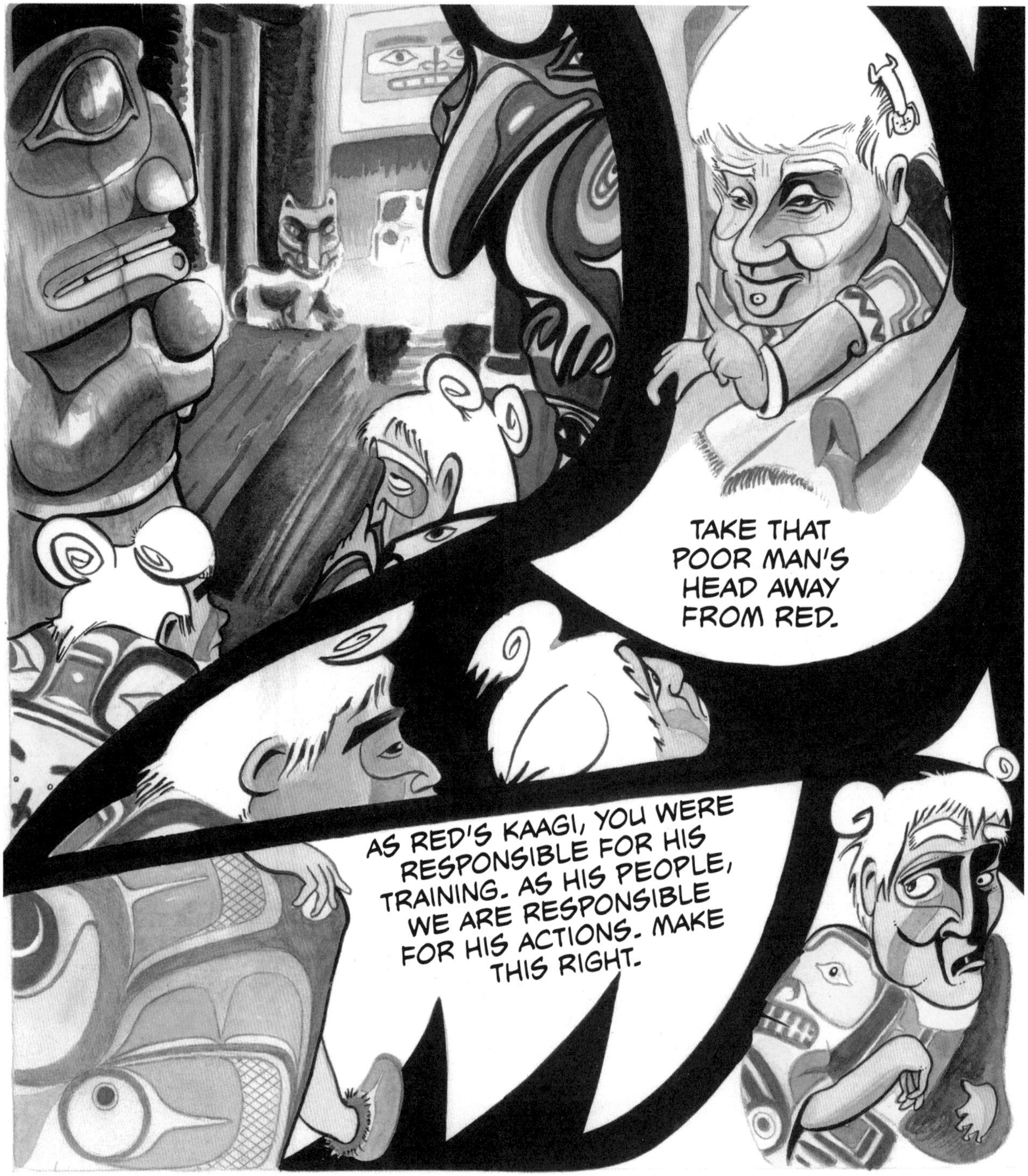
TAKE THAT POOR MAN'S HEAD AWAY FROM RED.
AS RED'S KAAGI, YOU WERE RESPONSIBLE FOR HIS TRAINING. AS HIS PEOPLE, WE ARE RESPONSIBLE FOR HIS ACTIONS. MAKE THIS RIGHT.

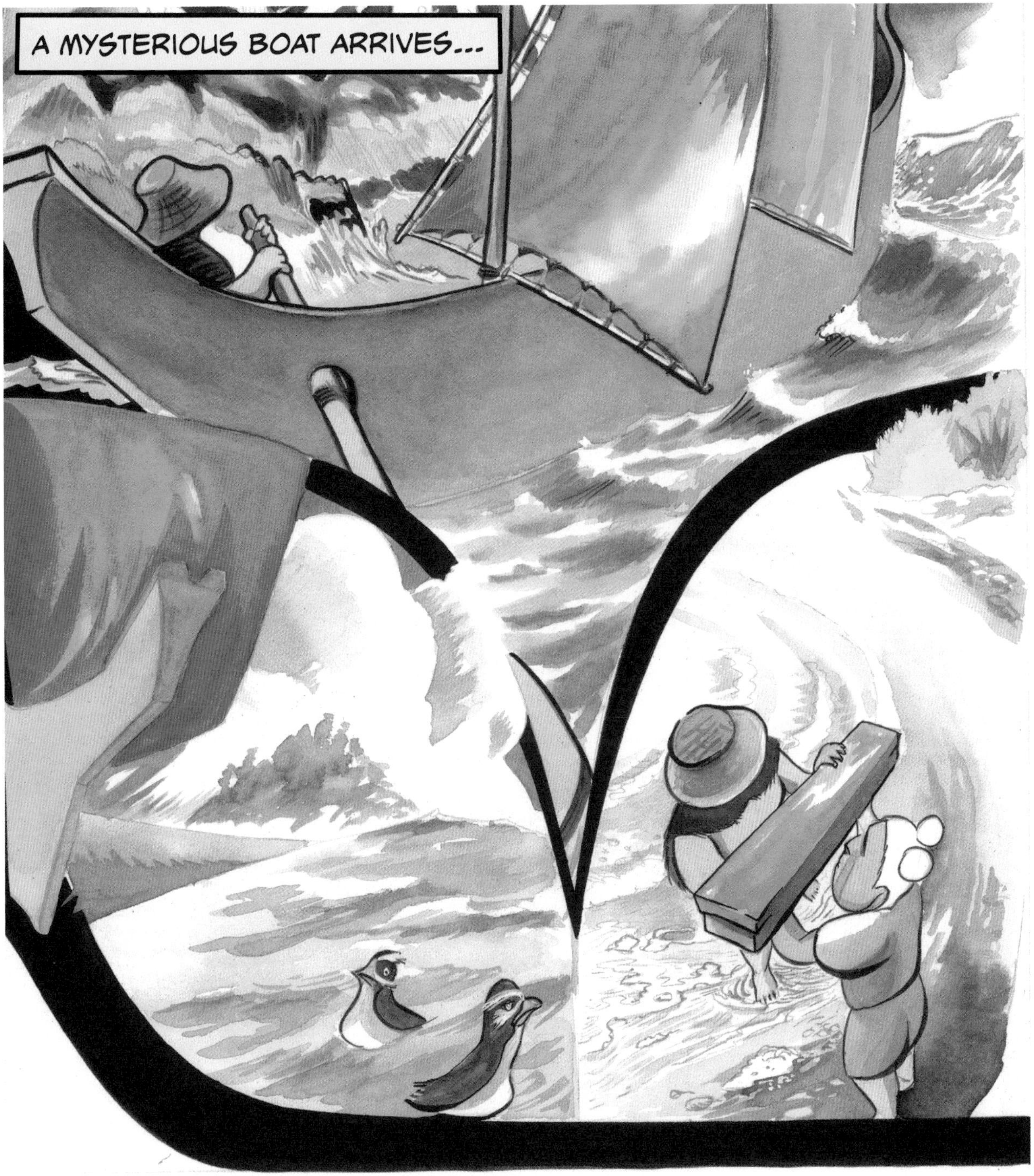
A MYSTERIOUS BOAT ARRIVES...

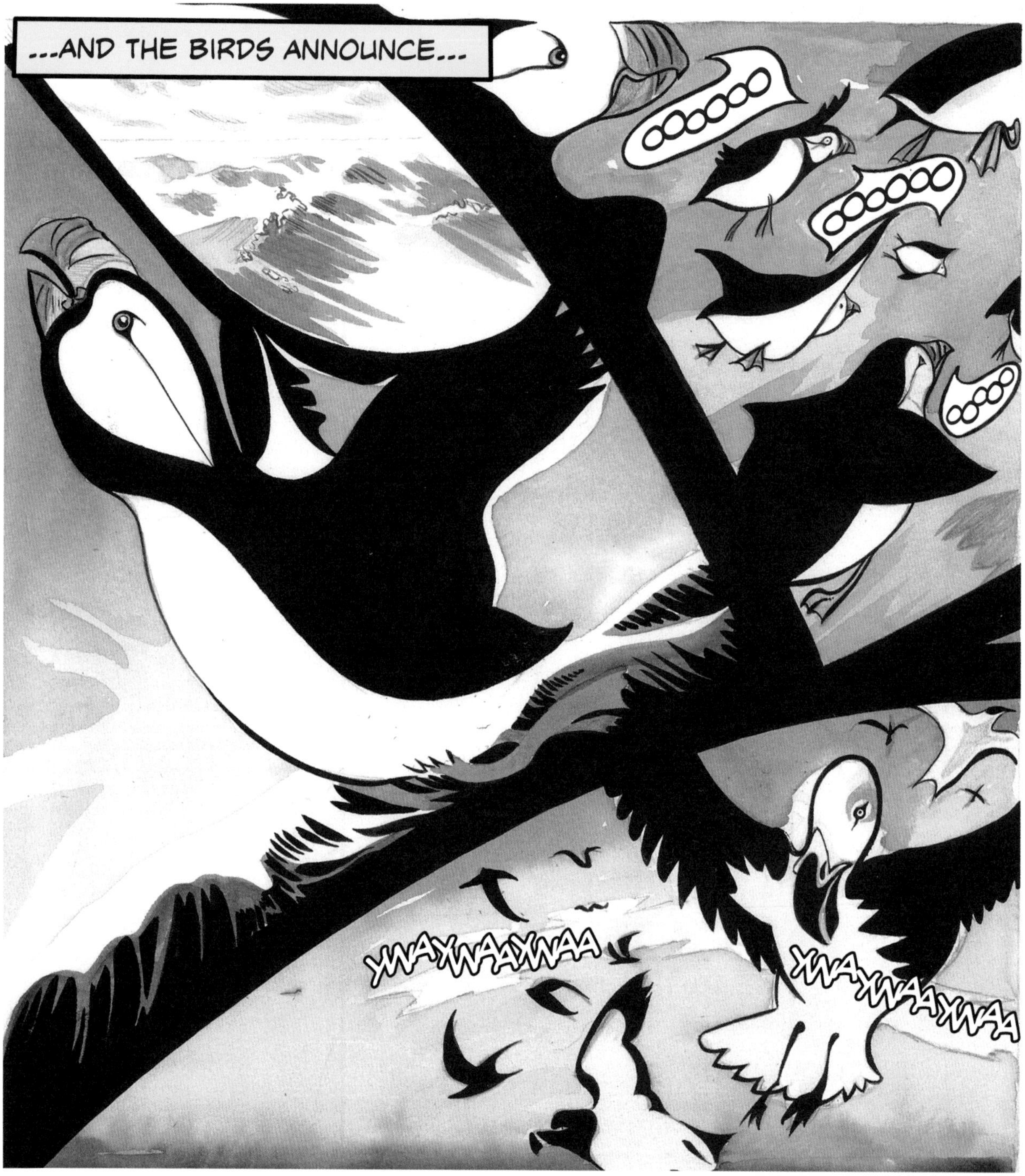
...AND THE BIRDS ANNOUNCE...
OOOOOO
OOOOOO
OOOO
YWAYWAAYWAA
YWAYWAAYWAA

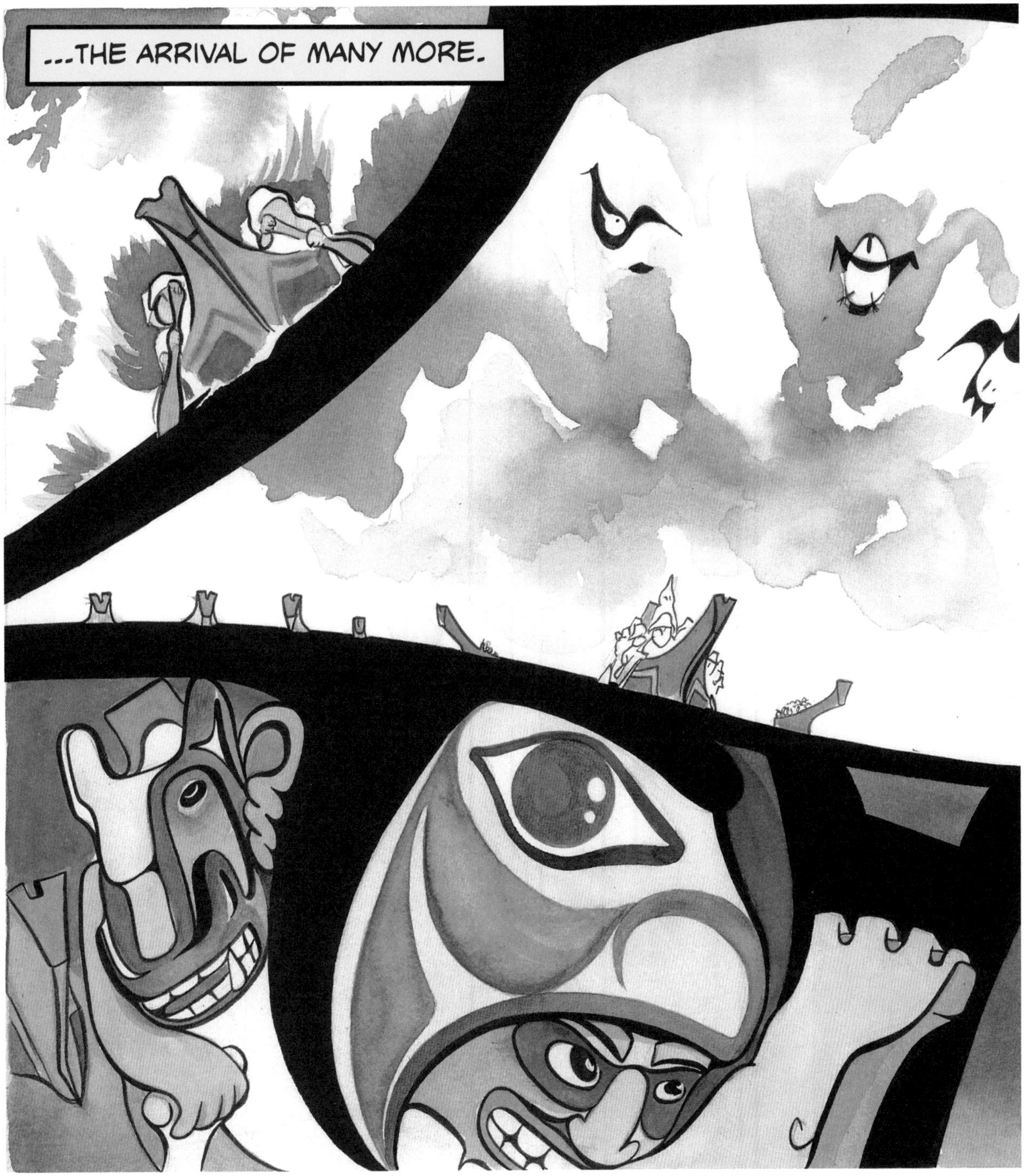
...THE ARRIVAL OF MANY MORE.

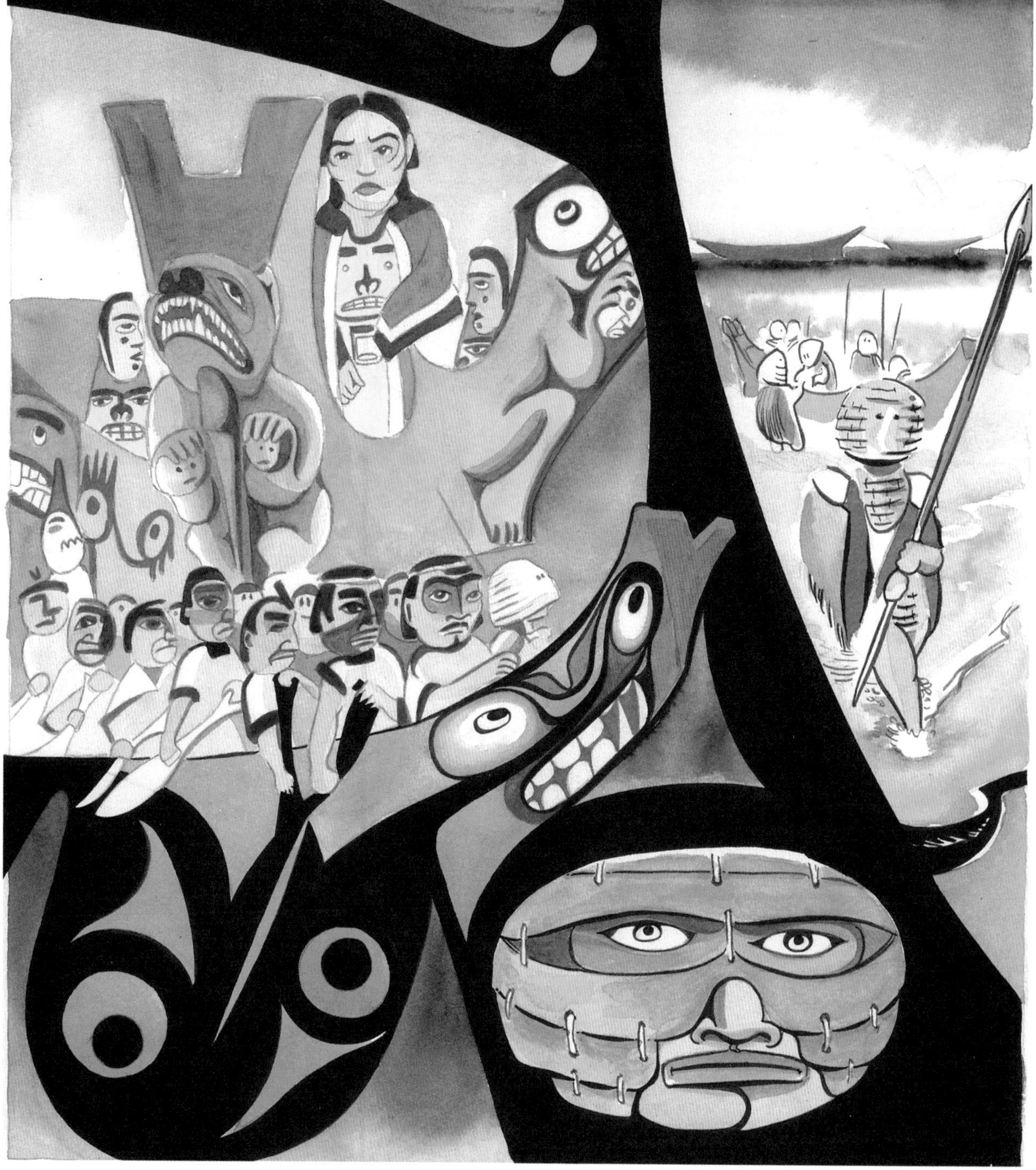

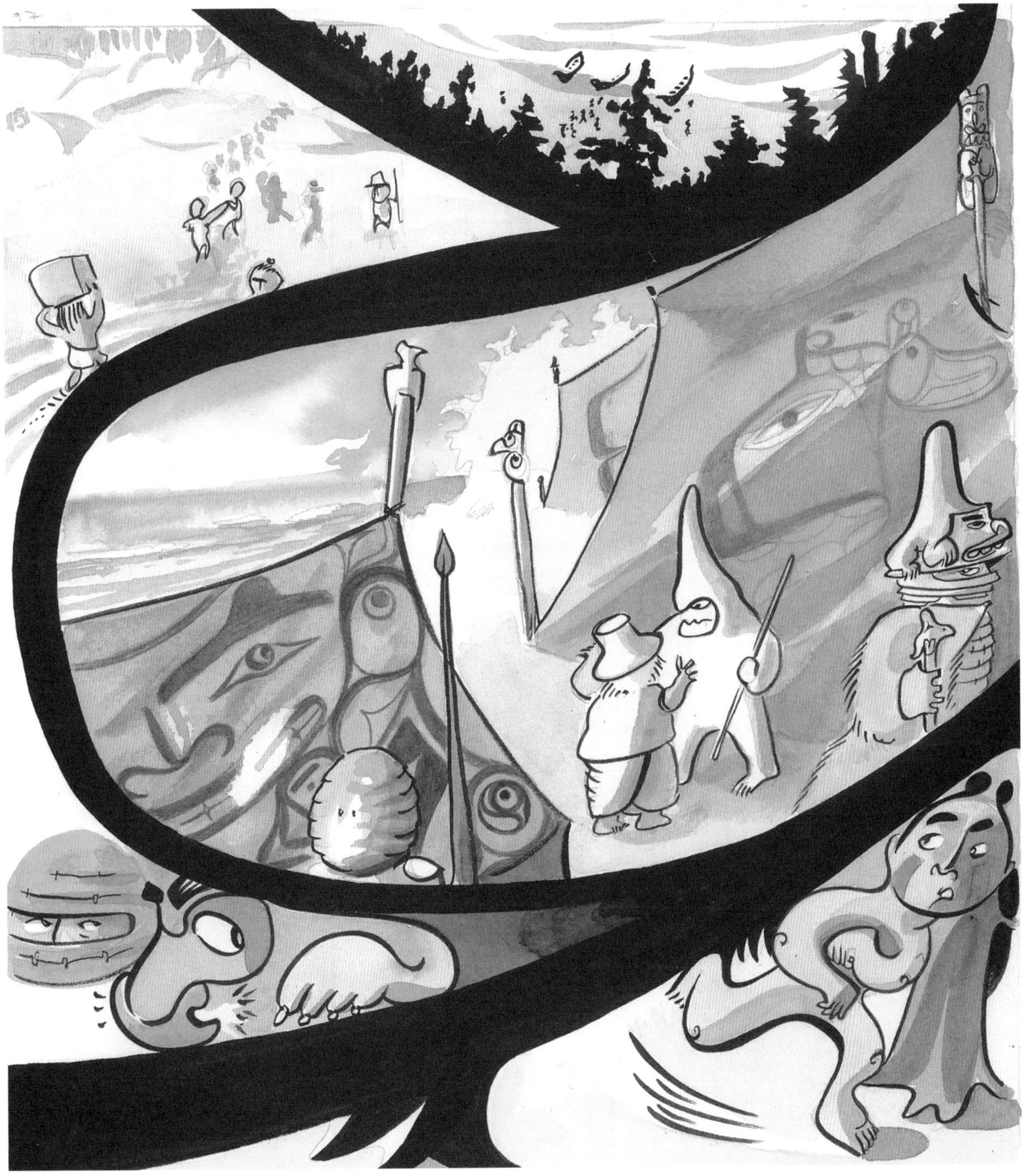

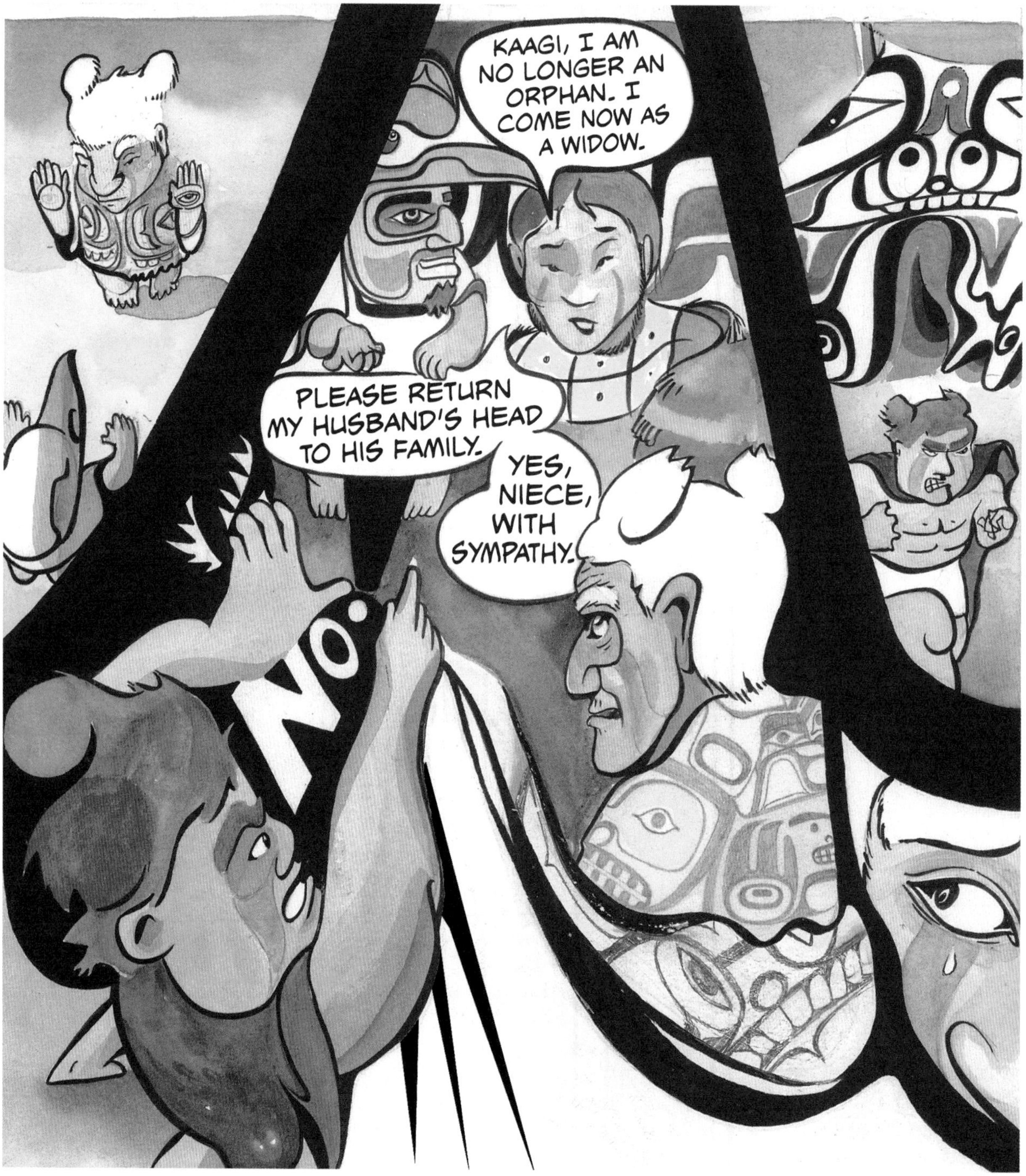
KAAGI, I AM NO LONGER AN ORPHAN. I COME NOW AS A WIDOW.
PLEASE RETURN MY HUSBAND'S HEAD TO HIS FAMILY.
YES, NIECE, WITH SYMPATHY.
NO!

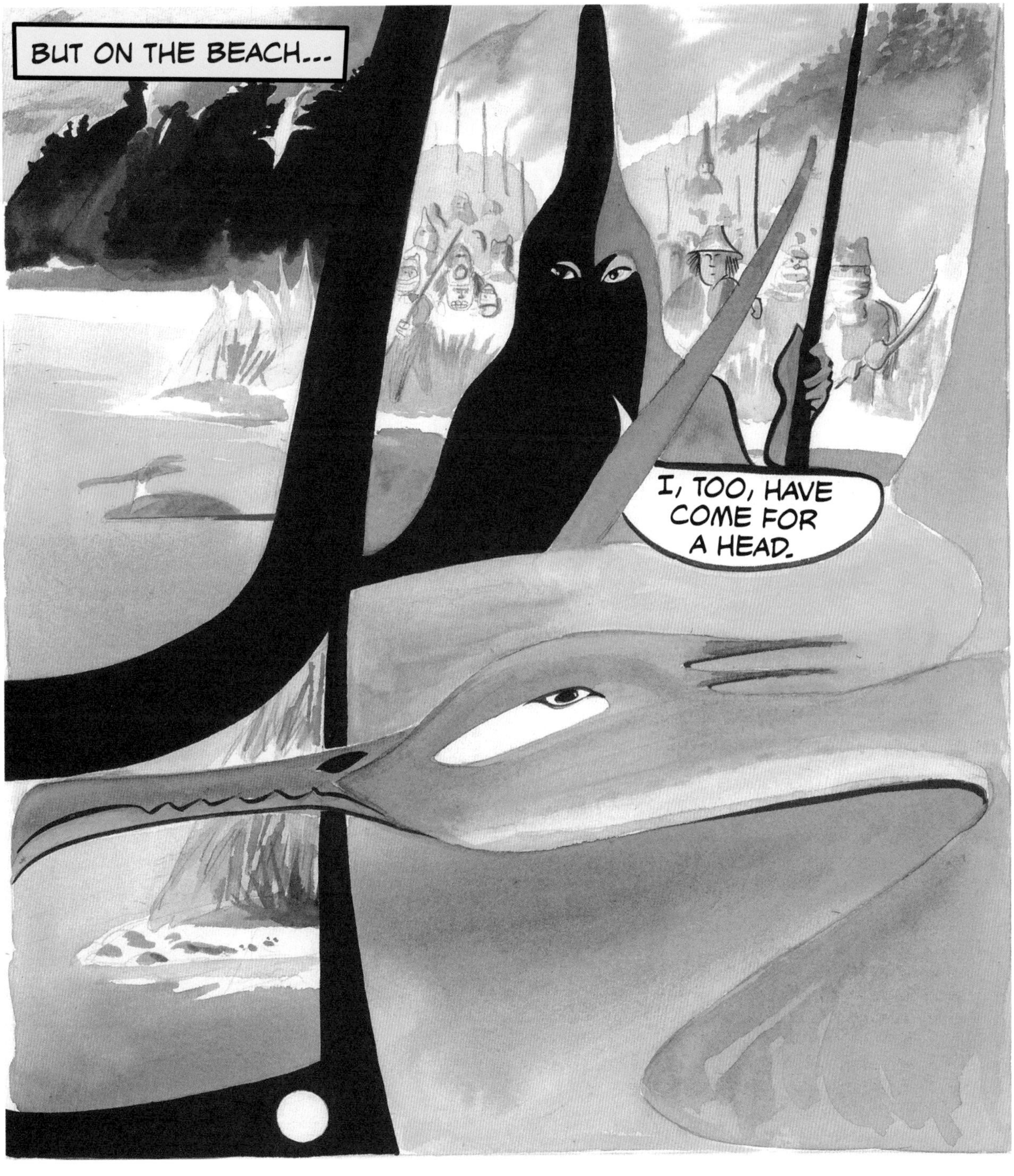
BUT ON THE BEACH...
I, TOO, HAVE COME FOR A HEAD.

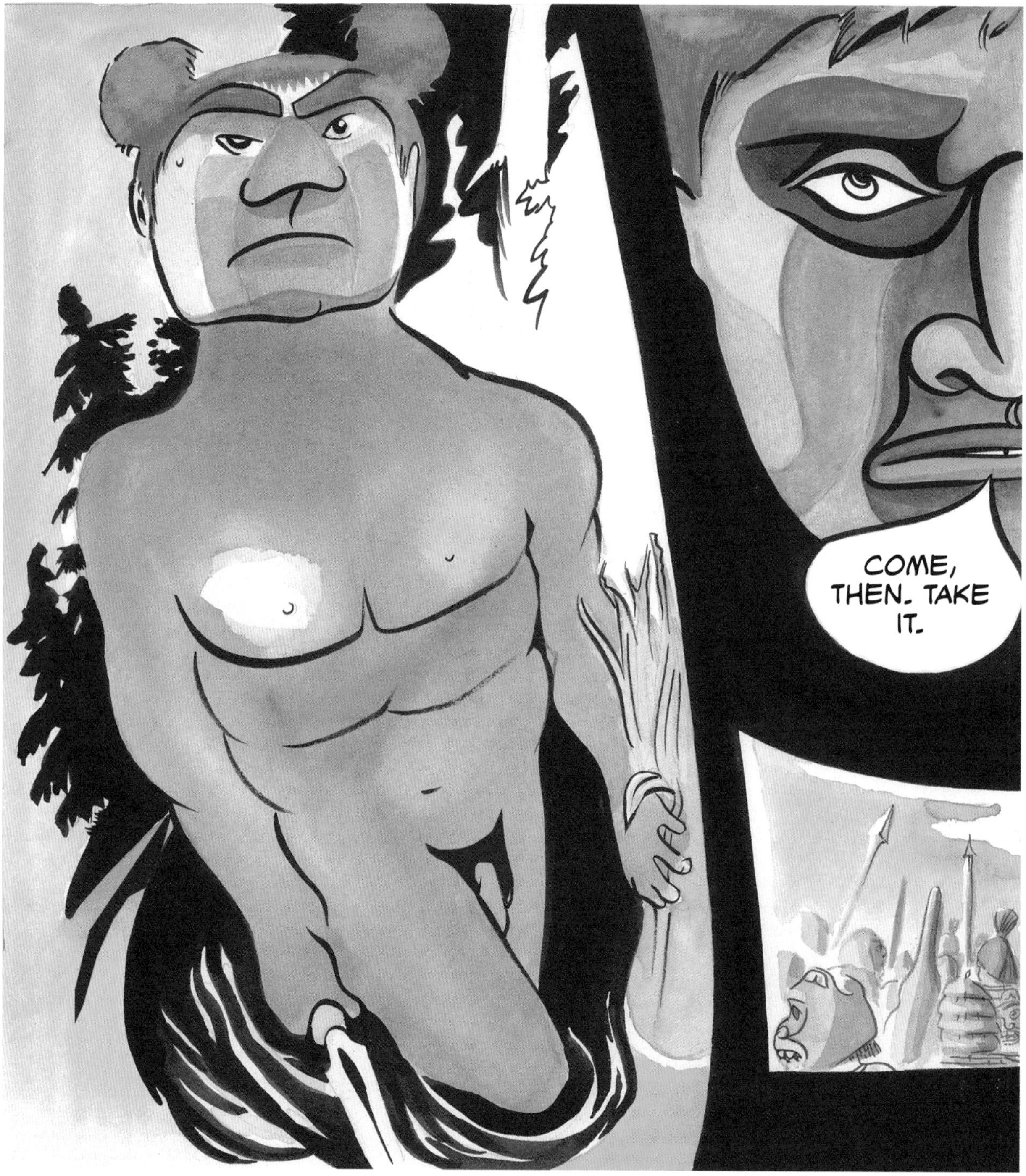
COME, THEN. TAKE IT.

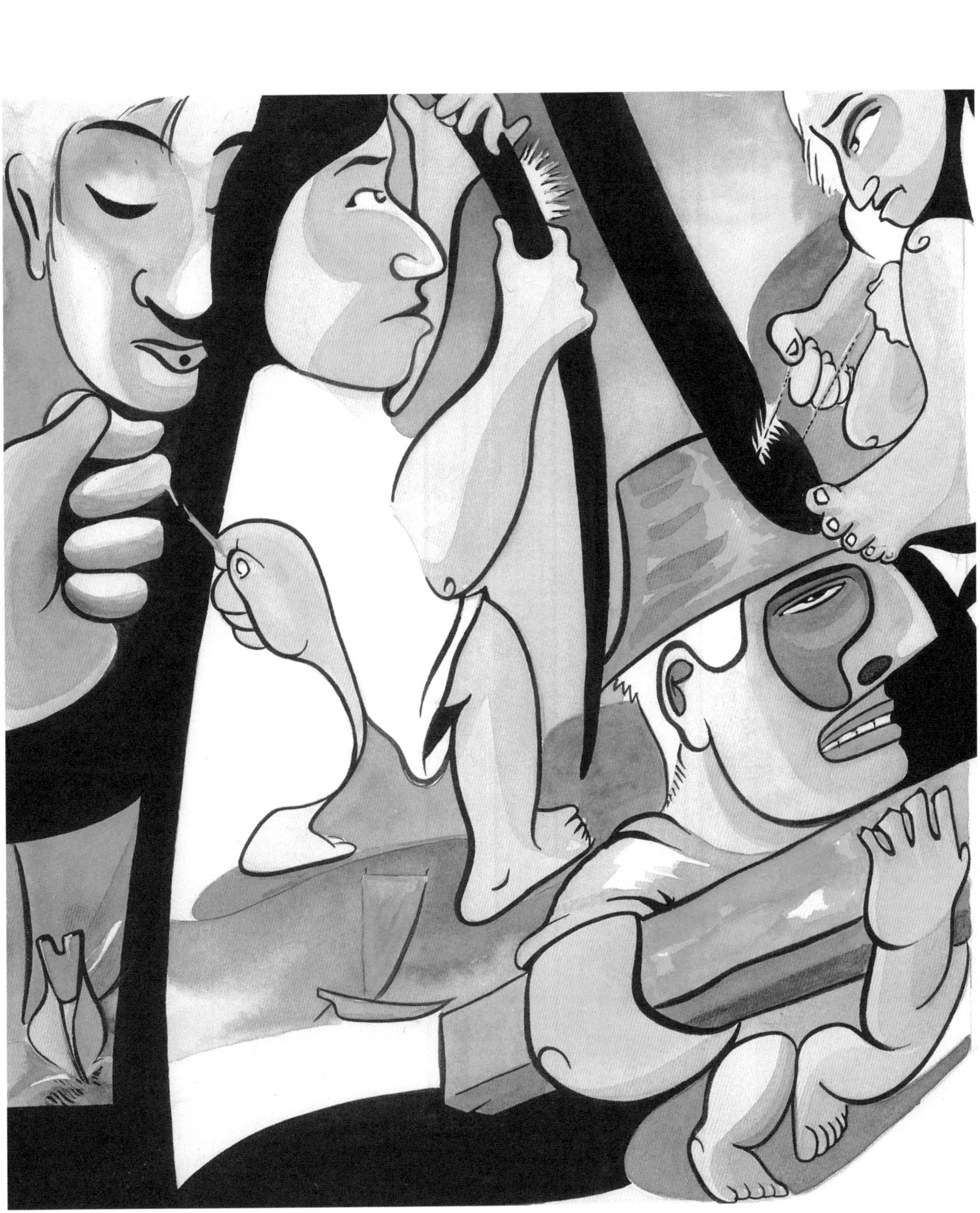

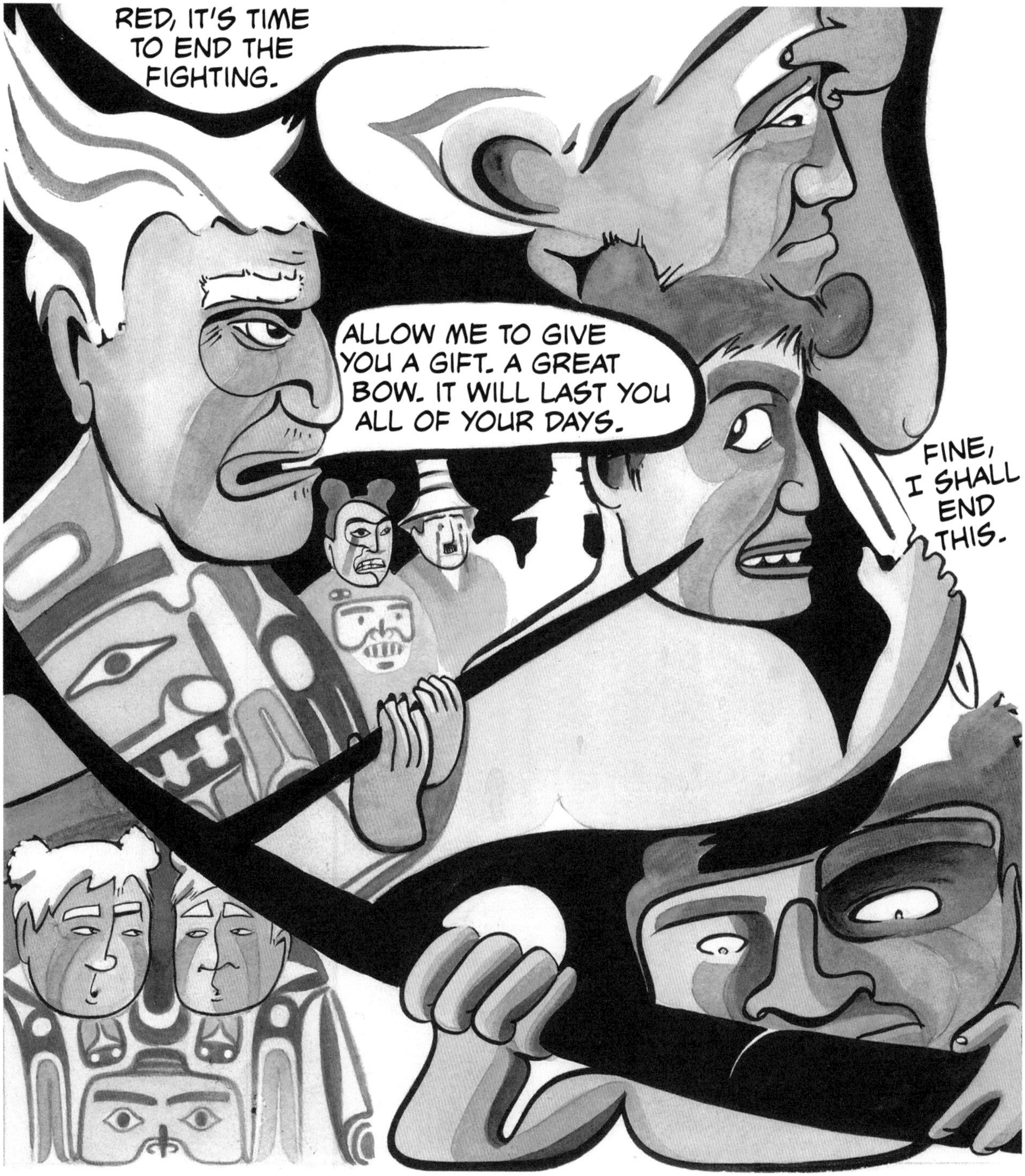
RED, IT'S TIME TO END THE FIGHTING.
ALLOW ME TO GIVE YOU A GIFT. A GREAT BOW. IT WILL LAST YOU ALL OF YOUR DAYS.
FINE, I SHALL END THIS.

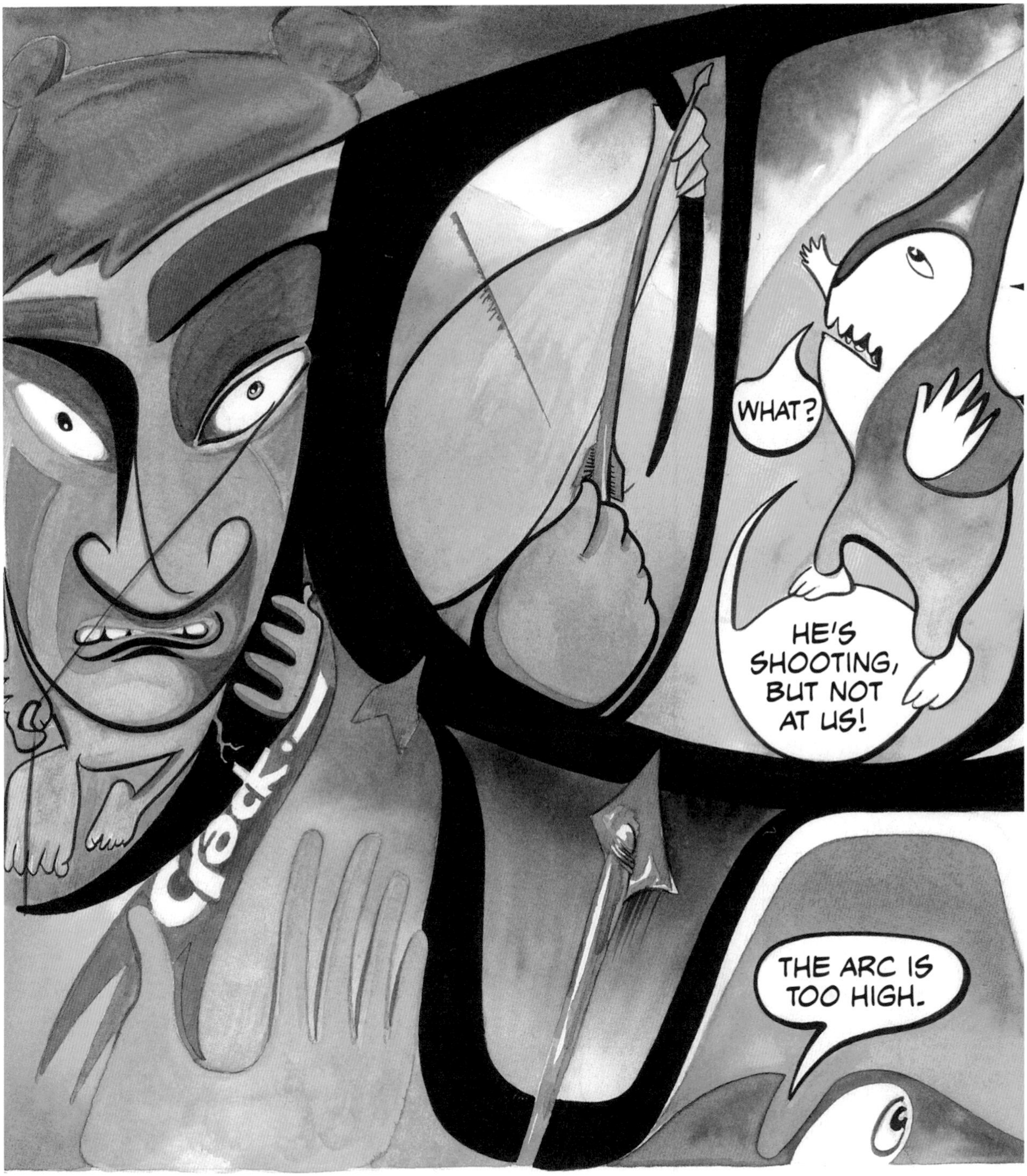

crack
WHAT?
HE'S SHOOTING, BUT NOT AT US!
THE ARC IS TOO HIGH.

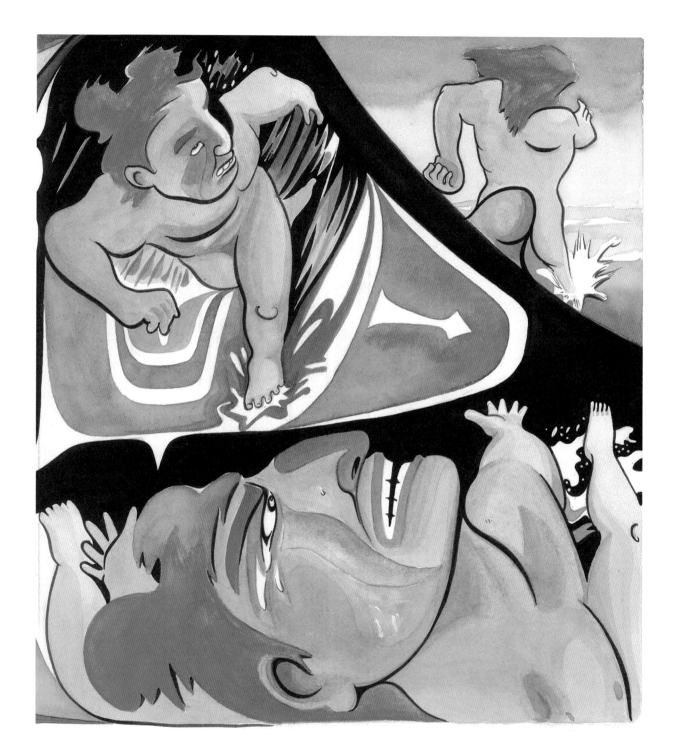

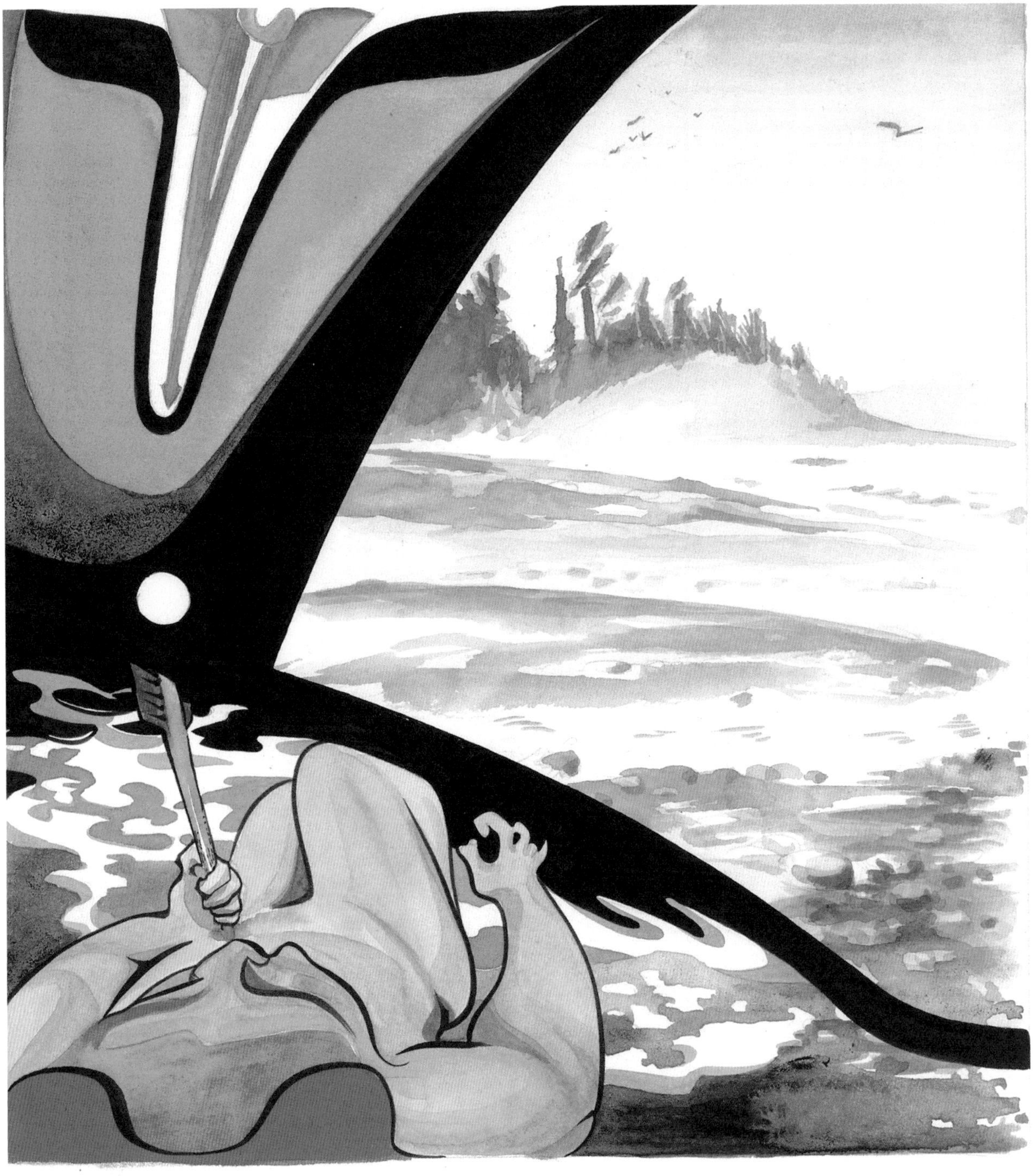

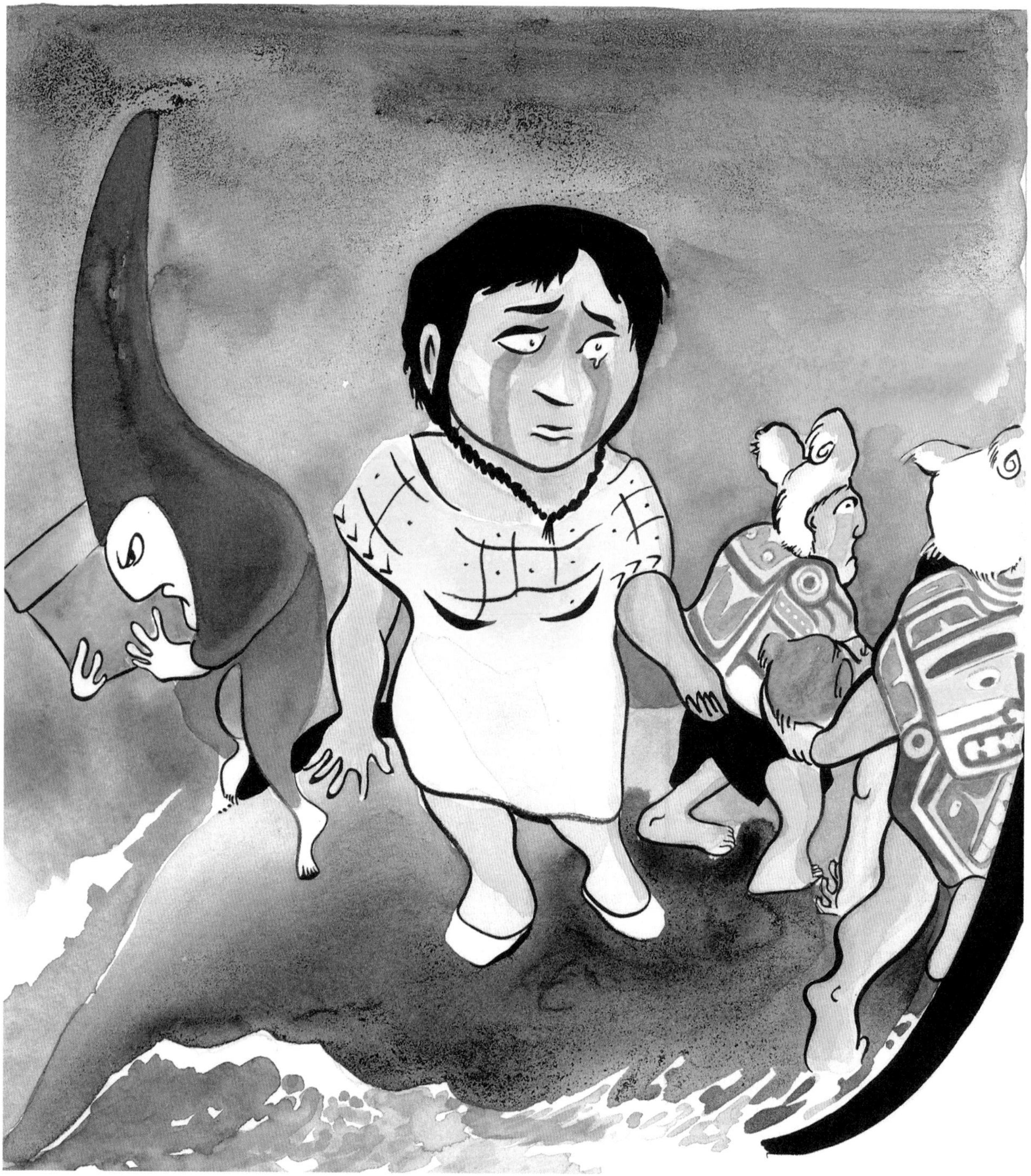

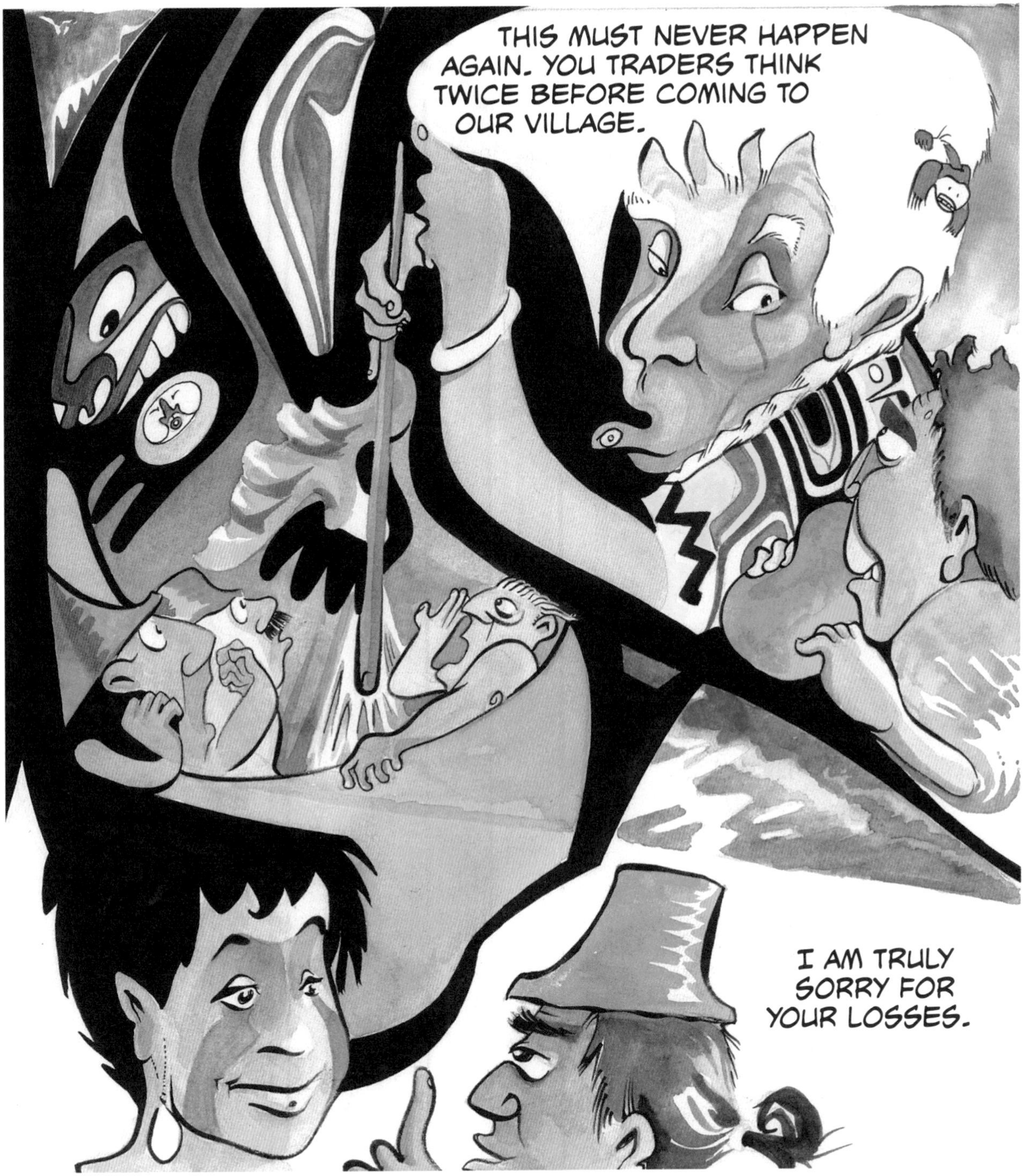
THIS MUST NEVER HAPPEN AGAIN. YOU TRADERS THINK TWICE BEFORE COMING TO OUR VILLAGE.
I AM TRULY SORRY FOR YOUR LOSSES.

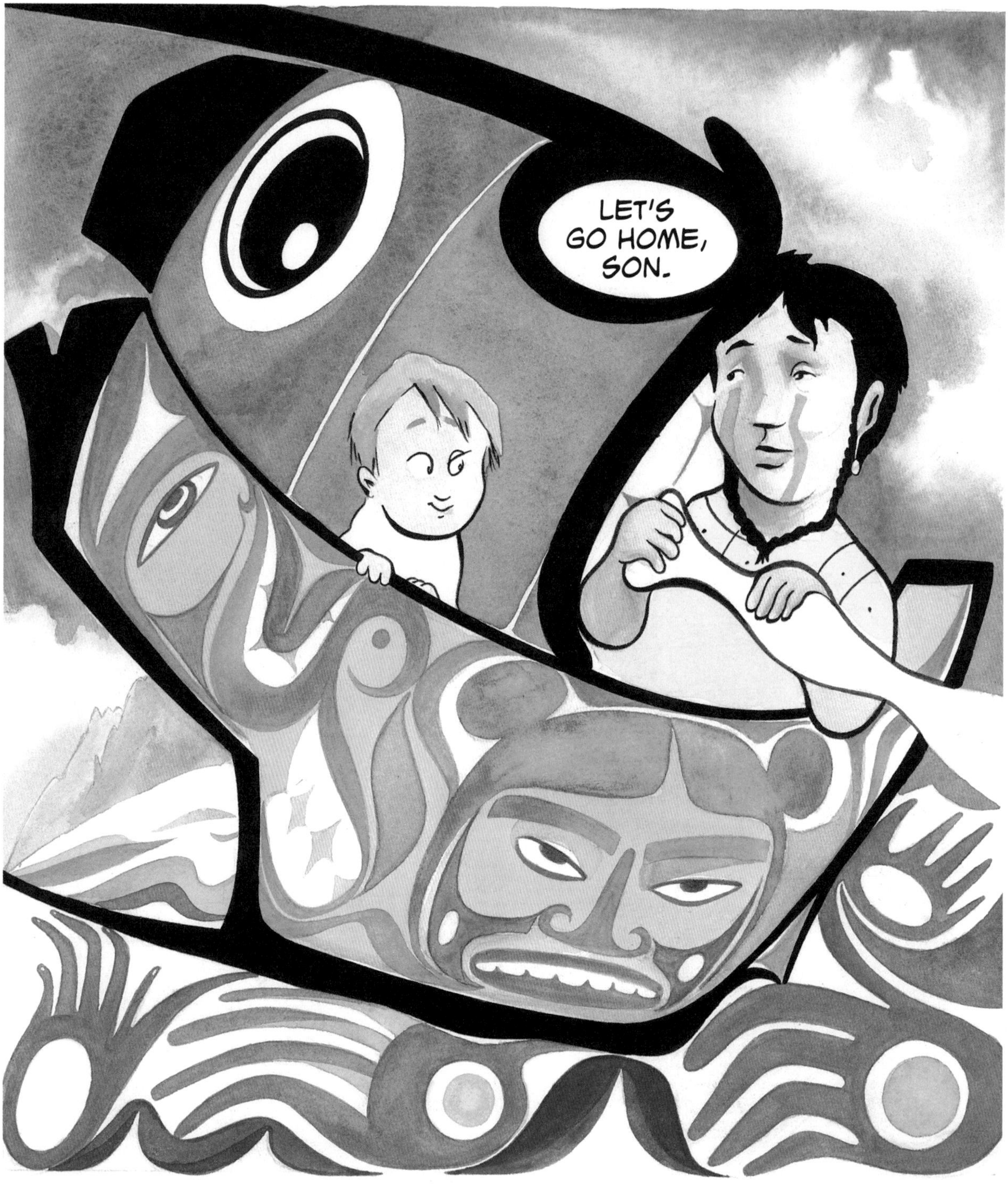
LET'S GO HOME, SON.

## ACKNOWLEDGEMENTS

TO BRUCE, EVER RESPECTFUL AND GENEROUS, WHO MADE THE SPACE BETWEEN HAIDA AND CANADA A PLACE OF CLARITY AND HONESTY;

TO TOM, WHO, IN THOSE LAST FEW MOMENTS WE EVER SPENT TOGETHER, TAUGHT ME HOW TO DIE;

TO NAOMI, WHO SHOWED ME HOW TO EMBRACE AGE, AND BABS, WHO IS STILL TRYING TO TEACH ME GRACE;

TO LAUNETTE AND TSUAAY, WHO EMBRACE ME:

I, THE POOR STUDENT, AM MUCH NOURISHED BY YOU ALL.

MNY

## OVERLEAF

*RED* IS MORE THAN A COLLECTION OF BOUND PAGES, SOMETHING MORE THAN A STORY TO BE READ PAGE BY PAGE. *RED* IS ALSO A COMPLEX OF IMAGES, A COMPOSITE—ONE THAT WILL DEFY YOUR ABILITY TO EXPERIENCE STORY AS A SIMPLE PROGRESSION OF EVENTS. TURN THE PAGE TO SEE THE ENTIRE WORK.

I WELCOME YOU TO DESTROY THIS BOOK. I WELCOME YOU TO RIP THE PAGES OUT OF THEIR BINDINGS. FOLLOWING THE LAYOUT PROVIDED OVERLEAF AND USING THE PAGES FROM TWO COPIES OF THIS BOOK, YOU CAN RECONSTRUCT THIS WORK OF ART

MNY

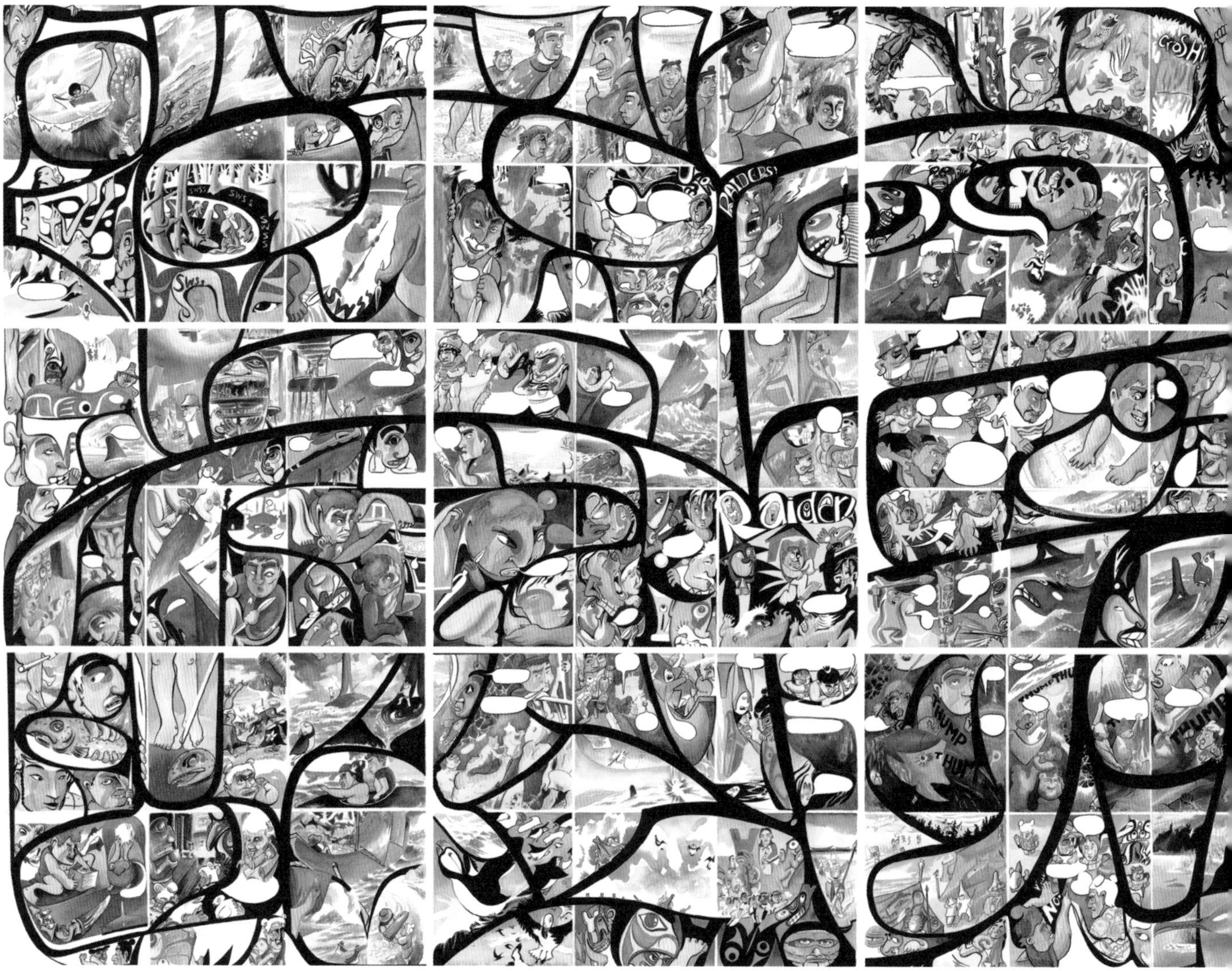

SPLOOS
RAIDERS!
THUMP
THUMP

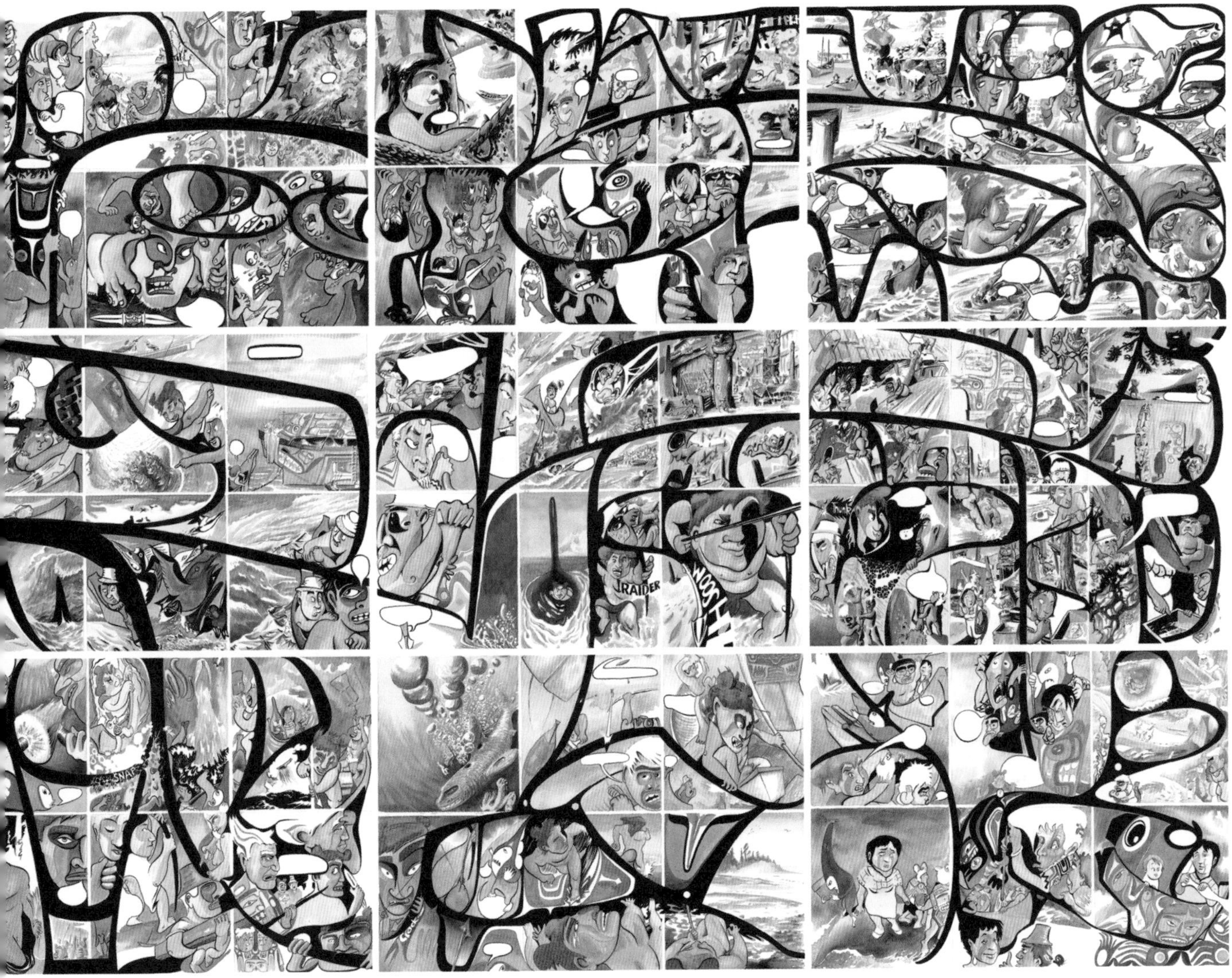
RAIDER
WOOSH
SNAP

MICHAEL NICOLL YAHGULANAAS (MNY) IS THE FATHER OF A NEW VISUAL GENRE CALLED HAIDA MANGA, WHICH REFRAMES CLASSIC INDIGENOUS IMAGERY AND NARRATIVES INTO POPULIST GRAPHIC LITERATURE. HIS ATTRACTION TO MANGA IS A NOD TO A HISTORY WHEN THE HAIDA VISITED AND ENJOYED JAPAN AND FELT WELCOMED AS FULL HUMAN PEOPLE IN CONTRAST TO THE ATTITUDES THAT LARGELY DEFINE CANADIAN COLONIALISM. A DESCENDANT OF PROMINENT ARTISTS CHARLES EDENSHAW AND ISABELLA YAHGULANAAS, MNY WAS FORMALLY INTRODUCED TO THE DISCIPLINES OF CLASSIC ICONOGRAPHY BY COUSINS JIM HART EDENSO AND ROBERT DAVIDSON. HE ALSO STUDIED WITH CANTONESE ARTIST CAI BEN WON.

HAIDA MANGA IS A GENRE THAT REFLECTS BOTH MNY'S INDIGENOUS AND COLONIAL HERITAGES AND IS INFLUENCED BY HIS LONG AND ACTIVE CAREER IN SOCIAL AND ENVIRONMENTAL JUSTICE ISSUES ON HIS HOME ISLANDS OF HAIDA GWAII AND THROUGHOUT THE PACIFIC RIM. HE SPENT MUCH OF THE 1980S AND 1990S IN PUBLIC SERVICE FOR THE HAIDA NATION, A CAREER MARKED BY A SERIES OF SUCCESSES AGAINST MINING, LOGGING AND POLITICAL INTERESTS.

IN 2001 MNY BEGAN TO EXPLORE THE BOUNDARIES THAT DESCRIBE "TRADITIONAL" HAIDA ART. HE BEGAN CREATING POP-GRAPHIC NARRATIVES AND RIFFING ON TRADITIONAL ORAL STORIES AND PAINTING TECHNIQUES, AND HE QUICKLY DEVELOPED THE DISTINCTIVE HAIDA MANGA ART FORM FOR WHICH HE IS INTERNATIONALLY KNOWN. HE HAS EXHIBITED IN ASIA, EUROPE AND NORTH AMERICA. HIS BOOKS INCLUDE *FLIGHT OF THE HUMMINGBIRD, A TALE OF TWO SHAMANS, THE LAST VOYAGE OF THE BLACK SHIP,* AND *HACHIDORI,* A BESTSELLER IN JAPAN. HE LIVES IN CANADA WITH HIS WIFE AND DAUGHTER, CLOSE TO THE TWO SISTERS MOUNTAINS ABOVE AN ISLAND IN THE SALISH SEA.

WWW.MNY.CA